# The Thresher Ghost



Spencer Compton

ISBN: 9798742785774

# CONTENTS

History has no conscience, no better self.
It is a lie told by a truth-teller.
It is the truth told by a liar.

# Part One:
# Los Angeles, 1963

# 1.

A flashing light beyond the surge and moments later a small launch glided out of the darkness. McCoy scrambled up off the wet sand onto the military-grade Zodiac, lurching past a light machine gun mounted at its bow.

Two men in navy blue jumpsuits pulled him aboard. The larger of the two, who seemed to be in command, sported a pistol strapped to his thigh. The right side of his face was deformed as if from a chemical explosion or a fire.

McCoy eyed the man closer. *Lost most of the mandible and its periosteum. Someone did a good reconstruction job.*

The other man revved the engines. The launch bounced over the waves, trailing a phosphorescent wake in the night.

"Smoke?" McCoy asked. Half Face shook his head.

McCoy lit a Tareyton on the fourth match and took a long drag. He wondered again about Hughes' "associate on the high seas" and what he'd "accomplished." Monkey glands, mineral water or megavitamins. These guys always have a gimmick.

And then he saw it.

A long, low island in the darkness. The moon glided out from behind a cloudbank and a black steel hull nearly a football field in length appeared. A green light blinked once from high atop her winged conning tower. The man at McCoy's side returned the signal, and the enormous underwater ship turned on her docking lights.

*A submarine from God knows whose Navy.*

The tiny launch bobbed in the waves while the man who'd been steering cast his bowline up into the darkness. A moment later, a rope ladder tumbled down, and Half Face gestured for McCoy to start climbing. "Use both hands, mon," he said.

McCoy could barely see through the spraying sea and inky dark. When he reached the deck, he staggered to the steel sail, climbed the mounted rungs to its top, then clanged down two more ladders inside. McCoy noticed there were no markings or numbers on the ship. Anywhere.

*Oh God, where am I?*

Los Angeles, California
August, 1962
One year earlier

Jack asked Bobby to check up on her so he drove out to Brentwood and brought her take-out Chinese. She wouldn't eat. She'd given her housekeeper the night off and lit votive candles all around her bungalow bedroom. Ella Fitzgerald was singing sad songs on the record player.

"Why do I only want what I can't have?" She swallowed a little girl sob. "He won't take my calls. He doesn't call me back." She was puffy-eyed and heartbroken in her white terrycloth robe. She tucked her bare feet under herself on the bed. Mascara was running down her cheeks.

"You think you're the only one? Half the time, he doesn't call me back." The whiskey was getting to him. Bobby laid a tennis-tanned arm across her shoulder and brushed her hair from her face. Her body scent overpowered her perfume; it was intoxicating. "Let me comfort you…"

Marilyn squinted pityingly. "You're his little brother." She lay back, pulling away from him. "I can't love everyone."

"I'm sorry. It's just that we're here. Alone…"

If Jack Kennedy appeared flawless, Bobby did not. Jack had a clear hazel gaze. Bobby's blue eyes wandered, searching for something better. Jack's face at rest was strong and peaceful; Bobby's dissatisfied, even cruel. Jack knew he was privileged; he was grateful for his father's connections. Bobby thought he had earned the dollar he found in his pocket.

He made what he hoped were soothing noises. *Another girl who wants Jack, not me.* She was rummaging in her purse for a pill bottle.

"Be a doll and get me a glass of water." She popped two Nembutals and swallowed them dry as he walked across the tile floor to the bathroom. Cicadas hummed outside the windows. She quickly dropped a Nembutal into Bobby's whiskey glass.

He was back, handing her a glass of water.

"Do you hear them? They're cicadas. Listen. It's so sad. The nymphs are born every seventeen years. They sing to attract their mates. Then they die. Isn't that beautiful?"

He smiled. Every moment with her was a performance. But Marilyn had moved on.

"I need you to do something for me," she murmured.

"Anything at all." He sounded hopeful.

She held up a suppository. A shy smile. "If I could sleep, I would relax." Her eyelashes fluttered. "And you might like that."

He eyed the four corners of the room. "Where did you get that?"

"My doctor. It's to help me sleep, but I don't like to give them to myself."

"What about the other pills you took? Did Dr. Feelgood tell you to take them too?"

"No. Another doctor. Dr. McCoy. But I sleep better with both."

Bobby rocked uncertainly on the heels of his Jack Purcells, fists jammed in his pants' pockets.

Marilyn turned on her knees on the bed and raised the hem of her white robe. She wore no underwear. Her smooth flesh glowed auburn in the candlelight. She bent forward with a sly grin. Bobby's heart was pounding.

"Right." He gulped his Scotch, then took the glycerin bullet from her. "I'll play doctor."

Moments later, they were curled up on the bed, her head on his chest. But the blood that had flowed to his groin no longer mattered. Bobby blacked out.

At 11:46 p.m., the beeping of the phone off the hook woke him. Nearly all the candles had gone out, but he could still see Marilyn, eyes staring wide open, clutching the receiver. Bobby groaned, fighting torpor, and sat up. He nudged her gently.

"Honey, you okay?" Drool slid down her chin, she was gasping for breath now. "Oh God…." He switched on a lamp. Her skin had a bluish tint.

Bobby stumbled out the door and onto the pebbled driveway. He wove his black Cadillac down Fifth Helena Drive. He pulled over at a pay phone on San Vicente and called Mickey Rudin, Marilyn's lawyer, at home.

"Get as far away as you can. I'll handle this."

Back in the car, on the seat beside him, lay the red leather diary he'd grabbed from Marilyn's bedroom. At Jack's request, he would burn it in a fire on the beach in Hyannis Port the next weekend.

Bobby turned the key in the ignition. An ambulance shot past him on Wilshire as he tried to put the car in gear, but his legs were shaking too badly, so he sat and breathed deeply.

In the few years left to him, summoning his courage would become commonplace.

## 2.

It was a shiny new decade. America shimmered with the promise of a handsome young president, who was a Harvard-smart war hero with a bold agenda and a pedigreed wife. The Second World War was over; both enemies and allies were now our trading partners. There was nothing the U.S. couldn't do. The moon would come to us and the world would fear the tail of our comet.

Sprawled in a coastal basin of lush green, golden light, and crumbling desert, purchased at gunpoint from Mexico, blessed with oil (if not water), California and especially Los Angeles with its neighborhoods named after hills (Hollywood, Holmby, Beverly—keep climbing) was our Mecca. In the 1960's, every image, every song, anything or anyone new or beautiful came from here or came to here like rain to earth. LA was the pulse of the American dream, even if it had no heart.

Poolside, Dr. Wiley McCoy took another toke of hash and rolled onto his stomach. *Does it get any better than this?* The sun was shining, it was a dry eighty-two degrees and The Chiffons were singing *One Fine Day* on the radio.

He was preparing a student lecture. He read aloud from his notes. "Magic is only that which science has yet to claim: poppies to morphine; mold to penicillin; hand washing and the germ theory. It is the space between miracle and cause and effect. It is the ever-peeling cosmic onion, orbiting for the good of mankind." *Yes, that's good.*

Ten palm trees, five on each side, reflected across the water's blue surface disappearing behind his roofline (designed to "mimic a French chateau yet retain a certain California sleekness"). McCoy smiled, recalling the real estate agent who showed him his house. Most of her clients were movie stars, she'd confided.

"Most of mine are, too." Eyes twinkling, he assessed her C+ boob job. "Just show me what you'd show them."

*One fine day, you're gonna want me for your girl....*

A successful surgeon at thirty-eight, he had a big house in Holmby Hills, a nifty fifty stock portfolio and a gleaming silver Jaguar XK-SS that smelled of leather and Canoe, his favorite aftershave. His patients were politicians, pro athletes, A-list entertainers, and television and movie moguls. He'd even treated Howard Hughes on occasion. And Marilyn (*poor Marilyn...*).

McCoy's female patients whispered that he looked like Steve McQueen, presently roaring across movie screens on his motorcycle in *The Great Escape*. McCoy was tall with a brooding look, perpetually fit from swimming fifty laps a day, every day, and graced with a compelling personality. People trusted him instantly. They told secrets and fears they normally shared only with a priest or a psychiatrist. He exuded concern and an obsessive dedication to healing. That said, the uncomfortable truth – and it did make him uncomfortable when he was drunk or stoned enough – was that much of his success was his prescription pad. His patients lived in a world of stress and calamity. They needed relaxation, sleep, freedom from the daily career warfare that was Hollywood Babylon. Dr. McCoy was there to help. Chloral hydrates to sleep, amphetamines to wake, and everything necessary (or desired) to survive in Tinseltown.

He'd been through bad times, too. Suzanne divorced him and took their son Stephen to live with her and the attorney she was sleeping with. When her drinking became too much, the shyster left them and now Suzanne was alone. Stephen was in a boarding school. Alimony and child support were the price of starting over. McCoy had married young, then chose career over family. Suzanne put on weight. He'd played around.

Sometimes, to play up his sensitive side to an interested woman, he would express regret that Stephen couldn't have a normal home life when, in truth, McCoy's limited child visitation rights (obligations?) gave him more time to play. Stephen seemed happy, even well adjusted. His fragile childhood would probably produce an extraordinary adult. *After all, I was the product of a broken home.* McCoy's patrician lawyer father died when McCoy was barely a teenager and left him to fend for himself with his overwhelmed mother in Manhattan. *Now that was hard and it hadn't hurt me.*

*As long as children are loved, they're fine.*

The blue reflection stirred. Katie Quinn stepped onto the patio, still on the phone, the wire trailing behind her high heels clacking on the tiles. She'd felt dizzy and anxious all morning. This conversation wasn't helping.

"No Tony, Spahn Ranch won't cut it. This is a PJ Lorillard commercial. We need a Western set, not a plywood dude ranch. What's *Gunsmoke* doing next week? Can we get stage 7? Even for a morning?"

Katia had been a Las Vegas magician's assistant, now, barely thirty; she was a TV commercial producer -- one of the few successful women in the business.

"So call them, Tony. Please. I'll love you forever, hon." She hung up the phone, rolling her eyes at McCoy. "Do I have to cut his food for him too?"

She tossed her blonde hair back, and undid her bright orange bikini top. She was hungry. She was always hungry. It was how she kept her figure.

"Simon's here," McCoy said without rolling over. "He sold me a lid." Simon Bolivar (*that can't really be his name*) was McCoy's pool man. He dealt cannabis and wore all white.

"Oh shit." Katie covered her chest and looked around. A car pulled away at the front of the house.

"That's him leaving." McCoy smiled.

The Ronettes were singing *Be My Baby* now. She tossed her top next to the Sunday *New York Times* piled on the umbrella-covered table. McCoy had started his morning reading about desegregation in New Orleans's schools, the letter to President Kennedy proposing a negotiated truce in Vietnam, and a U.S. satellite crash landing on the moon. The crossword puzzle page lay open. As usual, he'd completed it in ink.

He sat up. Katie's breasts were pale against her tan skin as she lay on the lounger next to his. He took another toke and passed the pipe to her. He had cut back on alcohol because it didn't mix well with cannabis. Sometimes he wondered if he should cut back on cannabis too.

"Stop staring." She inhaled the loamy smoke, adjusting her

sunglasses.

"It's a compliment." *She looks like a Playboy centerfold.* "You should have let them photograph you."

Katie had been approached by one of Hugh Hefner's scouts.

"Why? So you could feel good and my clients could think I'm a whore?" She primped, breasts swaying. "These will sag in a few years, but my bank account won't."

"That's why I love you, Katie. You're smart."

*No you don't.* She stuck her tongue out at him. *You just love fucking me. For now.*

He almost said 'I really do love you. I'm happy when I'm with you and a little sad when I'm not', but he didn't.

He would remember that.

They'd been together nearly a year. Content, but not yet trusting. Two professionals, too career-distracted to hear their hearts.

She leaned across him to turn up the radio. Bobby Darrin was singing about a fool in love. It made her sad.

"Can you rub oil on me?" he asked.

'Sure. Gosh, you 're burning up." Katie gently smeared Coppertone on McCoy's chest. He placed his palm on her thigh, peering at her over his Ray Bans. She followed his gaze to his madras trunks.

"Oh, look what I've done now…" Massaging the fragrant oil into his stomach, her fingers slipped lower. He pulled her close, kissed her. She tasted like cloves. He nuzzled her neck, enjoying the Chanel she wore behind each ear. Fighting back tears he didn't notice, Katia woozily watched the reflection in the pool of their lovemaking.

## 3.

Dusk after a day of rain. Cedars-Sinai Medical Center loomed overhead, an Art Deco cathedral. McCoy, still wearing scrubs, walked slowly across the parking lot, his PF Flyers sticking to the wet asphalt with every tired step. He'd been up at five, showered, shaved, kissed a still sleeping Katie, then drove to Cedars where he removed Mr. Zanuck's pancreatic cyst at 6 a.m. and visited patients' bedside until 11a.m., then held office hours until 4 p.m. and lectured Mo Breslin's interns on the resilience of the human liver until 6:30 p.m. and then rushed back to the operating room he'd been in twelve hours earlier to re-stitch a schizophrenic who'd pulled out his sutures in an attempt to touch his own stomach. McCoy was drained.

Inside his Jaguar was cool and dry; its leather smell revived him. He stopped at a light and put down the top, hoping wind in his face would keep him awake. He'd bailed on his plan to have a drink with Mo and one of his interns. He thought about calling Katie to tell her he'd be right home after all, but decided to surprise her. She'd complained of a stomachache when they spoke earlier. She'd cancelled her appointments and spent the day in bed reading *Gone with the Wind*.

He stopped at Schwab's in West Hollywood and picked her up a bottle of Pepto-Bismol and a tube of Ipana before heading home. He dozed off at a light on Beverly Boulevard and was jerked awake by a horn blast. An Asian woman in hair curlers was staring at him. She honked again when he turned off on Santa Monica. He'd forgotten to signal.

A green Mustang with a spoiler was in his driveway next to Katie's MG. McCoy was a great judge of Los Angeles vehicles. In show business, a car said more about a person than their face. This was an actor's car. Definitely. Sporty, but still domestic. Not a star, but a working actor. With an agent.

Who was visiting Katie? He crossed the flagstones to his bougainvillea-draped front door, which was jerked open by a muscular man who collided with him. McCoy caught the scent of Aramis.

"Hey," McCoy said. "Who the fuck are you?"

"Just leaving. Ciao." The Mustang spat gravel as it sped away.

Katie was on the stairs in her bathrobe. Her hair was mussed, lipstick smeared. She looked stoned and just-fucked.

"Who was that?" McCoy was exhausted, still dressed in his hospital greens and clutching the Schwab's bag.

Her eyes focused on him, "Jeff. He's a friend. An actor. He was just on *77 Sunset Strip*."

"He was in a hell of a hurry."

"He made a pass at me. I told him to leave. Then you showed up."

*Is she lying?* He studied her face, remembering the morning Suzanne told him she knew about Judy, the oncology nurse. *Christ! Is this happening to me now?!* He hurled the paper bag across the foyer. The Pepto-Bismol exploded in a pink splatter. Katie was back up the stairs. She slammed the bedroom door. Then locked it. He grabbed the banister, and vaulted up the stairs two steps at a time.

"Open the door, Katie."

"Not if you're going to wreck the room."

"I won't. I promise." *God, I'd like to though.*

Footsteps, a click, the door swung open. She was sitting on the unmade bed looking angry, as though he'd done something wrong.

"What're you so pissed off about?" he asked.

"Wiley, I don't feel well. Please...."

"How the hell do you think I feel?"

Her hand toyed nervously with the edge of a blue pillowcase. She backed into the corner as he grabbed the patchwork quilt and ripped the covers off. There was a wet stain near the center of the bottom sheet.

"Aw Jesus, Katie."

"Wiley, that's not what you think it is. I threw up..." She was hugging herself; eyes squeezed shut, like a kid making a birthday wish. "What do you want me to do? I can't stay here if you won't trust me."

"I don't know." His knees were shaking.

"Do you want me to leave?"

"No. I want you to marry me so we can have kids and grow old together." *Shouldn't have said that...*

Katie reeled into the bathroom. He could hear her getting sick inside.

Downstairs, he poured three fingers of J&B and lay back in the Saarinen chair he and Katie had bought together. He listened to the sounds of her packing. *If we break up, who gets to keep this chair?* He heard her make a phone call, then watched her lug her suitcase and an overstuffed shopping bag down the stairs.

"Cissy'll be here in a few minutes. I'm going to stay with her in Laurel Canyon."

"Good idea."

She stood in the doorway. "Jeff came over uninvited to return a script. He wouldn't leave. Finally, I had to tell him to." Katie's voice was quavering. "Oh Wiley. You're being a moron."

But he kept seeing Katie and Jeff rutting on the bed. He hated her. "I loved you," he said, baffled. Wrong again.

The doorbell rang. He wouldn't look at her. He heard the door opening and Cissy murmuring outside. He took another sip of his drink. A car started up.

She was gone.

## 4.

It was a full moon. McCoy flicked on the pool lights. The water was dappled with dead leaves and insects. He hadn't been for a swim since Katie left. He dipped the long-handled net into the water. Inside, Dave Brubeck's *Brandenburg Gate* was playing on the hi-fi. Its soaring piano always made him sad.

He scooped out leaves and made a pile for Simon Bolivar to deal with in the morning.

No cooking smells, no piles of scripts and Hollywood Reporters, no girly clutter in the bathroom. The house felt empty. Her absence stung.

Chilly, he pulled his jean jacket collar up, sat down on a lounger and took another sip of Scotch. He'd gone back to booze. Not a good sign.

When McCoy moved out on Suzanne and Stephen, she sent him a greeting card. "It takes two hands to build a house. It takes love to build a home," was crossed out and "Bastard!" was written below.

Mist rose off the pool.

*You have failed at this twice now. Wise up. You'll always be alone.*

Inside, the phone rang, and he felt the dread and excitement he'd felt every time it'd rung for the past two nights, thinking it might be her—tearful, repentant. This time it was.

"Wiley?"

"Yes." His anger was back.

"Please don't hang up."

"I'm not going to hang up. Why would I hang up? Jesus, Katie...." He walked the phone back out to the patio like she used to do.

"Wiley, I'm sick. It's my stomach. I went to the doctor yesterday and he said I have to have an operation."

"What doctor? What kind of operation?"

"Dr. Morrissey...?"

"Sure. Phil Morrissey. He's a good man. What did he tell you?"

"He says I have to have my gallbladder taken out. There's stones in it." She sounded frightened and very far away.

"That's all right. A cholecystectomy's a simple operation. Like having your appendix out. Phil's a capable surgeon. He'll do a good job...."

"No."

"No?"

"I want you to do it."

"Katie. That's not a good idea...."

"Wiley, please. I don't want anybody else to touch me. You know how I am about hospitals and stuff. Please, baby. I'm sorry about what you think happened." Silence. "I'm begging you."

Was it over between them? He wasn't sure, and her helplessness was irresistible. *Don't do this. You shouldn't do this.*

"If I do this for you, and I'm not saying I will, it's because we used to be friends." *God, that sounded stupid.*

"We can still be friends." Her voice was tiny and scared.

He let that statement hang in the air, then made up his mind. "Now listen to me, Katie. Stay off your feet and get a good night's sleep. Did Phil give you anything for the pain?"

"Yes. I'm taking something every four hours."

"Fine. I'll call him in the morning and get your X-rays. I'll schedule surgery as soon as possible in the next few days."

"Okay." She was holding back a sob.

"I'll call you first thing. Don't worry."

"Wiley?" There was shame in her voice. "I appreciate your help."

"That's okay. Get some sleep."

He hung up and sat staring into the pool. *I'm a chump.* He

stood, stripping off his clothes. *I should not have said yes. No good deed ever goes unpunished.*

He dove naked into the water and swam his fifty laps.

Phil Morrissey called the next morning.

"You know her too well. Wiley. It's like she's family. What if you get emotional?"

"I won't. You worry too much. She's just another abdomen."

"You're an experienced surgeon, Wiley. But if she were my ex-girlfriend you'd be cutting her open, not me."

I know. You're right. "It'll be fine, Phil. Thanks for your concern."

McCoy looked over her X-rays that afternoon and, as he'd expected, concurred with Morrissey's diagnosis. Her gallbladder had at least three stones and her white blood cell count was way up. Surgery was necessary.

He pulled a few strings at Cedars, got her admitted to a private room and scheduled the procedure for 7a.m. the next morning

He stopped in that evening on his rounds. Ponytail, no make-up, Katie was sitting in bed performing magic tricks for her duty nurse. Baskets and vases of bright flowers were everywhere. *I should have sent some.* But then he remembered.

Katie was studying the cards fanned on the overbed table. Suddenly, she reached up and pulled one from behind the nurse's ear. "Six of spades. Is this your card?" The nurse gasped.

McCoy examined Katie. The scent of her Chanel caused a wave of sadness. She'd been reading *Time* magazine.

"The cigarette science gets scarier every day. I'm not going to produce any more tobacco commercials. When they call, I'll turn them down."

"That's brave. Lorillard's your biggest client."

"Sometimes change is good."

He ignored her pointed look. "You're pale."

"Am I? It's probably just the light."

He didn't look up from her chart. "No. It's you. But you're not yellow. You're lucky. This could've turned into jaundice."

He finished probing her belly with his fingers, then stood. It was awkward. He flashed a professional smile. "Get some rest."

"Don't go yet."

"No, I have to." He checked his Rolex.

"Oh Christ, Wiley, can't we talk?" Her eyes were moist. "I miss you."

She pulled the sheet up to her chin. He took her hand. Her nails were fire engine red.

He wanted to say "I miss you, too," but because she was his patient now, he said, "Listen to me. You need to get better... and we need some distance." He exuded disengagement, competence and reassurance: the doctor's trifecta. He would remember that.

*What am I doing? Call Phil Morrissey right now and have him sub.*

"I'm just so scared, Wiley."

"Of course you are. In a few days you'll be out of here and back to Emma." Katie was writing a screenplay about Emma Goldman, a 19th- century New York socialist and revolutionary.

"I'll take good care of you." He patted her hand. "Sweet dreams, kiddo."

Woozy with medication, Katie shuddered off to sleep.

## 5.

McCoy had just extricated himself from a pouting petroleum heiress so improved from her surgery that she was trying to order cocktails from her nurse, when the PA system blared: "Dr. McCoy. Fourth floor nurses' station."

It was Mr. Hurok, with severe chest pains. When McCoy put his stethoscope to the man's ribs, he screamed.

"Jesus, Doc. I can't...I can't...." The old man's eyes were glassy, skin moist, turning blue.

It took nearly two hours to stop his aorta from hemorrhaging. A graft, replacing the ruptured section with a Teflon component, attaching a tiny material tube onto the artery with minute stitches.

"It's like sewing a garden hose out of macaroni," McCoy said, sighing. Exhaustion blurred his vision.

It was 3 a.m. when McCoy finished speaking with a grateful Mrs. Hurok and shuffled into the doctor's lounge. No time to go home, rest, and change clothes. Falling asleep on a vinyl sofa, he thought again about asking Morrissey to sub in the morning. No, it was too late. It was – really, it was – a simple procedure. *I'm the best. I can do this in my sleep*, he thought as he floated into a dream.

He was running barefoot through a jungle pursued by naked men hurling spears and firing arrows at him. Suddenly, he tripped on a root and they were on him, lifting his arms, lashing his hands, then his feet to a long wooden pole. They dragged him through the underbrush to a hut in a clearing. The air stank of feces and dead leaves. They sank his pole into the ground so that he hung upright, suspended from his bleeding wrists.

Katie was on a platform in the center of the clearing. A shiny-muscled giant holding a machete, his chest striped white and purple, watched the other savages tie her down. They all wore green cotton surgical masks. The one with the blade raised it above his head chanting "J'ai eno, j'ai mau mau, j'ai eno evil!" McCoy struggled against his ropes, but couldn't get free. He screamed as the machete swung in a flashing arc onto Katie's abdomen.

"Dr. McCoy?"

A Black face covered in a surgical mask was pressed close to his. It was Marie Laveau, the scrub nurse who would assist him with Katie's cholecystectomy. He sat up, suddenly aware of his body odor.

Nurse Laveau made him uncomfortable. She always seemed angry, resentful. He'd mentioned it once to Doc Friday, the hospital's resident pathologist, a Jamaican.

"She's Haitian and from New Orleans. They're all like that."

"Oh, come on. You sound like George Wallace."

"I've heard her talking to Shongo, I've seen her taking chicken bones from the cafeteria garbage." McCoy looked incredulous. "Oh, she's a decent nurse and what she does on her own time is her business. But she's a voodoo priestess. That's her secret, white boy." He chuckled. "Voodoo."

McCoy stood and yawned. Nurse Laveau was staring at his hands.

"I'll be right in to scrub up. Please tell Dr. Selzer to sedate the patient as soon as they bring her in." *So I won't have to speak with her until this is over.*

"Yes, doctor."

She walked away, shoes squeaking on the linoleum. McCoy looked at his fingers as he scrubbed up and wondered what she'd found so fascinating.

Katie was already under from the Pentothal.

"Good morning, doctor."

"Morning Sam. Piece of cake today."

Sam Selzer carefully slid the hosed mask over Katie's face. He and McCoy had worked together many times. McCoy liked him. Nurse Laveau unsnapped Katie's gown to bare her chest to the waist. With a gauze square dipped in reddish brown liquid she painted Katie's right side from above her breast to below her navel, cleaning the area for surgery. Dr. Selzer squinted at a dial on a tank before him and adjusted the halothane valve. He smiled, satisfied.

*Sam's the best*, McCoy thought, stifling a yawn. *I'm glad he's with me today.*

"Ready any time, doctor," Nurse Laveau's eyes gazed at him above her mask.

"Let's go."

McCoy selected a scalpel. He felt Katie's flesh below her right rib with his free hand, pierced her with the cool blade. He cut a smooth longitudinal incision in her upper abdomen about six and a half inches long.

"Like butter," he murmured. "How am I doing, Sam?"

"She's breathing like a baby."

Nurse Laveau handed McCoy a clamp with which he held open the wound while he located Katie's gallbladder with his finger. He cut into the bile duct, then carefully removed four gallstones before draining it with a T-tube. Somebody spoke softly. He looked up at Nurse Laveau.

"Excuse me?"

"I didn't say anything, doctor."

McCoy looked over at Sam, who shook his head, then back at Nurse Laveau who was staring at his right hand. The hand that held the scalpel.

"Let's cut the thing out and close her up." He was fighting back a yawn.

McCoy located the part of the bile duct that forked off into Katie's gallbladder and severed it neatly with his scalpel.

"...eno, mau mau, eno evil...."

He glanced at Nurse Laveau. Her lips weren't moving at all. He looked down at the seething gallbladder. His wrist jerked like a fish on a hook and his scalpel nicked Katie's liver. *Oh Christ.*

His wrist moved again, like a spasm, teasing the blade into her duodenum. Blood spritzed onto his gown.

"Wiley!" Sam was peering into the wound. "What the fuck are you doing?"

"Get out of the light, Sam. Suction please."

Nurse Laveau placed the catheter tip into Katie's abdomen. Sam twisted the oxygen valve.

Beep...beep...beep....

The electrocardiogram was sounding at longer intervals.

"She's slowing down."

*Oh, my God.*

"Give me a suture. I'll fix this."

"She's losing blood, Doctor," Nurse Laveau said.

"She's hemorrhaging!

"Take it easy, Wiley."

"Fill her up, Goddammit. She needs blood!"

Nurse Laveau attached a fresh bag, squeezing its plastic sides to get it started.

Katie's skin was gray, clammy now. "Pressure's very low," Sam said.

*I've never seen bleeding like this. Why doesn't it stop? It's like she's a hemophiliac!*

Forcing himself to be calm, McCoy worked efficiently and quickly to stitch closed the wounds he'd made when his scalpel slipped. *Slipped?* He administered Dextran to expand Katie's circulating blood volume, but her state of shock was severe.

Her insides expelled blood faster than they could pump it into her. The electrocardiogram stopped beeping.

Katie was gone.

## 6.

Katie's parents, George and Mira, were waiting in the hospital solarium. McCoy had met them only once when Katie brought him home for dinner. They stood and smiled anxiously. Mira had spilled something on her dress; George was trying to wipe it. "How's our girl?"

"There was a complication," McCoy's knees were shaking. *Oh, God, how do I say this?*

"Do you mean... Katie's not okay?" Mira's face was suddenly red. George put his hands on her shoulders to steady her.

"No, she's not. She didn't pull through." He felt like a murderer.

Mira was struggling to breathe. Her husband helped her to the sofa. A nurse brought cups of water and tranquilizers.

"Take these. They'll help."

His heart pounding, McCoy carefully described what happened: he'd tried to suture the wounds, they'd kept the blood transfusion going, but it was no good. Katie had felt no pain, not even at the end.

"Something happened to my hand." McCoy was looking George in the eye. His voice cracked. Mira was wailing.

Her father whirled to face him. "I know you didn't mean to do it...but I hate you."

McCoy's exhaustion, and sorrow overcame his self-control. He began to sob. And then he just walked away.

Dr. Blackmar, chief surgeon at Cedars, told him to take a few days off, and he did, but it didn't help. He drove aimlessly in his XK-SS, out to Malibu, up towards Carmel, anywhere. Once, in the middle of the night, he started for San Francisco, but an hour out of Los Angeles he had to pull over, because he was weeping uncontrollably. He kept seeing Dr, Selzer and Nurse Laveau staring at him over their surgical masks, and then looking down again at his patient. He remembered Katie, smiling in bed in the morning. She liked to wake up first and watch him sleep. She always woke up happy.

He visited Janice Kelsey, a neurologist near Studio City. Could his wrist jerking have been an epileptic episode even though he had no history of it, and there was none in his family?

She examined him thoroughly.

"There's nothing wrong with you. Nothing physical."

He was dressed again and sitting in her office. "I didn't think so but I wanted to be sure."

"You need rest, Wiley. I'd like to prescribe a tranquilizer." *Serves me right.*

"No thanks, Janice. I'll be fine. I just have to understand what happened on that table."

"You've been working very hard. That can affect people...."

"You think I cracked under pressure? During surgery?"

Janice shrugged.

"I wish I could believe that."

He drove home, poured himself a Remy and sat on the sofa. The pool shimmered outside. *I should swim. I should drown.*

"*J'ai eno, j'ai mau mau...*" He was talking to himself. He stopped, frightened. He'd never done that before.

McCoy sat back in his womb chair and flicked on the TV. Bud Collier was giving a contestant a prize on *Beat the Clock.* Music segued to a beautiful model displaying her legs. It was a commercial Katie produced for No-Run stockings.

*I fucking killed her.* He took another sip of his drink. My knife shouldn't have slipped and, even if it did, she shouldn't have bled like that. We gave her vitamin K before she went under. She didn't have a blood disorder....

## 7.

He didn't go to her funeral. He sent flowers instead, red carnations, her favorite. He tried to compose a note to her parents but couldn't find the right way to say, "I'm sorry I killed your daughter."

McCoy's attorney called the next day. The Quinns were suing him, his malpractice carrier, and Cedars-Sinai Medical Center for two million dollars.

Doc Friday's autopsy report cited cause of death as "hemorrhaging as a result of two scalpel wounds, one in the liver and one in the duodenum, possibly accidental." Dr. Blackmar suspended McCoy's hospital privileges indefinitely and ordered an inquiry into Katie's death.

"I don't have a choice, Wiley. I'm sorry." The old doctor leaned in; bifocals perched at the tip of his red nose.

"I know. I understand." McCoy avoided his gaze. Blackmar *looked like Santa Claus but without a beard. Or presents.*

"You're lucky this isn't a murder charge."

"Yes, I'm lucky." *I'm lucky?*

"What the hell happened?"

"I don't know."

"Wiley, were you drunk?"

"Certainly not. It was seven in the morning."

"You know the rule: twelve hours from bottle to throttle. Were you drunk?"

"Did somebody say I was drunk?"

He hesitated. "No. But I had to ask again."

"I hardly ever drink," McCoy lied. "I was up all night with a vein graft and I was very tired. Maybe I was too tired. My scalpel...slipped, but that shouldn't have killed her. It was the bleeding. It wouldn't stop."

Blackmar held up the autopsy report.

"Your scalpel slipped twice."

"That's right."

"In all my years, Wiley, I've never heard of a scalpel slipping twice. Not in the same patient. You're an excellent surgeon. Up until three days ago, you might have been the best surgeon we had. We're all going to miss you, because unless you come up with something better than 'my scalpel slipped', your career in California is over." His eyes dropped. "The California Medical Board wants to schedule a hearing. Do you have a lawyer?"

"I have a lawyer."

But it was the last thing Dr. Blackmar told him that hurt the most. McCoy was standing to leave. Blackmar held McCoy's shoulder as he spoke.

"Did you know she was pregnant?" Their eyes met. "About five weeks."

*What?*" She never told me."

"She might not have known."

*Five weeks. It was mine. It had to be....*

An arrow through his heart.

*I couldn't forgive her for something she swore she didn't do. Then I killed her. And our child. How did I get to this place?*

When McCoy was ten, he and some boys were playing on the wharf where the Nantucket ferry docked, jumping from one cargo trolley to the next. McCoy misjudged his leap and badly cut his head. Blood everywhere. Dr. Merrick, a smiling New England G.P., cleaned the wound and stitched it shut.

*When I grow up, I'm going to be a doctor.*

The summer he turned sixteen, his mother took him to Paris (more a gift for her than for him). There was a small medieval painting at the Musee Jacquemart-Andre of a knight driving his lance through the heart of a dragon. For McCoy, the brave knight was a doctor and the fire-breathing dragon was ignorance and disease. He had marveled at the power of the image.

Andover, Dartmouth, then the College of Physicians and Surgeons at Columbia. In 1951, he began his residency. His first operation was an emergency appendectomy on a Bronx high schooler who collapsed in the E.R.

Nine weary months with the 31st Regiment, 7th Division near the front lines in west-central Korea: always hot and raining or about to rain; the stink of gunpowder, blood, dirt; so many wounded; a handful of medics; and the long nights, operating by truck light when the power failed again. Every life he touched convinced him that doctors were saints and saviors.

But now, ten years later, his science had failed him. Was he betrayed by magic or by his own hand?

*I was a doctor. I healed people. What am I now?*

On an angry impulse, he got off the elevator on the second floor and went to the nurses' station where a pretty Asian nurse sat behind the desk.

"Nurse Laveau's not on duty. I think she resigned."

"She quit?"

Her phone rang. "Try the office downstairs. They might know more than I do."

In administration, he was told Marie Laveau hadn't been in for several days.

"It's not like her. She's very reliable," the clerk offered.

"Ok. I wonder if you could help me then," McCoy smiled. "She asked me to let her know about one of my patients, and he's not doing so well. He's been asking for her."

"I can give you her home address and phone number, Dr. McCoy, but I don't think it'll help. We've been trying to reach her since Tuesday."

Tuesday was the day of Katie's operation.

She wrote the information on a piece of paper. "You can have mine, too, if you want it."

He smiled awkwardly. *Don't you know I'm the one doctor no one should date?*

## 8.

Crickets were chirping in the pink twilight as he drove slowly down Marie Laveau's West Hollywood street searching for the house number. It turned out to be a small detached cottage behind a ramshackle rooming house with scrawny hedges. There were no lights on.

He parked around the corner and called her from a pay phone. He let it ring for a long time before hanging up. He thought about trying again in the morning, but no, he wanted answers tonight.

*What are you looking for? A doll with pins in it?*

Every modern medical bone in his body denied that supernatural forces could have caused Katie's death; but magic was the only explanation left (other than personal error, which was unthinkable) and McCoy clung to it like a beggar with a lottery ticket.

He walked to the main house driveway, and then kept on the grass embankment so his footsteps wouldn't be heard on the gravel as he hurried past the lit ground-floor windows. There was music and talking inside. A woman was singing along with Ray Charles.

He crept onto Nurse Laveau's tiny porch and tried the door. It was open. *Not good.* He pulled a penlight from his windbreaker.

*This is crazy. You could get arrested.* He slipped inside.

A familiar overpowering stench. He covered his mouth to keep from gagging. *Something or someone was dead.*

When his eyes adjusted, he flicked on his penlight and swept it around the dark room once before shutting it off.

An old sofa was against one wall flanked by two armchairs and a coffee table piled high with magazines. A dining set with plastic-covered chairs stood against the opposite wall with a mold-specked unfinished meal on a plate next to half a glass of wine.

McCoy crossed the room and peered into the kitchen.

Roaches skittered over the grimy counter and hid in a pile of plates in the sink.

He moved through the living room into the bedroom. The death stink was more powerful now. Whatever it was was close.

The bedroom looked as though someone left in a hurry: a beat-up wooden bureau with its drawers pulled out, and the closet door open showing an empty rack of bare hangers. There was a large brownish stain at the center of the unmade bed. He walked cautiously around to the other side of the bed, certain he'd discover Nurse Laveau's body on the floor, but there was nothing. He raised his dim beam to the half-open bathroom door. It was the only room he hadn't been in.

The light in his hand went out. He flicked the switch back and forth but it was no use.

Slowly, the hairs on his neck prickling, he felt his way in the dark to the bureau; he'd seen a pack of matches lying there. He was about to light one when the front door opened and the living room light went on.

"Maria? You in here?"

A woman's voice. It sounds like the one he'd heard singing in the main house.

McCoy stepped into the bathroom and hid behind the half open door. It was pitch black and humid, and the stench of rotting flesh stung his nostrils like sulfur. *Whatever it is, is in here with me.*

He listened to the neighbor walk into the bedroom and flick on the light. Her footsteps approached the bathroom, then stopped.

"Maria? You on the pot?"

McCoy kept still, resisting the urge to open the door and bolt past Nurse Laveau's neighbor out of the cottage and back to his car. The bedroom light finally went off. He heard the front door shut, and then feet crunching outside on the gravel.

Fingers moist with sweat, he had to strike the match twice before it lit, and even then it went right out, but not before he saw two yellow eyes staring up at him out of a black face floating in the blood-streaked tub. He willed himself not to scream and flicked on the bathroom light.

A black house cat floated spread-eagled on its back with its throat cut. It had been dead for several days. McCoy shuddered, switched off the light and headed out into the other room.

At the front door, he felt a sudden compulsion to take another look in her kitchen. He lit a match and walked back to the cramped, little room.

The icebox. A smudgy mark: something was written on the door. He lit another match. It was a large letter "T" finger-painted in dried blood. A knot was tightening in his stomach.

*Don't be ridiculous. You've gotten this far. Open it.* He gripped the dirty chrome handle and pulled. A scuttling sound. Something shattered on the floor as the refrigerator light went on. The icebox was empty save for a jar of mayonnaise that had pitched out and lay in shards at his feet.

## 9.

The next day, Saturday, he awoke bathed in flop sweat.

He drove out to Dolphin Prep School near Big Sur to visit his fourteen-year-old son. Dolphin was a school for problem kids, the problems mostly being that their parents had no time for them.

Stephen McCoy looked at his father sitting next to him on the lawn overlooking the ocean behind the junior dormitory. He seemed older since the "accident" even though it had only been a few months.

"Dad, I don't really like girls."

McCoy chuckled, lighting a Tareyton. "Well you're young, you'll get used to them."

"No. You're not listening. I don't like girls that way."

"Ok, Stevie. Well, give it time. I'm sure when..."

Stephen was squeezing his arm. "I don't like girls. I like boys." he whispered.

"Oh." *Ohhh...* Their eyes locked. "You're sure?"

Stephen nodded. Resolute, but fearful.

McCoy was blindsided. *What do I tell him?*

"It wasn't a choice, Dad. Like not going out for football or something. I can't change myself."

"It's all right." *Oh my God...*

"This is who I am, Dad." Stephen was crying now. "I haven't told Mom. I had to tell someone...." McCoy hugged him, kissed his forehead. He pictured the grandchildren he'd never really thought about evaporating into thin air. He thought about Stephen's now limited life choices in 1960's America; and the senseless mean people he would have to endure. McCoy squeezed him harder.

"It's all right, bud." Now there were tears in his eyes. Stephen pulled away. Passers-by were staring.

"Jesus, Dad. It's okay. I'm a queer, not a Nazi."

McCoy caught the absurdity and smiled.

*He'll need more courage than a Navy Seal to survive what the world has in store for him.*

"Thank you for telling me."

"Unh huh" The boy didn't meet his eye.

"I'm proud of you."

"No, you're not. Don't say that."

McCoy looked at the son he'd thought he knew. "But I am."

"Just don't make a big deal out of it. And don't tell Mom. Ok?"

"Sure. I guess..."

*I failed at marriage. I failed at medicine.*

*How can I not fail at fatherhood?*

## 10.

McCoy's phone rang while he was shaving. He almost didn't answer it. Calls these days were usually too depressing: his lawyer with bad news or unpleasant questions about the malpractice suit; Mira Quinn once in the middle of the night, drunk, asking for her daughter. The towel slipped off his waist as he bounded into the bedroom and grabbed the receiver on the fifth ring. It was a middle-aged woman's voice, one of Howard Hughes' secretaries, summoning McCoy to the billionaire's side at the Beverly Hills Hotel. With Hughes, it was always urgent.

"Can you tell me what this is about?" McCoy asked wiping lime-scented lather off his cheek.

"He didn't say, Dr. McCoy. He just needs you. Immediately."

McCoy recalled the first time he met the billionaire. What is it about celebrated people that makes them glow and stand out in the crowd as though they were Hollywood lit? Texas tall, slim, with shiny hair and a debonair mustache left over from the 1940's, Howard Hughes had that pomaded aura. But the truth unpacked quickly. Scars, some twisted at the lumbar region and up to the shoulders explained the pin-prick irises and swallowed gasps, as the pain in nearly every movement rocked him, and made him long for relief or death.

In July 1946, Howard Hughes cartwheeled to smithereens the first prototype of his XF-11 reconnaissance aircraft on a golf course in Beverly Hills. He survived with a crushed collarbone, broken ribs and third-degree burns, and the price paid was near constant pain for which he sought relief from doctors, herbalists, quacks and finally, in 1961, from Dr. Wiley McCoy. By then, celebrity pain management had become McCoy's most lucrative sub-specialty.

A one-time prospect for the Los Angeles Rams, now a hunky parking lot attendant at the Brown Derby, told Howard, after he failed to climax in a limousine back seat blowjob, that he should see a doctor. "Really, Daddyo. You're in a bad way."

Howard was pressed akimbo into the black leather seat, sweating, wan, trousers puddling around his ankles.

"I wrecked my knee in a pile-up. The owner liked me. He sent me to see his doctor at Cedars. Fixed me like that!" The boy snapped his fingers and grinned. McCoy had given him a two-week regimen of codeine and Demerol with methadone, then weaned him off of the needle cocktail. He was "cured."

A different secretary had contacted McCoy's office the next day. A house call to Bungalow 4 at the Beverly Hills Hotel followed, where, as best he could, Wiley examined Hughes, buck naked except for black socks, while he talked on the phone. Then McCoy studied Hughes' X-rays.

The forty-six-year old's body had a put-back-together look, like a crumpled marionette. McCoy watched him pacing gingerly around the suite's living room, wincing when something within hurt. His mustache masked a burn welt on his upper lip. His pupils, perpetually dilated, watched McCoy from under a glistening brow as he shouted into the telephone. "The peas are grey! Tell the chef or whatever he is that peas are supposed to be *green*. Like the color of money. And they should all be the same size. Not big peas and little peas jumbled together." Hughes voice rose in intensity. "Am I making myself clear, Bill?!" He slammed down the phone and looked at McCoy. "I'm sorry. I can get overwrought." The billionaire sneered. "But if not me now, who when?" His eyes glowed in triumph.

"You may get dressed, Mr. Hughes. I think I can help you."

Hughes considered the proposition. "I'll stay naked. It's my house." He stood, hands on his hips, appraising Wiley. His penis was slightly erect. "What makes you think you're different from the other doctors who've tried to help me?"

McCoy steepled his fingers. "Many of my patients are high-functioning prominent individuals who choose to lead demanding lives even though they suffer from near-debilitating physical or emotional pain. I'm the reason they're high functioning, Mr. Hughes. I understand pain. I served in a MASH unit in Korea. I only wish I had then the drugs I can prescribe today. There's a whole new world of relief out there, Howard. May I call you Howard?"

Hughes sat in an armchair and crossed his legs. "Please do."

"I can take the edge off of your discomfort and keep you clear-headed, or I can eliminate your discomfort and let you sleep. Those are the outer limits. Once I determine your medication tolerance, you'll tell me where you want to be."

McCoy took an alcohol rub out of his black bag and swabbed Hughes' forearm. He tore the wrapper off a disposable syringe, then administered a slow injection. He patted Hughes' shoulder.

"I have one rule, Howard."

"What's that? I don't like rules." His eyes were glassy now.

"I have to see you no less than once a month. I will not treat you if I cannot see you. Will that be a problem, Howard? I know you don't like to see people..."

Hughes' smile was a dreamy smudge. There was a tap at the

door and William Gay, fortyish and dressed in beige and a white short sleeve shirt, wheeled in a cart with a covered silver platter. McCoy walked to the door.

"Good night, Howard. I'll call tomorrow to see how you're doing." But Hughes ignored him, transfixed by the steaming mound of same-sized green peas before him.

Now, years later, McCoy selected a white shirt, lightweight gray flannels, Gucci loafers and a brass-buttoned blue blazer. No tie. His bag was packed with fresh ampules and BD PlastiPaks, the latest in disposable syringes. *God only knows what he wants....*

McCoy recalled an incident only a few months after he'd begun treating the billionaire.

"I need fresh blood, Wiley. Good blood. You follow me?"

"Of course, Howard." It was always best to agree with him. Hughes peered at him, flinty eyed over his famous black mustache.

"It's gotta be type A, negative West Coast college-educated white man's blood."

McCoy took a deep breath, then chose his words carefully.

"There is no data to support the idea that replacing your blood will improve your health. With all due respect, Howard, consult anyone. That's what they'll tell you."

But Hughes insisted, and his money was irresistible, so McCoy called around and found a pathologist in Salt Lake City to administer the unorthodox blood-gathering program.

Hughes spent over ten thousand dollars each month for a complete transfusion, flushing out his old blood and pumping in new, until after about six months he realized the futility (or grew bored or distracted) and discontinued the treatments

## 11.

Hughes' Cadillac was parked outside Bungalow 4. Two of its tires were flat. A large man in an ill-fitting suit led McCoy into the sun-streaked living room. Hughes sat behind a black lacquer desk stirring his coffee. He was pomaded and freshly shaved in a dark blue suit with a shimmering silver tie.

"Good morning, Dr. McCoy." His silky Texan voice turned

even a simple greeting into a command. "Long time no see." A hungry smile.

"Hello, Howard." McCoy quickly assessed Hughes' condition: good color, eyes bright. "What's going on?" He exuded concern and competence.

Hughes led him over to facing red brocade sofas separated by a white marble table. Bill Gay wheeled in a beverage cart. McCoy noticed Hughes was barefoot as he took off his suit jacket and handed it to Gay. When he leaned close, he smelled like licorice.

"I'm going to tell you a story and I know you'll tell me what you think." He was rolling up his sleeve. "You're not a suck-up, Wiley. May I call you Wiley today? After what happened, I'm a little uncomfortable calling you 'Doctor'."

That stung. He valued his famous patient. *Have he lost him too?*

But Hughes didn't go there. Instead he told McCoy a story.

Hughes had met a man—a sort of scientist and mystic—who claimed he could make Hughes immortal. "Now how about that!?" He smiled confidently, like a man about to patent pantyhose. Then an uncomfortable silence. McCoy noticed Hughes' toenails were curling and discolored.

"That's it?"

Hughes nodded expectantly. McCoy swabbed the billionaire's proffered forearm with alcohol. *Why are guys with too much money never content?* "Look, Howard, whoever this guy is—he's a fake. There's no such thing as eternal life or life after death." He jabbed the needle.

Hughes winced. "Until there is...." He stroked his mustache blankly. "I'd be grateful if you'd meet with him. He's a very persuasive man. Half-Haitian, half-Cuban."

"And all fraud." McCoy applied a Band-Aid to the injection site.

"I've heard about your recent difficulties and I'm sorry."

"Thank you. I'm sure it'll all be straightened out."

"Maybe. Maybe not. You killed a patient." Hughes smiled dreamily. "That's hard to forgive."

Hughes lay back on the sofa, his pain managed now. "I need you to be open-minded. Curious. Non-judgmental." He waved his hand grandly; his gold pinkie ring glistened in the sun. "I'd like you to keep working for me, and I'll pay you well."

"I don't understand."

"Wiley, I have spent the past fifteen year trying to outrun constant pain. I have sought relief from celebrated doctors, of which you are...were... one...." He groaned, grabbing the sofa arm to sit up. Gay helped him sip orange juice. Hughes wiped his dripping mustache with the back of his hand.

"He had the XF-11 dream again last night," Gay whispered, rolling his eyes.

Hughes exhaled a sob. "That fucking dream!"

It was always the same: first the dropping needle on the oil gauge, then the juddering and sudden loss of altitude. *Golf course, steer for the golf course!* But...too late! Impact, flames, crawling out of the broken hatch, his pant leg catching on a glass shard. Then Sergeant Durkin, lifting him under the arms, saying, "Okay, buddy. Okay, buddy..."

Hughes leaned forward in his seat holding McCoy's gaze. "I am a victim of serial pain management. I take one painkiller, or a combination of painkillers, and become addicted. So I switch to another set, then get hooked on that. It's never-ending."

McCoy's shame must have shown on his face.

"Look at me, Wiley. I'm a guy who doesn't settle. In the hospital, I didn't like my bed so I designed a better one for burn patients. Now everyone uses it. Everyone. I founded the Howard Hughes Medical Institute: hundreds of doctors and researchers. But it hasn't helped me. Western medicine is limited by its self-imposed horizons. There's more out there than painkillers.... Please help me find it." Another sip of orange juice.

"All right, Howard. I'll have a look. But free of charge my advice is to forget it. Pain and death are part of life. You can't change that."

"I can change whatever I want, sonny!" Hughes snapped. Gay began massaging his shoulders, flashing McCoy a "see what I have to deal with" look. The billionaire exhaled, became calm again. "You may see things that'll surprise you. Things you can't explain." He paused for significance, and then farted quietly "That wasn't me." He leaned close over the table. "Never ever discuss me or my activities with outsiders." His pupils were tiny now. McCoy wondered if he should reduce the dosage.

"Well I wouldn't...."

But Hughes was staring out the window now. "You know, after you've seen what my associate on the high seas has accomplished, you might want to stay and work with him." A hopeful pause. "I'd like that very much."

*Would you? You're barking mad.*

"You'll meet him tonight," Hughes said cheerfully.

*On the high seas?*

McCoy was dismissed.

## 12.

A pink Los Angeles sunset smudged to darkness as one of the tycoon's staff of ex-movie stunt drivers drove McCoy to an isolated stretch of beach above Malibu, then wouldn't get out of the car. As Gay had instructed, McCoy, in sneakers and jeans now, walked down to the sea alone. A bare sliver of moon lit the sky. The Zodiac delivered McCoy through the darkness to the submarine with no markings.

*Oh God, where am I?*

McCoy descended into a brightly lit control room.

Welcome aboard, Dr. McCoy. I am Romulo DaVinci. I command this vessel."

Romulo was tall with nearly pretty features framed by straight black hair, cut short, military fashion.

McCoy shook his proffered hand automatically. "Where am I?"

A gracious smile with sharp little teeth. "Welcome to my home, Dr. McCoy." He bowed like a seigneur.

The compartment was hung overhead with pipes and cables. Screen-peering, dial-turning technicians, some seated, some standing, all were wearing the same jumpsuits as the men in the launch. The crew looked global: Filipinos, Asians, Hispanics. None of them met his gaze. *Are they afraid? Ashamed?* McCoy couldn't tell.

The sonar, radar and radar-jamming equipment all bore the Sperry Rand Corporation logo. At the control room's center, two identical leather-padded swivel seats with straps, like deep-sea fishing chairs, faced a pair of aircraft-type steering yokes. McCoy couldn't identify the rest of the equipment, all blinking multicolored lights, beeping and whirring over the hum of the HVAC system. The processed air had an electrical/mechanical smell.

*Must be a covert Navy operation. But why don't the uniforms look right?*

"Very impressive." *Christ. That sounded stupid.*

"Let me give you a tour. We have much to discuss." McCoy followed Romulo down the long narrow passageway, chilly from the air conditioning. "She's 278 feet long and 21 feet wide. She displaces 3,700 tons of water and takes a crew of up to 112 sailors and officers to operate her," he explained as they descended to the level below, "including you of course."

*Me?* McCoy tried not to look startled. Hughes must have told Romulo he'd already agreed to work with him. *The presumptuous bastard.*

They entered a relatively large compartment. Two Navy-issue armchairs flanked a sofa. There were magazine racks and a metal table for ten against one wall. Two noisy sailors, one with Rasta curls down his back, sat playing cards with piles of money on the table before them. "This is the officers' wardroom. I may convert it into a laboratory with an operating theater. That is, if Mr. Hughes...." Romulo was staring at him. "But you must be wondering about my work."

"I am," McCoy replied. Romulo's casual cheerfulness amazed him. He was like an IBM recruiter taking a promising grad student on a mainframe tour.

"There isn't a medical researcher in the world who wouldn't want to be standing where you are now...."

*Here we go*. "Unh huh...." McCoy smiled thinly.

"You think I'm mad or perhaps pathetic." A modest fanged smile. "That's all right. You have no reason to believe otherwise. Mr. Hughes told me you're an excellent surgeon. You will appreciate what I'm going to show you."

They walked along the middle deck aft of the crew quarters, sometimes passing chest- to-chest with seamen heading the other way in the narrow passage. Romulo described how he'd learned leaf medicines and spells from his Cuban mother and rudimentary modern medicine, human anatomy and basic surgery in the United

States Navy. McCoy was only half listening, distracted by brightly colored movements, then scratching sounds from the darkness over the ceiling pipes.

The sounds ceased as they entered sick bay. McCoy admired its efficient design. Cabinets and storage drawers lined the bulkhead; there was an operating table at the center of the compartment.

A fluttering sound overhead. *A bird? On a submarine?*

Romulo had rolled up his jumpsuit sleeves and was scrubbing his hands in a stainless steel sink. "What I'm going to show you is very basic. With better equipment...Well, you'll see."

McCoy watched Romulo remove several radio transmitter parts from a cabinet and attach them to wires running out from beneath two large objects covered with wet cloths on the operating table. He switched on the transmitter, and took out three bananas, still in their skins, and an orange from a small refrigerator. "They must be chilled to below 50 degrees to work." He partially pulled back the cloth covering the larger of the two objects revealing more wires in a large pan of liquid, which he plugged into the fruits.

*The miracle of fruit salad?* McCoy was grinning until Romulo removed the smaller of the wet cloths.

A grotesquely enlarged human heart, like a football, floated in a beaker of clear fluid. Plastic tubes ran from it to beneath the other wet cloth. The heart was beating, pumping blood through clear plastic "veins." McCoy got goose bumps.

*That's not possible.* He scanned the table for the inevitable evidence of trickery. *Okay. Nothing yet.*

Romulo removed the second cloth gingerly; it clung to the ears of a severed human head: a white man in his late thirties with a large hematoma on his right cheek. His long dark hair had continued to grow post mortem and hung like a wet curtain over his eyes. Romulo pushed it aside. Large leaves were pasted with a muddy substance over each eye like some prehistoric party mask. Romulo picked up a microphone connected to the transmitter. The blue dead lips quivered.

*Oh sweet Jesus... The poor bastard is alive!*

Romulo spoke into the microphone: "J'ai eno, J'ai mau mau..."

The lips of the sad face repeated barely audibly: "J'ai eno, J'ai mau mau..." as though from far away, and the words were familiar to McCoy.

"Stop it!"

Romulo lowered the microphone. "I'm sorry. Did I frighten you? I've been working all week with the muscles in his mouth and throat. I've even achieved mastication, although without a digestive tract ...."

"Did you kill him?"

Romulo looked puzzled. McCoy crouched, peered under the table beneath the head. Nothing: no cables, no mirrors, no puppeteers. It wasn't a trick.

"My crewmember lost his life, but I've been able to grant him an extension of sorts." Romulo looked modest as though he'd done something clever.

"How much of his nervous system is intact?" *What nervous system? He's just a head and a heart. And... fruit?*

"He feels nothing. I severed his cranial nerves, except for the accessory nerve so he can speak. I regret you find it cruel."

*From which zip code in hell did this guy spring?* "I'd like to return to shore now."

"As you wish." Romulo primly led him out of the compartment. They retraced their steps in silence. "You and I both know that you couldn't replicate what I just showed you."

"You're experimenting on human beings. You're at the very least committing atrocities that the Nazis—particularly Dr. Josef Mengele—were condemned for. I want nothing to do with you."

Romulo stopped. "I am not Mengele. Mengele was a sad butcher who maimed and killed children, Gypsies and Jews. He accomplished nothing. I am an immigrant, and like all immigrants, I do the work no one else will. Your American Medical Association is restrained by regulations and ethics that hold back progress. My ethics are those of the striver—I wish only to succeed. Mr. Hughes understands. I'm sorry you don't." He hesitated. "How to put this..." Then, forging ahead. "It's unfortunate that we didn't meet several months ago. Perhaps I could have... helped you."

*Why you little prick.* McCoy pretended to ignore the reference to Katie's death.

"What does 'J'ai eno, J'ai mau' mean?" He could hear the fear in his voice.

A condescending moue. "Those are words you may hear. They

are not for you to speak." He led McCoy back up to the control room. "Please tell Mr. Hughes what you've seen." His lip curled. "And explain it any way you can."

Out of sight in the now empty sick bay, a feathery shape dropped from the ceiling onto the operating table, its talons scrabbling for purchase on the stainless steel surface.

The half-faced giant sped the Zodiac back to the beach. McCoy watched its navigation lights disappear out to sea, then vomited in the dunes.

## 13.

Hughes' driver was waiting in the locked car, windows rolled up. He drove McCoy straight back to the Beverly Hills Hotel.

"Sit down, Wiley. What did you think?" It was nearly midnight. Hughes was in his pajamas and a torn monogrammed bathrobe. Again, the bare feet.

"Howard, I don't want anything to do with this."

Hughes sniffed. "Do you know what ship you were on?"

"No. And I wasn't going to ask."

Hughes eyes were mischievous.

*No.... Of course! Strange uniforms, no markings....*

"The *Thresher*?" McCoy asked.

"I arranged for her transfer. She's going to serve a greater purpose. One which I'm sure you, as a man of science, will appreciate."

"Appreciate? I'm going to 'appreciate 'a hijacked nuclear submarine where God knows how many people died so Dr. Bizarro can make fruit salad with fingers and lips?"

A few months ago, when the American nuclear submarine *The Thresher* disappeared, the world had watched the headlines for two days, hoping that her crew might be saved. Instead, the search vessels brought back the remains of an apparent implosion deep beneath the sea. It was a national tragedy.

It was a hoax.

"That witch doctor is harvesting human body parts for experimentation," McCoy protested. "Howard, you've built a legitimate medical research institute. Don't risk everything you've accomplished for a ghoulish quack."

"So you were convinced, eh?" Eyes twinkling, Hughes walked to the bar, his overgrown toenails clicking on the marble floor.

"I'll admit Romulo's got impressive parlor tricks. But that's not medical progress. And he's crossing ethical lines. He could ruin you."

Hughes dropped ice cubes into his glass and reached for a green glass Coca-Cola bottle.

"Ethics?" He smiled innocently. "Do you mean the kind of ethics that say doctors shouldn't murder patients? You'll be interested to know that the attending anesthetist during Miss Quinn's operation will testify that you were drunk while performing surgery. He seems to think you murdered your ex-girlfriend on the operating table because she left you for another guy. You do mean that kind of ethics?"

McCoy stiffened. Shutters in a long-darkened room flung open, letting in the light. Now he understood. Katie's death wasn't his fault. He hadn't screwed up. Some external force had caused his wrist to jerk, and if that was far-fetched, so was a dead talking head, but he'd seen it!

*I'm trapped.*

"Where's this going, Howard? Are you blackmailing me?"

"I won't waste your time with nuances, Wiley. You've always been straight with me in your bullshit doctor way and I respect that." A sip of his Coke. "Here's what I want. Work with that Cuban doctor..."

"He's not a doctor."

"Whatever he is. Help him. You've got Western medical training and experience. He talks about leaves and spells and I don't know what. You can save him time with the fundamentals so he can get to the big picture. I want you to live aboard the *Thresher* and do what Romulo DaVinci requires. You'll report to me periodically in writing, and I'll pay you $50,000 a year. If you can prove to me he's a fake, well then keep my money and come on home. All will be forgiven. You have my word. Of course, this is confidential, and if you ever try to jump ship and go to the authorities, who'll never believe you—you'll be eliminated." Hughes crunched an ice cube. "Immediately." He gazed out the window at glittering Los Angeles. "You'll have to drop out of your Beverly Hills world for months at a time without a trace, except for a bank account of course, but you might be pioneering the future of medicine." He raised his glass in a toast. "And it beats the hell out of your alternatives."

"And what might they be?" McCoy was fascinated. *Can this get any worse?*

"A malpractice suit, which I guarantee your insurance carrier will lose. Your California medical license will be revoked, and you and your ethics can go elsewhere. If you can find a place that'll have you."

"I'll still have to face a malpractice suit unless I just disappear, and then I'll be a fugitive."

"I will settle your problems in your absence. Out of court." Howard smiled expansively, twisting the gold ring on his little finger.

McCoy thought of Suzanne and then of Stephen. Without his child support and tuition checks, they'd be lost. Suzanne was alimony dependent, not that he cared so much about her, but Stephen....

*So much for financial ruin.* He wondered how much Hughes knew. "Did you arrange for Katie Quinn to die on my operating table?"

Hughes rubbed his mustache, puzzled. "Let's not get paranoid, Wiley. I may be taking advantage of your circumstances—that's good business sense—but I'm not a murderer."

"What about Nurse Laveau?"

"Who's that?"

McCoy believed Hughes, or rather he believed in his ignorance. The man was too much of an egotist not to try to impress him with his manipulations if he'd arranged Katie's murder. Other forces were at work, darker ones, and Hughes may only be a cog in the wheel. *Just like me.* Perhaps if he worked with Romulo aboard that submarine, he'd find a way to clear his name and get his life back.

*I am Saint George. And this is my dragon.*

"All right, Howard, but I have to make some arrangements. And it's $60,000 a year, not fifty."

But Hughes was staring at a housefly buzzing against the

window. "Gay—Get in here! They carry disease... Please kill it for me, Wiley." His voice was thin with fear. McCoy crushed the insect with a single swipe as Bill Gay rushed into the room. Hughes put down his drink. "It's settled then." He took McCoy's arm affectionately. His focus shifted. "It's time the grown-ups were in charge. The employers, the corporations who give every Tom, Dick and Harry a job. American industry makes this country great, not New Deal Democrats who want to take care of lazy people, who want to give anyone with a pulse the right to vote. Someday a corporation with an agenda will be able to give money to a politician who will help carry out that agenda. Period. All perfectly legal."

"Voters will never stand for that."

Hughes chuckled. "They'll never know. They'll be voting based on television ads. Whoever buys the most ads wins. That's how democracy should work. Did you know that if you can attribute an idea, no matter how mean-spirited, to the Bible, some voters will think you're a caring person and take your side. Bill here's a Mormon. He knows about that."

Gay smiled evasively. "Mr. Hughes started a think tank to methodize what we call proof-texting. We use a Bible verse taken out of context to support a point." He looked heavenward. "Some of our references are very creative."

Hughes gripped McCoy's arm as Bill held the door open. "Corporations have to organize. If we don't, we could find ourselves with another Catholic president. Or worse. Good night, Doctor." He edged away from the closing door. "Bill will call you in the morning."

McCoy drove his Jaguar back to Holmby Hills a little too fast. He thought about his patient, now employer. *How can anyone so frightened be so bold at the same time?*

## 14.

True to Hughes' word, Gay telephoned the next morning. McCoy was to be paid $60,000 a year via monthly deposits into a bank account established in the name of a corporation in which McCoy would be the sole stockholder. He would work one month aboard the *Thresher* followed by one week's shore leave. Expenses, bonuses and salary increases were "at employer's discretion" and there was a confidentiality clause that ended with the words "enforceable in a court of law or otherwise." There were no names and no signature lines. It was a "Memo of Understanding."

To the outside world, Bill Gay was Howard Hughes. (Robert Maheu, an attorney and ex-CIA employee, was Hughes' only other bridge to reality, and, according to Maheu, they only spoke by phone. They never ever met.)

In 1947, a mere multi-millionaire Howard Hughes was searching for an office manager. Frank William Gay was invisible as beige. His friends, all Latter Day Saints, called him Bill, the closest thing to a nickname his personality could inspire. The word "cool" was just coming into coinage. Gay wore a short sleeve collared shirt, cuffed high-waisted pants and a butterscotch crew cut. He was not cool.

During their job interview, Hughes told Bill, "I need someone to arrange my affairs." Hughes' six-foot four-inch frame slouched precariously, size twelve feet up on his desk, he studied the blinking twenty-seven-year-old frozen before him like a rabbit in a garden. "You drink alcohol?"

"No, sir." Gay's gaze was direct. "None of us do. Mormons don't drink."

"Good." He'd already been told that, otherwise he never would have invited Gay to meet him. After a few more blandly answered questions, Hughes decided he liked the young man and offered him the job.

"But I want to be a school teacher." Gay was looking doubtfully around Hughes' cluttered inner sanctum: movie posters, futuristic airplane designs, blueprints and photos of actresses were pinned to a bulletin board. The building they were in was a nothing two-story stack on Romaine Street in Hollywood. But the pay Hughes offered was good, along with Hughes' proposed three-month trial period after which either of them could call it quits with "no hard feelings," so the two men shook on it. Gay would never work anywhere else for the rest of Hughes' rocketball life.

At first, Gay's responsibilities were coffee and soda runs, answering phones, organizing Hughes' office clutter, and nobody minded him. He was courteous, and always ready to help, often when no one else was. Naturally, Hughes came to rely on Gay. He saw and heard nothing, yet, over time, learned everything, and Hughes trusted him.

"You like working for me, don't you, Bill?"

"You treat me fair." That was Gay's standard answer to Hughes' monthly inquiry.

"But you don't think I'm a sinner or anything?" Hughes studied Gay like a hawk over a still lake, hoping a fish would leap out.

"God has a plan for each of us. Working for you seems to be his plan for me."

Now, Gay and his loyal Mormon guard were the cocoon in which Howard Hughes breathed, ate and slept. Gay carried out each and every one of Hughes' wishes and kept the world at bay. Like all smart men working for even smarter men, Gay had convinced himself that he was in charge. It was a mistake with a long fuse.

McCoy met several times with his lawyer. He left him a letter in a sealed envelope explaining the circumstances of his going to work aboard the *Thresher* and his worst suspicions about Romulo DaVinci and Howard Hughes. The letter was only to be opened after McCoy's death or six months from the time he'd last been heard from. He set up a trust fund for Stephen and funded it with Hughes' first check drawn on the account of a machinery company in Seattle. Rather than lying to Suzanne, who'd see right through him, he told her nothing. He wrote his son a separate letter:

> Dear Stephen,
> I'm writing to tell you that I have to go away for a while. The government has asked me to volunteer for a top-secret mission, and because I love my country almost as much as I love you, I've agreed to do it. Please believe that I would never leave you if I didn't have to. You're everything to me.
> I want you to work hard at school. Think of me when you can and know that I'm thinking about you. Tell your mother not to worry, her check will always be in the mail,

and show her this letter.
You'll hear from me when you do.
Love, Dad

He had no way of knowing that Stephen would angrily tear up the letter a few days later, convinced it was a lie and that his father was abandoning him for being gay.

The night before he shipped out, McCoy met Doc Friday for a drink at The Shady Alibi Room, a dive bar in Culver City. A few students were singing along with The Drifters' *On Broadway* at the jukebox. A TV over the bar flickered black and white footage of President Kennedy at the Berlin Wall. The pathologist sat waiting in a corner booth. McCoy ordered a J & B. He felt old.

"I'm going to take a vacation," McCoy said.

"Good. Smartest thing you've said in weeks." Doc was chewing peanuts and eying a girl in tight Madras pants. "Where to?"

*To hell.* "I don't know. I haven't decided."

"You should go for a cruise. The sea's very relaxing." McCoy searched Friday's face for irony. There was none. He thought about Stephen's confession last week. Now he wanted to confide, to unburden. He thought about Katie and felt suffocating guilt. Her loss was a pillow held over his face.

"You ok, buddy?" Friday was squeezing his arm.

"Yeah. Fine." He swallowed hard. *They've made me a murderer. Now they're shanghaiing me onto a hijacked submarine to take me God knows where to do God knows what.*

"Maybe I will," McCoy said finally. "An ocean voyage might do me good."

## 15.

His phone was ringing as he walked in from the carport.

"Wiley?" It was Doc Friday. "I thought you should know. Marie Laveau's dead.

*Wait? What?*

McCoy rushed past the night nurse at reception and took the elevator down to Doc Friday's basement office. "The Vault" was the heart of the pathology department. It was both a morgue and a dissecting room. It had a long neon-lit hall with an aisle between two rows of four stone slabs, each with a drain and a delicatessen-type scale suspended above it to weigh body parts as they were removed from corpses.

McCoy hated the place. *It's like the loser's locker room after a game.* He walked through the rows of sheet-covered, toe-tagged cadavers to the slab where Doc Friday was working.

Marie Laveau's corpse was on its back. There was an entrance wound nearly two inches wide in the left side of her neck and an exit wound, only slightly narrower, just below her right jawbone. The pathologist was examining the tip of her tongue with a forceps. McCoy cleared his throat. "What happened?"

Doc Friday looked up. McCoy had the fleeting impression that he was frightened but then his features relaxed. "She took a carving knife and rammed it through her neck. Severed her jugular."

"How do you know it was a suicide?"

"Her hand was wrapped around the knife when I found her."

"*You* found her?"

"She did it here in the morgue ...."

McCoy flashed on her squalid kitchen and the intuition he'd had before. "Did she leave a note?"

"No. Well...."

"Well, what?"

The same fearful look crossed his face. "She wrote something on the floor...in blood."

"Oh come on. People don't really do that."

"Look. She wrote a number."

Friday held up the corpse's bloodstained fingertip.

Does that mean anything to you?"

"Seven deadly sins? Seven days in a week?" McCoy shook his head. "That's all I got."

Flashbulbs popped as a police photographer snapped photos. A detective with a badge clipped to his belt hurried over to where McCoy knelt by the smudged chalk circle next to the body outline. "Crime scene, you can't be here." He hustled him past a uniformed officer putting yellow tape across the doorway.

McCoy's legs were rubber again as he walked back to his car. 45

Marie Laveau hadn't written a "7" on the cold floor. It was a "T."

*Now why in the world of voodoo would she do that? What does "T" mean?*

It all had to end. He closed down what was left of his practice and rented the Holmby Hills house to Robert Vaughn, an actor who would later play the *Man from U.N.C.L.E.* on TV. At Hughes' suggestion and because McCoy liked hotels steeped in history, McCoy took a room at the Chateau Marmont overlooking Sunset Boulevard where he swam in the old pool each morning, got stoned and read *One Flew Over the Cuckoo's Nest.* Waiting to be summoned.

# Part Two: Haiti, 1939

# 16.

In 1939, Madonna and Victor were living in Haiti in a one- room shack near the edge of the forest, which many called *la jungle noir*. It was a hot morning and Madonna was splayed in the grass eating a coconut Victor had cut up before heading down the dusty path to the Garde d'Haiti police barracks in Saint-Marc. Madonna had shiny black hair, olive skin and a hump. She had dozed off in the humidity and when she awoke, a small naked boy stood staring at her. Two, perhaps three years old, with tangled and matted dark hair and crusty bare feet. He lunged for a piece of coconut and Madonna grabbed his little hand before he could run away. He hissed like a snake. She smiled, offering him the sweet white meat. There were scars and barely healed scrapes along his arms and legs and his ribs stood out. The child was starving. Could he really live alone in the jungle?

"Where is your *madre*?"

A grunt from the mouthful of coconut.

The boy considered running, but when she held out more coconut, he ate it greedily. She backed into her hut, gesturing for him to stay, and returned with a cup of water, which he drank, never taking his frightened eyes off her. A sheet of rain crossed the clearing, spattering them in its path. Madonna gestured for the boy to follow her into the hut but he hissed again, then took off running into the dark trees.

Madonna had been unable to bear Victor a child and she worried that she was barren. Their courtship and marriage had been passionate. But still no baby came.

When Victor returned from his three-day shift and had taken off his dusty uniform and sat in his chair, Madonna told him about the boy. When she finished her tale, he took her hand and, looking into her eyes, kissed it before she hobbled off to wash the beans for dinner. It pleased her that he knew she was sad. Later, while Madonna whispered incantations and stitched one of her talismanic amulets by candlelight, Victor rummaged outside. Soon he was hammering something.

In the morning, the biscuit she left outside on the table was gone. She saw that Victor had built a toy truck out of flat pieces of wood and a coffee can and added thimbles and bottle caps for wheels.

When she rose at dawn, that too was gone, along with a small plate of red beans. Later, she saw the boy through the window watching the hut from the edge of the jungle.

That night, a quarter moon casting only enough light for those with a purpose. The boy's cries grew louder as he approached the doorway dragging his foot. Madonna crept out of bed carefully so as not to wake Victor and unbolted the latch.

She calmed him with guava juice and Victor's leftover dinner, which the boy ate with his filthy hands while she wrapped his swollen ankle tight with fabric straps. By sunrise, she had bathed him in soap and kerosene for the lice, cut off his pungent, hair and placed him, with a few slices of pineapple, in her laundry wagon for a trip down the hill to Saint Jean Baptiste and Mass with Father Feliciano.

After the Mass, they stood outside the little chapel with Father Feliciano. "And who's this?" he asked, patting the child's bottom. The priest listened warily as Madonna explained how the boy came to them and Victor nodded helpfully for emphasis. All the priest's parishioners were either current or past Voodoo believers. His peasant flock worshipped side-by-side gods.

"Victor finally spoke. "Can we keep him?"

There had been no reports of missing children in the village and even if there had been, their fate could have been far worse than to be raised by a raven-haired hunchback and a wobbly policeman.

"I think it is God's will." The priest said and smiled, pleased to have his moral authority confirmed.

"What shall we call him?" Madonna asked.

Father Feliciano looked down at the little boy. "He was probably raised by a wolf. You should call him Romulo," and he made the sign of the cross.

When Romulo was little, Madonna often stayed up late knitting while he slept in the little room next to the closet and Victor lay on the sofa, dreamily puffing on his cheroot. Madonna would sit peacefully, her needles clicking, dreaming of the day when she, her husband and her son (for she thought of Romulo as her son) would all live on a beautiful boat with a small chapel in the bow and a room full of books. In this fantasy, she and Victor had another child – a beautiful girl with smooth skin and straight graceful limbs. Madonna's greatest fear was to give birth to a child deformed like herself. In her prayers, when she asked God for this miracle of a little girl, she always included her vow to strangle any creature that might come out of her with a hump.

And then her belly swelled up.

Madonna's body was not given to child bearing; her stooped posture and crab-like walk were not improved by a stomach hanging over onto her thighs. As the day for her delivery grew closer, she became more anxious.

On a hot afternoon with sunlight streaming in through the bedroom windows, Dr. Miro and his midwife delivered a baby girl. She sucked air and cried when she was slapped. Before she fell asleep, Madonna counted all ten toes and fingers and gently felt the baby's perspiring pink back: smooth and straight.

When she awoke, Victor smiled tenderly and kissed her

They named their daughter Aurora for the hope and renewal of dawn.

## 17.

Madonna knew that no child of a hunchback was safe in Haiti; Aurora's body parts would command a premium. Word of Aurora's birth spread quickly among the practitioners of *la science* and a month hadn't passed before the giant Johnny Christ in his dusty suit and foot doctor boots came to call.

"I will buy the child. She is no use to you," he said as he and Victor were drinking *clairin* at the table in the grass, man to man, while Madonna listened from the kitchen with a pounding heart.

"My daughter is not for sale." Victor put down his empty glass a little too forcefully. It banged on the table. Johnny rubbed his grizzled temple with the back of his shovel-sized hand.

"Another man will only steal her for the same purposes. At least I offer *la monnaie*. This time," he added menacingly.

"Because I am a guard with the police, I have a pistol," Victor said, standing up. “I am going to get it. If you are still here when I come out, I will shoot you in the knee, by accident.” He disappeared into the house.

Johnny Christ rose, tipping over his chair, and lumbered away. “Your children will cause great harm someday. They are a plague! Best to drown them.”

Mosquitos nipped ferociously that night while Madonna put Romulo and Aurora to bed.

“Our children are in danger, Victor. We must leave Haiti. You can’t shoot everyone in the knee.”

Victor and Madonna packed up and made the all-night ocean journey with their children aboard a fishing trawler to Santiago de Cuba where they and settled into a large rented room in a shabby “American-style” boarding house. Victor’s uncle Ernesto worked as a waiter at one of the new tourist hotels. As chance would have it, Uncle Ernesto had recently died and Victor took over his job at the Hotel Lincoln.

One morning, Madonna heard screaming from somewhere near their house. The shrieking was coming from the little shed behind the calabash tree where Victor kept his tools and sometimes hid his liquor bottles. She crept over to the wire-mesh-covered window and peered inside. His hands spattered with blood, Romulo stood at the work table, sewing a long thin needle with black thread through a quivering orange and green feathered pile of dirty brown fur. The little animal (or was it a bird?) screamed again, and Romulo poured clear liquid onto a grimy cloth and held it to where the creature’s head seemed to be. It stopped moving, and Romulo returned to his task. Occasionally, he paused to chant in Creole.

When she’d taught Romulo her spells, she’d hoped he wouldn’t use them for wicked purposes. Madonna was a *mambo* and had practiced *la science* ever since she was a little girl; she learned her *pouins* and potions from her father, a Haitian leaf doctor descended from the last king of Benin, who sat on a throne of human skulls. But Madonna’s magic was good magic, the power to heal and cast out evil spirits. Alas, Romulo only wanted to know spells for power or seduction or how to strike his enemies dead. He showed an unhealthy interest in *zombis*, too, even after Madonna told him that it was all just stories to frighten children. Still, he persisted until she gave him her recipe for mambo paste, the legendary potion that was said to bring back the dead. It had never worked for her; her heart wasn't in it.

"You must believe, *Maman*, otherwise the *loa* won't grant your desires." Romulo was only repeating what she'd told him many times, and he was right. She just didn't want to believe in such grisly things. Years before, she'd joined the village church. Jesus Christ asked for more faith but less blood, and Christianity was a religion of sunlight and joy. She was tired of dancing around squalid fires in the forest at night.

The creature Romulo had assembled healed, and Romulo called him Remus: the stocky, short-legged body of a hutia--a long banana rat--with the wings and powerful beak of a parrot, grafted onto the rodent by Romulo's mystical surgical hands. Now the friendless boy had a pet.

He will be a doctor, Madonna hoped, a great doctor, and he will learn to use his powers wisely. But she knew she was wrong.

Romulo was dark-haired and olive-skinned, with long limbs and graceful hands. His was a sinister beauty, like the apple and serpent in one. Much to his mother's chagrin, he'd cultivated a sneer and taken to chewing sugar cane, which sharpened his teeth, and gave him a feral appearance. At school, he paid attention only to what interested him, drawing extraordinarily precise anatomical sketches of humans and animals (or combinations of both). His teachers feared him. "Your son never learned to read," Signora Alba told Madonna. "He just knew." She crossed herself and leaned closer. "He can speak and write English and French. Did you teach him?"

Madonna shook her head, wishing she were proud of him.

Now at seventeen, his father dead of drink, Romulo was an infamous village troublemaker. He couldn't keep a job, and yet he always had money for cerveza and gambling. His mother suspected him of stealing and worse.

By thirteen, Aurora had matured into a willowy beauty with arresting blue eyes. Like her foster brother, she kept no friends for long. Aurora and Romulo had become fiercely protective of each other and, although they never let on to anyone, shared intuitions and thoughts. For her mother's sake, Aurora pretended to be a Catholic, but inside her was a confused moral compass. Remus wouldn't go near her. Aurora was the only human he feared.

There was a ruined church off a footpath in the forest where Aurora liked to sit in the evenings in the lone scarred pew before the space where the altar had been.

Tonight, bored and curious, Romulo had stealthily followed her. Squatting behind the collapsed confessional, he watched Aurora strike a match, then light a candle, a look of peace on her face.

Romulo grimaced: a bat lit on her shoulder like an epaulette.

He hurried to her. Something bumped him from behind as he grabbed her hand. A bat lay twittering on the floor; it shrieked to warn its congregation. A cloud of tiny red eyes enveloped Romulo as he ran, dragging Aurora from the church.

"You must never go there again at night," he told her, gasping to catch his breath. "Bats are filthy. They can make you sick."

Romulo hugged her. *There's something very wrong.*

As can happen when two objects or ideas appear before us, because of the angle of the light or the intensity of concern, we see only one and overlook the other. So Romulo feared for his sister and for her destiny. With no idea why.

She didn't tell him about the wound. She noticed it the next morning: two tiny puncture marks on her shoulder. Red and angry. Then chills and a fever. After a few days, she felt better; the wound healed. She forgot about it.

Madonna found a tortoise on top of her bedroom closet two years after Victor's death. It was an evil spell to place a tortoise carcass so, and Madonna went into a rage when she discovered it. Dr. Miro said liquor and a bad liver killed Victor – but now she knew the truth.

When Romulo came home for supper, Madonna accused him of planting the tortoise death spell to kill his father.

"Papa was a drunk, Mama," Romulo said, "*Cerveza, Clairin*--whatever he could get. He drank himself to death. The doctors told you that. He and I fought sometimes..." He bumped his fists together. "But I didn't kill him."

Tears welled up in Madonna's eyes. "He raised you and he loved you. You murdered him."

Romulo hesitated, then came to a decision. "No. He was a coward and a drunk, mama."

Madonna put her head in her hands. "If I am your curse, mama, you are mine. You don't know whether you're a Catholic or a voodoo priestess and I'm not sure what the difference is." He pushed open the torn screen door. "I should leave. Aurora will take care of you. If you're right, and I'm something evil, it's time I sought my mayhem."

Madonna and Aurora watched open-mouthed as he disappeared into the humid night.

## 18.

Romulo walked the seven dusty miles into the business district and found Mr. Collins early the next morning in a restaurant. Collins was a tall, friendly American he'd met a few weeks before at a cock fight, who wanted to know all about him and never let on anything about himself. He worked at "this and that" and always had money for food and cerveza. He gave Romulo breakfast, a few pesos and the address of people who'd take him in.

Romulo soon became one of the locals purchased by the C.I.A. operatives who took orders from Agent Collins (who took orders from Howard Hughes) twenty miles inland from *Cochinos* Bay, a strip of coral-laced beaches about a hundred miles west of Trinidad - the "Bay of Pigs". Romulo was to help organize local village men after U.S. troops landed to liberate Cuba. He was to be part of a civilian brigade of sympathetic Cubans to ally with the invading forces and march on Havana after the American air strike.

On April 17th, 1961, there was no U.S. air support, and the liberating army was shot to pieces on the beach. In the first town they entered, Castro's police arrested Romulo and others like him and threw them into prison along with hundreds more suspected insurrectionists.

Romulo languished in Havana's central prison for two weeks.

One morning, he was kicked awake and dragged from the building. A truck drove him away. Romulo grinned through his filthy beard. He wasn't going to be killed; they were taking him somewhere.

At the government dock, he was pushed aboard a fishing vessel which headed across the Windward Passage towards Haiti. By nightfall, Romulo was in *Le Negra*, a 19th-century Haitian prison.

Two guards dragged him out into the courtyard and turned a hose on him. One of them, Leo, a bear-like mulatto, handed him a torn dry shirt and a pair of pants. He marched Romulo back inside, past rows of crowded cages filled with jabbering prisoners and finally to a cell at the end of a long hall. It was almost a perfect ten-foot square, with a window high up on the west wall, which Romulo could see out of if he hoisted himself by the bars over the window opening. Two bunks were bolted to the opposite wall, and the inevitable metal can rested in the corner, buzzing with flies. When he urinated into it, he noticed fresh feces floating in the water. He assumed the lazy guards hadn't bothered to change the can.

He awoke at sunrise to the aroma of incense. He got up to drink from his water jug. His naked feet felt something on the floor - a pile of ashes. Next to them someone had sketched what looked like a "T" and something else that Romulo had obliterated with his footsteps. Whatever message had been left was gone.

"Guard! Guard!" Romulo shouted. No one came.

Near dusk, Leo opened the door and placed a bowl with green bananas and fish stew inside.

"Who was in this cell before me?" Romulo asked. Leo was swinging the door shut, pulling his machine gun out of the way.

"The one who is still in it." Leo replied as he hurried away, keys jangling, down the long corridor.

Romulo made himself stay awake, waiting for whatever occupied the cell with him to show itself.

Half-asleep, he peered around his cell. Something stirred in the bunk above him, and an arm dropped over the side and hung, inches from his face. He grabbed it and pulled with all his might. A human form came hurling down but vanished in midair the instant before it would have hit the stone floor.

Romulo slipped off his bunk and rushed towards the sound. The voice shrieked. Suddenly, he was clutching the shoulders of a naked elderly black man who'd re-materialized, urinating into the metal container.

Romulo wrapped his hands around the old man's throat, who screamed again, disappearing, then reappearing like a flashing light.

"I won't kill you if you tell me who you are and stay so I can see you."

His captive nodded frantically, eyes bulging. Romulo released the man's neck. The man said: "I am Baron Zabop, the mightiest sorcerer alive. You may call me Papa."

"Papa Zabop?"

The old man grinned, nodding.

"If you're such a mighty *houngan*, why are you in prison?"

"The President put me here two years ago. He said I tried to poison his cousin. I didn't even know he had a cousin, but I like it here. *La Negra* is my *houmfor* and the prisoners and guards, my *societe*. They pay me to cure their illnesses and cast out their *loupgarous*."

"I'm no stranger to *la science*."

"I know about you, Romulo. My *loa* told me in a dream. Do you have any rum or cigarettes?"

"I have no money."

"You've been sent to me for initiation, *hounsi canzo*. Someday you shall leave here with complete *connaissance*."

There was a loud implosion. All four walls of the cell suddenly were covered in fire. Romulo spun around, terrified, as sheets of flame closed in on him. He heard Papa Zabop's voice over the roaring inferno: "Don't be afraid. What you do not fear cannot harm you." Romulo could hardly breathe. His shirtsleeve flared up. Screaming, flailing his arm to smother the fire, he fell to his knees. The instant before he blacked out, there was a burst in the atmosphere, a roaring in his ears; but he didn't lose consciousness. He'd been pulled from his body, floating through the flames with no sensation of heat or pain. When he spoke, his voice was Papa Zabop's voice, "J'ai eno, j'ai mau mau, j'ai eno evil," he sang, and the sounds of the swirling inferno blended in harmony.

Papa Zabop laughed. The fire became a stream, like water from a hose, and rushed down towards the center of the cell, visible again at the periphery of the inferno. The old sorcerer stood, his mouth wide open sucking in the flames, which heaved and rolled from the air down his throat and were gone. Romulo dropped from the ceiling of the cell on the tail of the last streak of fire.

He came to, slowly. He found himself sitting on his bunk listening to Papa Zabop who hovered in midair before him

"I have told you the names and showed you the forty-nine

leaves and tree barks you will need. Do you remember them? What is *laloi*?"

"*Laloi* is a tonic. It purifies the blood and is used for *saisissements*, burns, piles and madness. It can drive off evil spirits," Romulo replied, hardly having to think.

"Someday your knowledge will surpass even mine," Zabop said huffily.

"What is my destiny?"

Papa Zabop giggled, rocking back and forth and shaking his grizzled head. "You are the element of water, baptized in fire. You are life and death. Time will end, and the world will be what it shall be."

Romulo thought for a moment, and then phrased his question carefully. "Am I evil?"

"There is no evil. There is no good. There is only water, fire and air." A smile teased Zabop's lips. "And rum."

One rainy morning, Romulo awoke to a gecko flitting across his face. His cell was empty. It was barely light outside. The door swung open and Leo walked in.

"You've been released."

They gave Romulo a cheap cotton shirt, a blue-gray sharkskin suit (sleeves too short) and black shoes with pointed toes that somebody had already worn.

Aurora met him outside. Her blonde hair and pale skin glowed in the morning light.

"I've been dreaming of this day," she said after she hugged him. They walked down the already bustling street towards the Iron Market with its reek of uncleaned *pepe* mackerel, and wafting scents of nutmeg, ginger and anise.

Remus followed above, fluttering from rooftop to rooftop.

She watched Romulo devour a plate of dried fish, plantains, rice and beans in the plastic tablecloth restaurant off her hotel lobby. Thin and pale, hair cropped short, accentuating the shape of his head; he looked older than his twenty-three years.

She bought him a pack of Kools. He lit one and inhaled gratefully.

"How did you get me out?"

"I used our savings to pay off the prison commander."

Romulo laughed. "Thank you. I'll repay you someday."

"With what? Magic?"

He moved into the room across from hers. Remus lived in a tree by the *carrefour*. At first, Romulo earned money loading cargo at the docks, but his arms and back weren't built for it. The head of the stevedores Johnny Christ pulled him aside. "No more work for you. You drop too much." He frowned, wiping his mouth. A flaming crucifix was tattooed on his huge forearm. His eyes narrowed. "I know you... Why?"

Christ was twenty years older than the day he tried to buy Aurora from Victor, a lot heavier and just as mean.

Romulo shrugged. "I don't know you."

Christ watched him walk away. "How's your sister?" He shouted.

Romulo didn't look back.

Aurora was serving drinks at a local bar, a rowdy place with a lightbulb-strung dirt garden and cable spools for tables. Romulo pulled her aside during her break. "I lost my job." He had to speak loudly to be heard over the music. "The body parts merchant who tried to buy you from Mamma and Papa recognized me at work."

"Don't worry." She spoke into his ear. "I met an American official, and he knows a man in the State Department who'll help us. He likes blondes," Aurora posed seductively, a hand on her hip, laughing. "I'm meeting them both tomorrow."

Romulo felt protective but also useless. "Be careful."

A black 1955 Thunderbird was parked away from the streetlamp at closing time when Aurora left work. Johnny Christ watched her cross the deserted street before starting his engine.

After a block or so, the car pulled alongside Aurora, its tinny radio playing a popular version of *Haiti Cherie*. As she turned into the alley leading back to her hotel, the Thunderbird crossed in front of her and Johnny Christ climbed out. He grabbed her arm and pulled open the rear door. Aurora kicked him hard in the groin. Christ barely blinked.

"That won't work. He has no balls." Romulo said as he stepped out of the shadows with Remus perched on his shoulder.

Christ grinned. "So the weakling comes to his sister's defense. Are we going to fight now?"

"No need."

"What is that?" Christ squinted at Remus. Remus launched off

Romulo's shoulder and, in a feathery flash, flew across Christ's throat, tearing it open like he was shredding paper. Christ sank to his knees, trying to hold back the red spurts with his hands.

Aurora met the two Americans for lunch. They ignored her and talked about baseball throughout the meal. It was as though she wasn't there. Finally, the State Department man nudged her and said "I know what you want, sweetheart, but... do you have the money?" He named a price.

Romulo sold Johnny Christ's Thunderbird to a dealer in Trader's Alley. The next afternoon, Aurora brought $5,000 in cash to a small American import/export company with an office in Port au Prince where she and Romulo posed for wallet-sized photographs. "Who shall we be? It's up to us," Aurora pondered dreamily. By evening, Romulo DaVinci and Aurora Lee were both naturalized passport-carrying U.S. citizens. Two days later, they put Remus in a carrier box with holes in it and flew to Miami.

When Aurora went to the ladies 'room at Miami International Airport, Romulo took half their money and got on a plane for New York. He left a note inside her valise, which she recovered at the TWA lost and found counter:

> Chere Aurora,
> I'll write to you at the Miami Post Office in care of General Delivery. I heard my destiny call, and it only had one seat. Trust no one. I will help you.
> Romo

## 19.

It was July. Manhattan was hot and sticky. Romulo lived on the streets of the Lower East Side and in the parks, sleeping in alleyways or on benches and panhandling with the drunks and hippies on East Eighth Street during the day. Remus kept to the overgrown areas of Central Park, high in the trees, and filled his belly with worms from the reservoir banks and garbage.

Winter came early. By late November, the parks, which had sheltered Romulo all fall, were swept with icy winds and covered in soot-stained snow. Still, no destiny had arrived.

Reluctant to wait for his future any longer, Romulo joined the U.S. Navy that afternoon. He wanted to see the world.

He rode a bus with thirty other recruits to basic training in Great Lakes, Illinois. Remus came with him in an old suitcase in which he'd punched breathing holes. A fidgety young man in a denim jacket sitting next to him glanced down at it from time to time.

"Is that a cat you got in there?"

Romulo ignored him.

The young man had a baby face, almost pretty, with blond hair. He offered Romulo a piece of gum.

"No, thank you."

"I said, is that a cat?"

"Very much like a cat."

The boy chomped noisily. "If it's not a cat, what is it?"

"It's a griffin. They're extinct."

"Ohhh. I'm Murphy. Whitey Murphy."

Romulo shook his hand. He felt calluses and strength.

"You Puerto Rican?"

"My name is Romulo. I'm from Cuba, but I'm American now."

Whitey popped a bubble. "I'm going in for submarines. The pay's the best there is in peacetime."

Romulo lit a Kool, but didn't offer one to Whitey.

"What's 'extinct' mean?"

"It's when a species doesn't exist anymore."

"You know a lot for a guy who's just off the boat."

"I have a great curiosity."

"Well, you know what they say."

"No, I don't. What do they say?"

"About curiosity and the cat?"

Romulo looked baffled.

During boot camp, Recruit Company 69, some two hundred men in all, lived at the naval training center just outside Chicago on Lake Michigan. Romulo and Whitey were fifteen bunks apart in the same barrack. They learned seamanship, navigation, knot tying and the Navy's ranking system. Romulo was selected for the Hospital Corpsman program. With *la science* and the lessons from Papa Zabop lurking at the back of his brain, he graduated first in his class and was assigned to the Navy Hospital at Portsmouth

Naval Shipyard. Whitey, awaiting a submarine posting, was Romulo's bunkmate. Whitey went into town in search of liquor and girls whenever he could. Romulo kept to himself, reading medical textbooks in his free time and helping Remus find mice.

Captain Hollander, the chief medical officer on the base, was a drunk. He'd been in the Navy for twenty-three years and that, as he was fond of saying, made him "a career drunk". Romulo hated to watch him operate. He always left scars much larger than necessary.

As a hospital corpsman, Romulo's duty was scrubbing down the operating rooms and cleaning the instruments. Sometimes, he got to observe a surgery from the gallery overhead, sitting next to officers serving their medical internships in the Navy. He envied their opportunities. *If I'd had a fancy education, I'd be an officer too, and then a doctor.*

But Romulo was learning. Fighting sleep, he read late into the night beneath a blanket by flashlight, memorizing human anatomy and studying the science of the brain.

One morning, Whitey noticed how tired Romulo looked. "Take one of these tonight. It'll help you concentrate." He gave Romulo a black capsule.

"What's this?"

"Black Beauty. If you can't burn the candle at both ends, you might as well light the whole thing up."

Romulo took the pill and studied straight through until breakfast. His reading speed increased, and he seemed to absorb more information.

On a hazy night in July, 1962, Whitey and Romulo drove into Back Bay to meet a man who'd told Whitey over the phone he'd pay a thousand dollars to have a meeting with them.

At South Station, Whitey waited on a far bench.

A crowd newly arrived from New York swarmed towards the street doors. A tall sandy-haired man in a tan suit sat down next to Whitey.

Outside, Romulo pulled their car up, and Whitey and the man got into the back seat. Romulo spun around and held a 45 to the man's groin.

"This is a federal agent. He's the one who let me go to prison."

Collins didn't flinch. He'd recognized Romulo. "Easy, amigo. I don't work for the government anymore, and that Cuban disaster wasn't my fault. Everybody got screwed." He smoothed his hair with both hands. "Maybe I can make it up to you."

His teeth had been capped too large, Romulo thought, and he looked older. Perhaps it was his pale skin. Collins had a tan when Romulo knew him in Havana.

"Whitey, you drive. I want to sit with my old amigo. He's going to talk his ass off to save his life."

As they drove through downtown Boston, Collins explained that he worked for a powerful individual who wanted to make friends in the Navy Yard; friends he could trust and who'd be well-paid for their loyalty when the time came. Romulo studied Collins' face in the erratic illumination of passing headlights, store windows and flashing neon.

They let him off in the North End. He pushed an envelope into Romulo's hand. Romulo considered shooting him in the back, but Collins' offer was intriguing, and the money was good. Too good. *What is trust but a temporary truce?*

"Jesus Christ! There must be five thousand dollars in here! Whatta we gotta do? Kill people?" Whitey was shaking his head.

The rest of the summer was hot but uneventful. Collins communicated twice: once to ask if a certain destroyer was departing for Honolulu as scheduled and once to advise Romulo where to pick up his next "friendship" payment.

Romulo asked to set up a small laboratory in which to perform "textbook" experiments. Captain Hollander, who viewed Romulo's medical education with the zeal of a drunken missionary, allotted him a storage closet with a sink.

What fascinated Romulo was the origin of life. No textbook or monograph could explain it. For centuries, both brilliant and aberrant minds had been experimenting on unluckier living organisms, yet no one could identify what started it all. *How did the light get in?*

But Romulo had knowledge of sciences beyond the ken of both modern and ancient medicines. He'd learned the powers of herbs and dead things, and of looking at the full moon in a certain way. He could heal deep wounds with cicca bark and meld flesh. Papa Zabop told him stories of men come back from the dead with the mouths and genitals of leopards, of children—little girls—

transformed into creatures with the lower bodies of fish to swim ahead of the war boats and warn of the enemy, their throats opening and closing rows of red gills as they bleated their frightened messages. Here, in his tiny laboratory amid mops and buckets, Romulo used science and magic to investigate genesis—the spark of life.

In early fall, Collins made a suggestion and gave them another envelope of money.

Romulo and Whitey put their names down for submarine duty.

## 20.

Life swept Aurora up. She'd gotten control of her tears in Miami Airport and her sadness and fear turned into anger at Romulo, and by extension, at all men. As she sat on an airport bench, she became aware of two thirtyish women who had been watching her from the next gate and were now approaching.

"Would you like to be in a pageant, honey?" the taller one asked. She was auburn-haired and quite beautiful, in sunglasses and a slash of red lipstick.

Her chunky friend with short red hair and pointy earrings sat down next to Aurora and said, "You might win some money. Do you have a talent? Can you sing or dance?"

"Don't worry about the talent part, Maisie. She can recite a poem or something. Look at her—she's perfect!" the first one said.

Aurora had never been called "perfect" before. She liked these ladies.

The taller one, whose name was Trish, suggested Mai Tai's in the airport bar "to cheer you up, honey." After an hour of drinking, Aurora had learned all about the two friends and they had learned next to nothing that was true about her. Trish and Maisie were married to two land speculators who had come to Florida to buy as much of the Orlando area as possible on behalf of a mysterious employer. "Whoever he is, he's crazy," Maisie said, draining her glass and waving for another round. "It's all swamp out there and our guys are buying thousands of acres for him." She shook her head.

"What brings you to Florida, Rory?" Trish liked calling her that. Aurora sounded so formal.

"I was traveling with my brother. I decided to stop and visit here for a while."

"Where're you staying?"

"I'll get a hotel room, then figure it out."

"Unh unh. You're staying with us. Isn't she, Maisie?"

Maisie raised her glass in a toast. "To Rory and the pageant!"

It was nearly dinnertime when they pulled up next to a red Corvette in Trish and Maisie's driveway, a dirt road off another dirt road with no other houses for miles. A large German shepherd ran up barking to Trish's VW Beetle, as they opened the doors. "Oh, be quiet, Reverend King!" Trish rubbed the dog's big ears as he slobbered on her. Then he saw Aurora and froze. "He's Duane's dog. You like dogs, Rory?" Aurora smiled. King dropped to his belly and crawled to her, then stopped, prostrate at her feet. Trish and Maisie exchanged puzzled glances.

A shirtless man in shorts with a crew-cut and six-pack abs stood grilling hamburgers on the deck of a ranch house while his large-bellied friend slept in a lawn chair. A Confederate flag hung over the door. "Woo hoo, chiquitas! Just in time for dinner!"

Trish rushed up to Duane, the shirtless one, and gave him a hug. He twirled her in his strong arms. "This is Rory, hon. She's gonna stay with us in Lizzie's old room for a while and guess what? She's gonna be in the pageant!"

Duane flashed a welcoming smile.

"She's perfect!"

Sandy, the other man stood up and kissed Aurora's hand. "She's the prettiest white lady I've ever seen."

Maisie and Trish brought out beers and lit citronella candles. Over burgers and ribs, Duane explained what the pageant was. "You see Sandy and me are here in Orlando on a top-secret real estate project." Sandy put his hands to the sides of his head and wagged his fingers like mouse ears. Duane wagged back and the two had a good laugh.

"Trouble is," he said, "hardly anyone lives here. Which means there's not enough workers, not enough homebuyers. So another part of our job is to get the right kind of people..."

"He means *white* people," Maisie stage-whispered with a wink.

"...to move here."

"To the swamp!" Sandy crushed his beer can and let out a belch.

"The pageant is a beauty contest to promote our new neighborhood by showing off all the pretty girls who live here." "The right kind of pretty girls." Maisie winked.

"But I don't live here."

"The pageant's in two weeks. You'll stay with us 'til then. You live here."

"Is there a prize?"

"Five hundred dollars and you get to ride in my Corvette in the parade."

"If I win."

"Oh, you'll win, honey." Maisie put her arm around her. "There's no girls here prettier than you."

*But I'm not white, you idiot.* "So who decides who wins? And what's in it for you guys?"

"She may be pretty, but she's not stupid," Duane chuckled. Maisie kicked him under the picnic table.

"Our minister, our mayor, the guy who owns the hardware store and Duane are the judges." Trish slapped a mosquito on her arm.

"And you care because...?"

The four looked at each other, then at Aurora sitting with her hands folded in her lap.

"Okay, okay." Sandy popped another beer. "We're running a betting pool. So far, there's over five grand riding on this." He shrugged. "People are bored out here."

Finally she nodded. "All right. But if I win, it's a five-way split."

Duane snorted and gave Trish the evil eye.

"And I'll throw my five hundred dollars into the pot." The mood lightened.

"That's fair." Sandy was nodding.

Duane shrugged okay. Maisie turned up the radio, blasting Little Eva, and she and Trish began twisting in the candlelight, screech-singing "Do the locomotion, do the locomotion with me!"

Near dawn, while the others slept, Aurora searched their house. In the front closet, was  a loaded shotgun with several boxes of cartridges and two hooded white robes crudely made from sheets.

In the living room, which stank of ashtrays, there was a locked strongbox on a desk by a pad of form real estate contracts and a notary stamp. Upstairs, save a baggie of pot, an asthma inhaler and a letter from Maisie's mother begging her to visit her dying father, Sandy and Maisie's room held little interest. But in Duane and Trish's bedroom, a loaded Colt 45 lay by snoring Duane's side of the bed alongside an open 35mm film can with white powder and a razor blade.

Back in Aurora's room, King was asleep at the foot of her bed.

## 21.

On an unseasonably warm morning in late November 1962, Romulo and Whitey reported to Lieutenant Commander John Wesley Harvey, skipper on board the U.S.S. *Thresher*. Romulo was assigned a berth as Chief Medical Orderly and Whitey was First Machinist's Mate. They knew that agent Collins and his mysterious employer had arranged for them to be stationed on the same vessel. They had no idea whether or how many others on board were similarly placed.

Romulo worried how Remus would take to submarine life but Remus seemed okay, and even allowed members of the crew to pet him. Many of the sailors had never seen a griffin before.

In February, Romulo was ordered to give a ship's tour to a visiting officer. It was agent Collins with a regulation Navy buzz cut, wearing a commander's uniform. As they walked through the giant ship, Collins asked after Whitey.

"Let me make this easy, *Commander*." Romulo held his gaze. "I've known Whitey for less than two years. He likes women, he doesn't like men, which is what you want to know. He's too dumb to be an officer, which is why I trust him. He does what I say."

"Why do you always begin conversations in the middle?"

They were approaching the bow. Wearing radiation badges and cloth boots now, they squeezed into the nucleonics room. The humming nuclear generator caused the black rubber decking to vibrate beneath their feet as they eased past a row of technicians monitoring gleaming machines bearing General Dynamics

Corporation badges. No one paid any attention to Romulo and Collins talking in a corner of the neon-lit compartment.

"You want this ship, don't you?" Romulo asked.

Collins looked away, nodded at an officer with a clipboard who saluted back.

"You're doing it again." Collins sighed.

Romulo leaned close. "I know how to get her. I know her inside and out."

Saturday night, in the bar of a bowling alley in Watertown, as Collins sipped beer out of a paper cup and glanced over Romulo's shoulder from time to time at three girls who threw mostly gutter balls, Romulo described his plan. When he finished, Collins let out a long burp.

"What makes you think the guy I work for gives two shits about your plan?"

"Because if he's smart, he'll see that it can work."

"Suppose he's not smart?"

Romulo leaned closer. "I'm not just offering him the submarine. You've heard something about my experimental work at Portsmouth. It was very successful."

Collins crushed his cup. "I don't know what you're talking about."

"Tell your employer that I'll deliver the *Thresher* according to my plan. I'll also guarantee him eternal life."

Collins, whose gaze had drifted towards the laughing girls again, looked back. "You wanna run that by me again?"

"Eternal life."

"What's that, a magazine subscription? Be serious."

"I am serious. Let me show you."

Romulo unlocked his car trunk, pulled away a canvas covering and showed Collins a severed human hand that wiggled its fingers like a typist on Romulo's command.

Naturally, Howard Hughes was curious about Romulo after hearing Collins' report and Romulo was eager to finally meet Collins's mysterious employer. After passing muster with three security guards, Romulo and Collins were ushered into Hughes' penthouse at the Ritz in Boston. Barefoot in slacks and a white shirt, Hughes extended a welcoming hand to the young man in the

U. S. Navy uniform.

"I'm Howard Hughes," he said. "Collins has told me a lot about you. I understand you can help me procure the *Thresher*."

"I am without ruth," Romulo said, pretending to struggle with his words.

Hughes frowned.

"He means he's ruthless," Collins added helpfully.

"Hello, Mr. Hughes. I am honored to meet you."

"Sit down. Sit down," Hughes grumbled, "Collins, get this man a rum and Coke."

Collins drifted into the other room.

Romulo and Hughes appraised each other as Hughes crunched an ice cube. "So... You're from Haiti." Romulo nodded helpfully. "And they let you into our Navy?"

Romulo leaned closer in his chair. Hughes had cotton balls between each of his newly manicured toes.

"I like money, Mr. Hughes. And I have unique ideas to sell."

Hughes laughed, "I love an immigrant with a vision. Guys like you made this country great." He grinned at Collins, lurking in the doorway. "Burgers from room service!" Collins picked up the house phone. "Con fritos!" Hughes winked at Romulo.

As they talked and ate, Romulo began to admire Hughes; he was self-centered and brilliant, qualities Romulo saw in himself. Romulo's plan to seize the *Thresher* impressed Hughes. He'd thought through every detail and he was an okay guy, *for a spic.*

"What's this I hear about eternal life?" Hughes was licking ketchup off his fingers. Romulo heard the skepticism in his voice and chose his words carefully.

"I can bring a man back from the dead." His dark eyes bore into Hughes. "You need never fear as long as I'm with you. If you're injured, provided your brain or heart isn't destroyed, I'll heal you. When your body grows old, I'll put you in a new healthy one and you can live *siempre*—forever."

Hughes rolled his eyes, then took a sip of his Coke.

"You're not a doctor. I've checked. Your formal medical training is about the same as a nurse's aide. Pardon me, Mr. Foreign Guy in a U.S. Navy uniform. How will you be able to do all this?"

Romulo leaned back, smiling. *This is going perfectly.*

"I'm skilled in *la science* and voodoo, the ways of my people. By applying these arts to modern surgery and anesthesia, I've developed a new kind of healing. But I need help. A proper laboratory. Without the technology, I can go no further."

Romulo paused, watching Hughes. *He's taken the bait.* "Please continue."

"I'll give you eternal life, but you must give me the means to continue my work."

"And the *Thresher*?"

"She'll be yours if you do as I ask."

Hughes studied Romulo carefully. He was intrigued.

"Let's get the boat. Then we can talk about the rest of it. I'm interested in what you've told me. I need to think it over."

Romulo was nodding.

"The hijacking will be according to my plan?"

"That's right. But can you command a submarine?"

"I can with the right crew."

"You'll have the right crew."

Romulo's smile left the billionaire wondering who got the better part of the deal.

## 22.

Aurora heard Sandy and Duane drive off after midnight the past two nights, not returning until close to dawn. Tonight, she would find out what they were up to.

Pleading a headache, she'd gone to bed early, leaving Maisie and Trish to their beers and their gin game. Shortly after 11:45 p.m. by her watch, she slipped downstairs and climbed into the trunk of Duane's Corvette, concealing herself under an old blanket that smelled like earth and gasoline. She didn't have long to wait. She heard approaching footsteps, then the trunk swung open.

"Hey, what'd you put in here?" Sandy dumped what felt like pieces of wood—paint stirrers?—next to her. Then a sloshing can of liquid.

"Nothing."

Duane climbed into the driver's seat. Sandy slammed the trunk.

The gasoline stench became overpowering as they drove away.

Smooth roads with occasional traffic for about twenty minutes, then a rougher surface with fewer cars, then bumpy dirt and near silence. Duane turned off the headlights—they were driving in the dark— then, finally, the engine. The car glided to a stop. There was only the sound of cicadas chirping in waves.

Sandy opened the trunk. Peering over a corner of the blanket concealing her, Aurora watched the two men staple the pieces of wood into cross shapes, then soak them with gasoline. They must have made nearly a dozen before they carried them off, laughing and shushing each other like schoolboys.

Aurora climbed out of the trunk. The Corvette was pulled over on a country road—more like a track. Small, shabby houses with boarded-up windows and garbage in front yards lined both sides. Somewhere, a baby was crying. Up ahead, she could see Duane and Sandy, dim shapes driving their crosses one at a time into the ground in front of each home.

*Those little bastards.*

Duane had left the key in the ignition.

A few hundred yards away, she saw the first cross light up. Then running footsteps, and a second cross burst into flames. They were working their way back to the car. Quickly.

Aurora started the engine, turned on the high beams and cranked up the radio. Martha and the Vandellas blasted out: "LIKE A HEATWAVE, BURNIN' IN MY HEART..."

A dog started barking. House lights went on. She threw the car into reverse and swerve-turned to point it in the direction she'd come from. "CAN'T KEEP FROM CRYIN'! IT'S TEARIN' ME APART." In the rearview mirror, she watched a large shape in a ragged bathrobe grab Duane by the arm, then punch. "IS THIS THE WAY LOVE'S SUPPOSED TO BE? IT'S LIKE A HEATWAVE!" Someone tackled Sandy at the knees. A screaming woman turned a hose on him.

Aurora gunned the Corvette back along the dirt road all the way to the highway. It was a pleasure to drive.

Trish was sleeping face down tonight, snoring beneath her sleep mask. Aurora carefully lifted the strongbox from the bedside table and tiptoed back to the bedroom doorway--where Maisie stood holding a pistol.

"I'm sorry, Rory. Did I disturb you? You know, I don't think you're very grateful. We took you in, fed you and now here you are swipin' our strongbox."

Trish moaned and rolled over. "What's goin 'on?" Aurora smiled at Maisie. "The gun's not loaded."

Yesterday, Aurora had removed its bullets and nestled them beneath the charcoal briquettes in Duane's barbecue grill. Just for fun.

Maisie squeezed the trigger. Click.

Behind her, King appeared panting outside the door. Aurora pushed Maisie, sending her tumbling backwards over the dog, then bolted down the stairs, clutching the strongbox. She heard an approaching siren and saw flashing lights in the rearview mirror as she peeled Duane' Corvette out of the driveway and sped off.

## 23.

Early on April 10th, 1963, a sunny but windy day, Lieutenant Commander Harvey took the *Thresher* out of Portsmouth harbor on a shakedown cruise to conduct deep-diving tests. The submarine rescue ship *Skylark* accompanied the nuclear submarine.

220 miles east of Boston, and 55 miles south of the comparatively shallow waters of the continental shelf, Commander Harvey ran the *Thresher* into a deep dive in 8,400 feet of water. On the surface, *Skylark* stood by into 40 knot winds and high seas. It was 9 a.m.

Whitey's legs were like rubber as he opened the forward compartment door and slipped into the reactor room, where crewmen wearing protective clothing were monitoring engine functions as they supplied nuclear power for the dive. Whitey's fingers worked furiously to strip off his shirt. No one noticed him hurry to the railing around the core and handcuff himself to it. Twelve sticks of dynamite were taped around his torso and a small radio-activated detonator was clipped to his belt. A sailor in the breeder section looked up.

"Hey, that guy's not wearing protection."

A deck above, Romulo stepped into the control center and

approached Commander Harvey, a stocky silver-haired officer poring over a chart. A few feet away, the helmsman sat strapped into a padded leather chair gripping a steering yoke set between two semicircular banks of hooded dials.

"Gyro and S.I.N.S. are checking out. Fathometer's steady."

Harvey grunted.

Romulo cleared his throat. "May I have a word, skipper?"

"Certainly not, sailor. Get back to your station." Harvey returned his attention to the blip of light that was the *Thresher* moving beneath the plotting table map.

"I'm holding a transistorized detonator. There's a man in the reactor room wearing twelve sticks of dynamite."

Harvey looked up.

"Would you like to make history?" Romulo asked him.

"What the devil do you want?" The skipper glanced around the compartment. None of the other officers had noticed anything.

Romulo dangled the detonator device in his right hand. The intercom lit up. "That'll be the reactor room to confirm what I just said. Tell them to do what the man wants and not get excited."

Harvey picked up the receiver and listened. His voice quavered. "Do as he says. Stand by for further orders."

"Let's take a walk into the radio room. Smile, please. It may be your last chance."

Officer Sparks stood up and saluted when Romulo and the skipper entered. Romulo handed him a piece of paper.

"Do what this man says," Harvey growled.

"Yes, sir."

"Contact *Skylark* and read that to them," Romulo ordered. Sparks radioed the standby rescue ship on the surface. He adjusted his glasses and read from Romulo's handwriting. "Experiencing minor difficulty. Have positive up angle. Attempting to blow. Will keep you informed."

The blast from Romulo's .45 caliber handgun blew the top of Sparks' scalp into the ventilation grid. Romulo flicked off the transmitter.

On board *Skylark*, the radio operator copied down the message and sent it to the bridge. Captain Zebrowski read it and frowned.

"Anything else?"

"Radio operator reports hearing an explosion just before the

*Thresher* went off the air."

The Captain frowned again."Run a Gertrude check every fifteen minutes. It's probably nothing."

"Yes, sir."

The seaman saluted and returned to the radio room. For the next two hours, *Skylark* attempted to contact the *Thresher* every quarter hour.

Fathoms below, Dr. Hunter was puzzled. A number of the crew had drawn black crosses on their foreheads. He stopped the Executive Officer, Kool Silver, the *Thresher*'s Jamaican-born second-in-command, outside of sick bay.

"Is today Ash Wednesday or something?" Hunter asked.

After a glance at his watch, Silver produced a pistol from inside his shirt and squeezed the trigger. Hunter's stomach came apart in his hands. A muffled gunshot nearby, then another farther away. All over the *Thresher*, Hughes' men, identifying themselves by the black crosses on their foreheads, were neutralizing the rest of the crew. By 10 a.m., it was done and the *Thresher* was speeding west towards the zone marked "Explosives Dumping Area" on Navy charts.

Of the two hundred souls who shipped out on the *Thresher* for her maiden dive, some thirty-seven men were immediately deemed unreliable, paid $1,000 cash each and asked to wait with their bags packed in a compartment near the torpedo tubes. Whitey locked the air seals and Romulo turned off their oxygen flow. Their bodies were eventually jettisoned to the surface along with selected "wreckage".

Every available vessel in the Atlantic fleet joined in the search while an anxious nation waited for news of the missing $45 million submarine. For the next two days, newspapers all over the world carried headlines about the *Thresher* until, finally, the destroyer *Warrington* found the oil slick Romulo had jettisoned, the red and yellow plastic glove (the kind used by the reactor section crew) and bits of plastic, all floating near George's Bank, a favorite shoal for Soviet fishing vessels. This led to worldwide speculation about Soviet complicity in the loss of the *Thresher* and a thorough, though clandestine, re-assessment of international fishing laws. It was all just as Romulo had planned.

A somber President Kennedy addressed the nation at cocktail

hour:

"The courage and dedication of these men of the sea, pushing ahead into depths to advance our knowledge and capabilities, is no less than that of their forefathers who led the advance on the frontiers of our civilization." How little he knew.

Hughes had made arrangements with Haiti's kleptocratic President for life Papa Doc Duvalier, still angry over the United States 'diplomatic withdrawal, and Romulo sailed the *Thresher* through the Bermuda Triangle into a discreet shipyard in Port-au-Prince harbor for refitting.

The Haitian boat builders were delighted to have work, and Papa Doc himself, in top hat and sunglasses, with his black-booted imperial guards at his side, came aboard to gleefully inspect the mighty submarine, so cleverly purloined from his enemy. Romulo felt smug about the difference in his circumstances since last he set foot in Port-au-Prince. He was tempted to go ashore and look around the city but elected instead to pore over Captain Harvey's log books and teach himself to command the ship. He came across the *Thresher*'s motto "*Vis Tacita*" (Silent strength). He smiled. Papa Zabop would approve, wherever he was. *Gardez silence.*

Work on the ship complete, she was rechristened with a bottle of champagne broken against her hull by First Lady Simone Duvalier's bejeweled and sticky-fingered hand. A fresh crew of Haitian sailors came aboard to replace the men killed in the mutiny (and otherwise). Ill-educated, raised on superstition and not enough to eat, the new crew quickly learned to fear and obey their captain. Rumors spread as fast as the smell of sweat in close quarters: the captain is a mighty *houngan* who needs no air to breathe and can control the weather; he is Papa Doc's illegitimate son; he is a CIA agent on a secret mission.

Romulo's voice was quiet but firm in the packed mess hall their first night aboard. Whitey, with a fresh buzz cut, and the ever-faithful Executive Officer Kool Silver stood on either side of him.

"I command this vessel because I *took* this vessel," Romulo announced. "There is no law but my law. If you disobey me, you will die."

Silver's huge arms were crossed. The rippling scar tissue that was half his face glistened as he looked over the crew. As though summoned, Remus fluttered brightly down and came to rest on Romulo's shoulder.

"Look around, he continued. "The faces you see who are loyal to me will send home money - lots of money." There was a rumble of approval.

"Those who are disloyal will have their bodies slit and stuffed with salt before I eat them."

"With pico sauce," someone shouted. There was nervous laughter.

Romulo held very still.

"I'm so glad you said that. Please step forward."

Hands pushed and shoved forward the man who spoke -- a portly young man with a ponytail. Romulo put his arm around him.

" You have given all of us an opportunity to experience the meaning of my words."

The man smiled uncertainly. The crew cheered him.

In an orange blue flash, Remus tore open the sailor's throat with his beak. The artery gushed and the men fell over each other to escape the blood spurting from his neck.

"Crew dismissed."

The *Thresher* headed back out to sea. What had begun as a mostly American assortment of submariners from the Midwest and the Portsmouth, New Hampshire area would be replaced one after another by mariners (or pirates, for that's what they were) from the desperate countries: Haiti, the Dominican Republic, Cuba, Senegal and South Africa. Port-au-Prince would be the rogue submarine's home base for many years, and Romulo would return to Haiti often.

## 24.

At the Miami Greyhound station, Aurora paid a homeless man in a Gators cap twenty dollars to drive Duane's Corvette north until it ran out of gas. She took a cab to a Howard Johnson's where she checked into a mostly orange room and opened the strongbox. It contained a film can filled with white powder, and nearly $4,000 dollars. She kept the money and flushed the powder down the toilet.

Aurora rented a sunny studio apartment with an ocean view in Miami Shores and enrolled in business classes at Barry University.

She wrote her mother:

> Mi Querido Mama:
> I am living in Miami close to the sea. I'm going to college. I think you will love America as much as I do. I miss you so much and there is nothing left for you in Haiti now that Papa is dead. I have worked hard and saved this money so you can buy a plane ticket. Come to America as soon as you can.
> I send you hugs.

She mailed a $500 money order with her letter to Madonna, then stopped at the post office's general delivery. Her heart soared. A letter from Romulo was waiting for her.

## 25.

Los Angeles, 1963

McCoy was told to bring only a change of street clothes and a few personal items. Everything else would be provided. One of Hughes' drivers drove him to another moonlit Malibu beach and dropped him off with his small canvas bag, a memento from his M.A.S.H. unit he brought for good luck. Two swarthy men in blue coveralls hurried him onto the Boston Whaler. They bounced across the waves for a mile or so to where the *Thresher* lay anchored. A scramble up the hull net, a climb up the sail tower, past her two periscopes, then down through two hatches by ladders to the nerve center of the air-conditioned steel tube.

Romulo and Silver were huddled over a video screen on the bridge. Romulo looked up, beaming, but pale with red-rimmed eyes.

"Well, look who's back! Welcome, Dr. McCoy. I see your principles have been compromised." Romolo hugged him like a lost son.

*What the...?* McCoy stood stiffly, breathing through his mouth to evade Romulo's body odor.

"Anchors aweigh, Silver," Romulo said as he took McCoy's arm. "We're setting sail for the Far East tonight. Watch the knee knocker." McCoy stepped over the bulkhead divider.

" Your quarters are this way. I haven't slept -- how long is it now, Silver? Thirty-four hours?"

"Thirty-seven, Captain. A tru tru." Silver followed them as they made their way through the mess hall. "I'm in the middle of an experiment," Romulo explained offhandedly. "I'm seeking the cure for sleep."

"Sleep isn't a disease. It's a healthy restorative state," McCoy pointed out.

"We waste a third of our lives doing it. Imagine if we could get that time back."

"I'd rather get some rest."

The crew quarters were on the middle deck, long rows of aluminum bunks, stacked three high. A privacy curtain ran the perimeter of each bunk; some decorated with flags, tie-dyed fabric—even a peace sign. A poster of Raquel Welch in a fur bikini brandishing a spear covered part of the bulkhead. Romulo led them to the next compartment—a small cabin with three stacked bunks, a desk with drawers and a fold-down sink. A set of sheets and a towel with a locker key lay on the bottom bunk.

"Lower bunks are for the higher-ranked officers." He eyed McCoy. "I've given you the benefit of the doubt."

"Thank you." McCoy tossed his bag on the lowest bunk. "What's in there?" A padlocked steel cabinet hung over the desk. "The latest and greatest antibiotics and sedatives from Hughes Pharmaceutical. Also anything with the word 'alcohol 'on it. You'd be surprised what a thirsty sailor will drink. Only you and I have the key."

McCoy nodded. "Do I have bunkmates?"

"Not yet. But you will." The whomping engine noise had grown louder. Silver caught Romulo's eye. "O.K. Back to the bridge. We're preparing to dive. Breakfast is at seven, doctor. We can discuss your duties then."

McCoy stowed his things in his assigned drawer, then stretched out on the bottom bunk. He closed the curtain around him. Wide awake, he opened the *TIME* magazine he'd been reading—an article about medieval health practices. His interest suddenly piqued, he read the words twice: "The letter "T" was often painted on the sides of a well or cistern as a warning that the village was infected with plague." *Is that what Marie Laveau wrote in her own blood? A plague warning? But the plague was eliminated over a hundred years ago...*

The engine rumbled at a different pitch; he felt his weight shift as the giant vessel tilted, then submerged. Dropping off to sleep, he thought about Katie. *She's been dead less than two months. God, I miss her.*

The Etta James version of *I'd Rather Go Blind* was playing on the stereo the night they met at a shoulder-to-shoulder party in the West Village. He was in New York for a conference, flying back to L.A. in the morning. Low sofas, candles burning, and too much pot smoke — he almost left, but then he saw her.

Katie was dancing alone to the music's sultry pain. *I would rather, I would rather go blind, boy, than to see you walk away from me.* She opened her arms wide as Etta James held the throbbing refrain. One nipple peaked over the top of her low-cut peasant blouse. Their eyes met. He could barely smile for being so smitten. But she could. They talked and laughed that two people from L.A. would meet in New York. She tied her hair back in a chignon while they spoke. Later, he walked her to her friend's apartment building. Outside, he asked for her number but made no move. "Sure!" Such a big smile—and she smelled so good. Chanel. Neither had any paper, so she wrote her number on his hand.

At 7:05 a.m., grinning like a mangled Cheshire cat, Ensign Silver whisked open McCoy's bunk curtain. "Day-O, Sunshine. Plenty a food in the mess!"

McCoy hit his head sitting up and cursed.

Silver gave him a tour of the ship, walking along the passageways, chest-to-chest with seamen passing in the other direction. "Wah gwaan. Beg yuh pass." If the Frankenstein monster were real and could speak, McCoy decided, its voice would be Silver's—a deep Rasta monotone with a Jamaican growl. Silver's vocal chords were damaged by the fire that melted half his face and all of whatever smile he might have had. But from the neck down, he was magnificent with a boxer's well-defined upper body and the agility of a panther.

The two men entered the supply compartment. "Small up yuhself." They had to duck their heads now walking on top of yards of stacked cartons: canned goods, produce and other supplies. "The more we bring, the longer we can stay." Silver led McCoy into the officer's wardroom. " Ova deh--one shower. You get two minutes a day of water. Use more—you get beat up. Stink—you get beat up worse."

Silver paused next before rows of orange life jackets attached to hoods.

"Steinke hoods. If you need to escape to the surface, put one on. The hood traps the air. Enough for you to breathe maybe six hundred feet. If you're deeper than that..." He was shaking his head. "Bumborass. Go to sleep, mon, and don't wake up." He pointed at the rungs and the hatch above. "Climb into the immersion compartment. Seal it behind you. When it fills with water, open the next hatch and swim out. Breathe regular. Shout 'Ho, Ho, Ho 'until you reach the surface. You might freeze or drown up there, but at least you won't be here."

McCoy was in charge of the sick bay, diagnosing and treating the various maladies 103 men in close quarters might suffer. He spent his days dispensing aspirins and Pepto-Bismol, stitching wounds and setting the odd break or fracture. His greatest challenge was monitoring the locked pharmacy cabinet. *I used to treat movie stars and millionaires; I wore Gucci loafers and cashmere sweaters. Now I stitch up tattooed thugs.*

> Dear Mr. Hughes,
> Life aboard the *Thresher* is a combination of U.S. Navy chain of command and a ruthless dictatorship. Romulo DaVinci is titular captain (although he seems to know little about seamanship and next to nothing about navigation). He relies on the Executive Officer Kool Silver, a Jamaican giant unwaveringly loyal to DaVinci, who he claims brought him back from the dead (I'm looking into this. Don't get your hopes up.) One of the crew told me that after the hijacking, those who refused to serve under

> DaVinci and his offer of triple pay and prize money (isn't that what it is?) were fed to the sharks through the torpedo tubes. You may wish to consult with your legal advisors because I believe that makes you an accessory to murder. Yours in malpractice, Wiley McCoy

His loneliness could not have been more complete. The men around him were broken toys– criminals, malcontents. There were no women; only sailor-ready whores in Haitian dive bars every few months. Slipping off to sleep was when he missed Katie most. The spooning, the wound legs akimbo—greater treasures lost than the kisses and couplings.

*I am the saint of lost causes. I look forward to stolen moments with a ghost. I breathe for both of us.*

He was haunted.

## 26.

It was March 1963. Hughes had Romulo flown into Los Angeles by helicopter, then driven at a frighteningly high speed to the Beverly Hills Hotel where he kept him waiting in the living room of his bungalow for almost three hours. Near dawn, an unkempt and barefoot Hughes burst out of the bedroom trailed by two aides. He hurried past Romulo without a glance and left the suite. Furious, Romulo stood up, wondering if he should follow.

But the bedroom door behind him was ajar. Romulo did a double-take. Hughes, who he had just watched leave, was standing peering out the window. He winked at Romulo.

"They've gone." He was dressed in one of his blue silk dressing gowns. He had a suntan; he looked good, practically as good as you'd expect a billionaire to look, Romulo thought.

"Who was that?"

"Brooks Randall, my double. He keeps the news hounds off my tail so I can get some work done." Hughes grinned mischievously. "Want to go for a drive?"

In the parking lot, they walked past a row of Cadillacs, Rolls-Royces, and Lincolns. Hughes stopped at a battered old Chevrolet and unlocked the door.

"I can't ride in those luxury cars. Too conspicuous." They climbed in and Hughes started the engine. The front seat smelled like potato chips. "How's the big boat?"

Romulo paused before he spoke. "I'm having problems with Dr. McCoy."

Hughes turned onto Santa Monica and headed for downtown Los Angeles.

"What sorts of problems?"

"He's surly, he doesn't do what I tell him. I don't trust him."

"Is he doing his job?"

"He's doing his job. But he doesn't mind his own business."
Hughes looked pleased. "Good. That's why I pay him."

"He could be dangerous. I want to work with somebody else, Howard...."

"Then you can work without me, my money and my submarine. You were a two-bit Navy supply clerk when I found you. I'm sure the job's still open." He looked at Romulo through hooded lids. "McCoy stays. You can't have everything."

The Chevy lurched as he braked suddenly, inches from the car in front of him.

"For a wetback, you're doing pretty good. Now I want you to listen to me."

Hughes squinted out the car window as though he could see a shining city on a hill. "Someday corporations with an agenda will be able to legally give money to politicians to carry out that agenda. That's how democracy should work and it will. Guys like me will get what we pay for and everyone'll be better off."

They sped past Grauman's Chinese Theatre, its garish arches glowing in the early morning light. The tourists hadn't arrived yet to crowd over the sidewalk stars and the handprints. Howard began talking about President Kennedy. The fury of his tirade made his driving even worse.

"He keeps screwin' up! We would have had Castro if it hadn't been for him. I could've rebuilt Cuba, set those Russian bastards back a few squares, but that hunky fucked us! God damnit, Romulo. Jack Kennedy's the reason you went to prison!"

Romulo recalled his toilet of a cell in Haiti and the caranques that crawled all over him. He began to share the billionaire's anger.

*But how to take advantage of it?*

"You're upset, Mr. Hughes. You should take action, otherwise your anger will cause an ulcer. Always take action." His penis stiffened perceptibly at the thought of violence.

"He used to date Gene Tierney, too. That pissed me off! Not that he got any while I was around. No sirree. But that suave mick sure as hell tried."

Howard pulled into the parking lot at the Brown Derby.

"I'm going to take action, goddamnit!" As he climbed out of the car, his robe fell open revealing stained boxer shorts. He tossed the car keys to an attendant.

"Forget this voter stuff." He gripped Romulo's arm so hard it hurt. "Within a few generations, with business backing the right leaders, the right laws will get passed, the right Supreme Court will get appointed. " Hughes' right eye was twitching now. "My money can make that happen. But first, we have to pop that son of a bitch! Let's get some eggs."

## 27.

Romulo's letter to Aurora contained ten $100 American Express travelers checks.

> Chere Aurora:
> I'm sorry I left you in the airport like that. I hope this money will help you.
> Are you enjoying America as much as I am? Have you had a hamburger from that Scottish place yet?
> Please write me in care of: President Duvalier, the Palace, Port-au-Prince, Haiti and tell me your news.
> Love, Romo

Aurora wrote back immediately:

> Dear Romo,
> I am a student.
> Thanks for the guilt money.

Are you dealing drugs or just taking them?

In his next letter to Howard Hughes, McCoy reported that Derek Ts'Me, a South Vietnamese Army medic with a specialty in anesthesia, had deserted under fear of execution by the corrupt Van-Thieu regime. Ts'Me had become too familiar with their opium smuggling connections to the CIA.

Early one violet morning, he paddled a raft laden with heroin through crowded, stinking Ho Chi Minh City harbor to where the *Thresher* lay at anchor. Romulo, who knew Ts'Me as a narcotics middleman and a dogfight enthusiast from the seediest dock bars, welcomed him aboard as third Medical Officer.

McCoy was grateful for the assistance.

His new bunkmate was a cheerful soul, sexually ambiguous, with a beatific smile and a fleshy Buddha's body. McCoy found him medically competent if ethically challenged.

*But who am I to call the kettle black?*

"I'm very happy to be aboard this pirate hospital," Ts'Me confessed one evening after dinner. He and McCoy were out on the conning tower. Ts'Me wore a silk bathrobe and smelled of cologne. He lit a joint, cupping his hands against the wind and passed it to McCoy. "I feel safe here."

"You'll get over that."

Dreams were his refuge. Katie didn't appear every night or if she did he couldn't always recall.

The settings varied: sometimes they sat by the pool in Los Angeles just talking like they used to do; another time, while shopping on Rodeo Drive, she insisted on teaching him Japanese, a language he had no recollection that she knew. And the sex was always good. So nearly real. "It's how spirits live on," she confided. "We come to those who conjure us in their dreams."

He always awoke in a clammy sweat to the sound of the ship's HVAC system punctuated with Ts'Me's snoring in the bunk above.

*I'm losing my mind to stay sane.*

New Orleans, The French Quarter

Caribbean architecture set in an ambling grid of stone sidewalks and palm trees, like a sweaty little Paris, with churches and squares named after Civil War generals, scoundrels and pirates and blocks of three and four-story brick houses hidden behind tall shutters to keep the hurricanes out. Romulo felt right at home.

It was his first meeting on Hughes' behalf with hairless David Ferrie, a failed priest but successful pederast, turned pilot and anti-Castro zealot. Romulo knew of him but they'd never met. In his reddish wig and pasted-on eyebrows, he looked like a snake dressed up for Halloween. Most of Hughes' missions were laugh-out-loud crazy, and Romulo had low expectations for this drink in a Magnolia Street bar to discuss a very dangerous idea.

"You see?" Ferrie said. "Everyone helps and no one *knows* they're helping." His long fingers cradled his bourbon glass. "Patriots have to *do* something. After what happened in Cuba...." He was shaking his head. One of his pasted-on eyebrows had shifted. "This can't be allowed to go on."

Romulo came away impressed by the research and detail the soft-spoken viper had set forth. His plan could work. Ferrie had the contacts; he only lacked the network which Hughes could provide. And, of course, the money. Best of all, there would be no accountability. No roads would lead back to Rome.

He was so lost in thought that he nearly passed by an old shopfront on Charles Street with a weathered wooden sign that said "Jo Jim Pharmacy." Mullioned glass windows displayed antique jars with handwritten labels. The wide plank floorboards squeaked as he entered to the tinkling of a cat's bell over the door. A young pharmacist in a white short-sleeved jacket was talking on the phone behind the counter. "Be with you in a moment," he said.

Romulo peered at the old apothecary bottles on shelves that reached to the ceiling. There were oddly named drugs, medicinal herbs, *gris gris* potions and obscure patent medicines. He could barely contain his joy. This is where he loved to be: at the crazy edge of healing.

"Can I help you find something, sir?"

Romulo was wearing his usual shore outfit, a light blue *Cubavera* shirt and linen trousers. He smiled. The pharmacist blinked at Romulo's sharp teeth.

"I'd be surprised, but I'll ask. I am looking for a *Sanjivani* plant."

"There's no such thing," the young man replied too quickly. His arms were pale and skinny. "It's only a legend."

Romulo first heard of *Sanjivani* from Madonna who had met a *houngan* who swore to the plant's reanimation powers. It grew in India on the northern slopes of Dunagiri, a mountain in Uttarakhand, and its fragrant yellow flowers and sappy milk could revive the dying. It was said to glow in the dark. Years later, Romulo heard about it again in Norfolk from a drunk Pakistani-American soldier during a poker game; he claimed the *Sanjivani* plant had brought his baby sister back to life.

"Some legends are true. I have heard that the *Sanjivani* can grow in Louisiana because the climate is like India's."

A senior pharmacist with little hair on his head but much growing out of his ears appeared as if from nowhere. "I'm sorry, sir. Although we carry a few harmless but perhaps helpful Cajun folk remedies, we stay away from discredited fantasy concoctions."

"I see. Well, thank you."

Through the shop window, the two pharmacists watched him round the corner and disappear into the bustling French Quarter crowd.

Floyd St. Cloud was lost in every way but geographically. Barely a high school graduate, after two years in the Army Corps of Engineers, he returned to St. James Parish to find his mother dying and no jobs worth having, so he went to work for his crazy uncle Jo Jim in his French Quarter drugstore for three dollars an hour, living frugally in the creaky attic room upstairs, where he lifted weights and masturbated over men's magazines he surreptitiously replaced on the store's periodical rack after use.

Floyd followed Romulo when he left the drugstore, all the way to his hotel at the edge of Jackson Square. He was waiting on a bench outside, watching the front door, hoping Romulo would reappear, when he nearly jumped out of his skin. Romulo was sitting next to him.

"Do you want to talk with me, or did you have something more brutal in mind?" Romulo asked.

"*Sanjivani,*" Floyd croaked, then cleared his throat. "I can get it for you."

"That's not what you said an hour ago."

"That's 'cause my uncle was there. He doesn't want to lose his license." Romulo was watching him like a lizard on a rock waiting for a fly.

"Go on."

"My grandpa worked in the sugar cane fields at Oak Alley. He and my grandma were sharecroppers who worked with the freed slaves who still cut the sugar fields because there was nothing else they were fit to do. My grandma used to tell me stories about the old plantations and about the slave doctor. His name was Merricq and the plantation owners paid him to take care of their slaves when they got hurt or took sick. Grandma said Merricq had been a surgeon in the French army and was particularly good at amputations. If somebody's leg got crushed, it was easier to just cut it off and let the stump heal, than to save it and nurse the patient back to health." He looked at Romulo and paused. "Dr. Merriq took a shine to my grandpa. He loaned him the money to open the pharmacy my uncle now runs. And my grandpa paid Merricq back every penny before the old doctor died."

"You ought to write a book," Romulo said as he stood up.

"Where are you going?"

"I don't want to read your book."

"Sit down. Sit down. I'm getting to the point."

Romulo slumped back onto the bench.

"So every time Merricq would amputate a hand or a leg, he'd take the body part and bury it somewhere because he believed it would be reunited with the patient in the afterlife." He leaned closer and lowered his voice. "My grandpa kept a box of Dr. Merricq's old papers and one day I looked through it and found a map. A map of where he buried the body parts. It had a ledger with dates and patient names and, in one corner, a notation: 'planted seeds on slope in strong sunlight. This will be the best crop ever.'"

"And you think 'seeds' refers to *Sanjivani*?"

Floyd looked around. "About a year ago, I borrowed Uncle Jo Jim's skiff and paddled out to where the map said to go."

"And?" Romulo's heart was beating faster.

"And what's it worth to you?" Floyd asked.

Days later, the *Thresher* anchored shortly after dusk about a mile off Mendicant Island, one of many small land masses along the marshy coast of Louisiana.

"Why have we stopped here?" McCoy asked Romulo when he stepped into the control room.

"To pick flowers," Romulo said as he pulled a pair of boots from the bulkhead cabinet and tossed them to McCoy. "You'll need these."

With Silver at the helm and Romulo and McCoy side by side, the Zodiac made the journey in the dark at high speed across Little Lake into Bayou Perot in slightly under an hour. Silver reduced speed as they headed out onto Lake Salvador.

"There he is!" Romulo pointed to the nearby shore where a light was flashing.

"I feel like a grave robber," McCoy grumbled. "What are we doing out here?"

"We are going to meet a man who may lead us to a place where *Sanjivani* flowers grow," Romulo said. "But you don't know what those are. And if I told you, you'd laugh at me."

The light flashed again much closer now. A figure stood on the shore. Silver cut the engine and the Zodiac glided forward, then bumped against the bank. The stranger waded a few yards out and swung himself aboard, taking a seat in the bow. He was red-haired with a modest Elvis Presley pompadour.

"I'm Floyd." He stuck out his hand.

McCoy shook it. "Wiley."

But Floyd was concentrating on the vast dark lake before them. There were no other boats or lights from houses. The Zodiac's searchlight flashed on, sweeping the still surface.

"There." He pointed towards a lone tree standing in the water like a stork. "Stay to her right and head for shore." They were moving along an alley of moss-hung cypress trees glowing silver in the blackness. The sounds of nearby creatures were everywhere. Here and there, particularly near the banks, dark shapes with red crescent eyes thrashed and their thick scaly tails slapped the water.

Floyd saw McCoy flinch and laughed. "It's peak mating season for the alligators. Don't worry--they're too busy making baby 'gators to care about us."

"Which way, mon?" Silver asked as they approached a fork in

the bayou.

"Stay right and shut down the engine. We're getting shallow now fast."

It was quiet with the engine off. McCoy could feel his paddle bumping into an alligator at almost every stroke. The water was churning with them.

Floyd smiled at his revulsion. "Alligators are cold-blooded reptiles. They spent the last few months sleeping underwater. Now it's warm outside, they're horny and hungry."

Romulo swung the searchlight across the black water, "You sure you know where you're going?"

Floyd was staring intently ahead. "Not much further now. Stay left." As the little boat turned, its port side dipped lower, nearly submerging itself. A dark shape about two feet long came aboard. Its fore-claws scrabbled against McCoy's boot top.

"Jeezum pees!" Silver raised his paddle to strike.

"He won't hurt you." Floyd said, grabbing the middle of the alligator's back and lifting it up like a puppy. "You're too big for her to eat." Floyd tossed it back into the bayou. "Now if you fell in and came upon a larger alligator and struggled with him, he could decide you were a threat and pull you under the water, holding you there 'til you drowned. That's how they kill."

"See that?" Floyd was pointing now at the glow emanating from around the curve, which grew brighter as they paddled through the turn. An unusually steep slope rose up from the left bank, which was embedded with row upon row of white flowers, each one luminescent like the tail of a firefly. Romulo was slack-jawed ecstatic.

"The *Sanjivani*," Floyd said with proprietary pride. "Just the way Dr. Merricq planted them."

Eyes alight, fearless, Romulo waded ashore and threw himself into the white flowers. A cloud of glittering pollen rose in the air like sparks from a fire. "Come on, McCoy! And bring that bag!"

While Silver held the Zodiac, McCoy and Floyd trudged up the bank with the bag of trowels and small paper bags. Following Romulo's example, they set about filling each with earth and carefully uprooted *Sanjivani* flowers. Romulo, laughing like it was Christmas morning, kept digging and packing. "You have no idea of the joy we have found, doctor." Then his eyes clouded over and he looked at Floyd. "Unless the myth has no truth to it."

"Hey, you asked for the flowers. I got you the flowers."

Fifteen minutes later, they pushed off into the darkness and carefully paddled back through the roiling alligator waters. Floyd was singing softly. "I got sunshine on a cloudy day. I got all the riches, baby...."

Romulo's paddle rose up and came down hard across the side of Floyd's head, knocking him unconscious into the water. Dark shapes came at him from several directions.

"Why did you do that?!" McCoy gasped. He tried to clamber out of the boat to help the man, but Romulo held him back. Floyd's blood-bubbling face broke the water's surface, coughing and heaving. A long ridge-backed shape glided alongside and nudged him.

"Help me!" Floyd's elbow jabbed the alligator as he tried to swim towards the Zodiac. Large jaws opened, glinting needle-like teeth, then closed on his shoulder and upper arm. Floyd tried to squirm away but the creature's tail thrashed. The alligator pulled down Floyd who kicked loose a boot as he submerged with his captor. All was suddenly quiet.

"You killed him!" McCoy yelled, diving on top of Romulo, his fist drawn back to punch. Silver's huge hand closed around McCoy's arm and restrained him.

"Should he go for a swim, too?" Silver asked Romulo.

"No. Just hold him." Romulo was looking past them at the ragged bundle that was Floyd breaking the water's surface with a gloop, then floating lifeless, face down, arms akimbo. The alligators ignored him now except for two that were having a tug-of-war with his discarded boot. Romulo paddled closer to the body and McCoy helped him pull it aboard. McCoy held two fingers to Floyd's neck, feeling for a pulse. His carotid artery had no movement.

"Dead," he said after a moment.

Romulo eased Floyd into a leaned-back position and gently closed Floyd's eyes. "I disagree with your diagnosis." He plucked a *Sanjivani* flower from its little bag, shook the earth from its stem, then placed it carefully between Floyd's bluish lips. The light from its petals cast an eerie glow on his dead face.

"You sick bastard!"

"That's no way to speak to a colleague, doctor. I'm only testing the merchandise we bought."

McCoy couldn't take his eyes off Floyd and the ridiculous flower in his mouth. *I've put my hands on enough dead people. That man is dead.*

Approaching Mendicant Island, Floyd's arm slipped off the side of the Zodiac, his hand trailing in the water. Fearing fish (or worse) might nibble the dead fingers, McCoy leaned forward to pull Floyd's limb back into the boat. His body was still in a state of primary flaccidity. *Rigor mortis* had not yet begun.

As McCoy leaned back in his seat, Floyd's hand gripped his forearm. McCoy and Silver gasped as Floyd pulled himself upright, coughing violently. Romulo seemed unperturbed. Floyd began vomiting seawater. The limp *Sanjivani* flower, petals now gray and lightless, fell onto McCoy's lap.

Romulo's smile oozed triumph. "Your patient is in some distress, doctor. You should help him." He paused. "Or do you think he's still dead?"

Floyd lay sprawled at the bow like a rag doll. His pulse was faint but steady, his breathing was shallow and the head wound where Romulo struck him with the paddle was bleeding again. He was very much alive.

Strapped in a canvas stretcher, they hoisted a woozy Floyd aboard the *Thresher* and passed him, dripping blood and seawater, along the corridor into sick bay. McCoy cleaned his wound, stitched it shut, and gave him a tetanus shot. Floyd moaned as McCoy listened to his heartbeat through a stethoscope. "I'm going to give him a sedative." He looked at Romulo leaning against the bulkhead, dreamily examining two bags of *Sanjivani* flowers. "Or do you have a botanical solution?"

"No," Romulo responded. "Your primitive care will be sufficient."

"And what should I tell him when he comes to and asks what happened?" McCoy released Floyd's wrist. His pulse was growing stronger

"Tell him he's lucky to be alive." Romulo looked thoughtful. "And so are you." He watched McCoy administer the sedative.

"I like him. Let's keep him."

Floyd St. Cloud became McCoy's second bunkmate.

# 28.

All summer long, Romulo, Collins, Gay, and Hughes prepared for the assassination. They selected Dallas because it was a city where President Kennedy had long been unpopular. Vice President Johnson and his wealthy cronies controlled the state of Texas and had individually expressed to Hughes their shared disgust with Kennedy's high-handed politics and his New Frontier. JFK would be hard to protect in Dallas.

"I know there are easier simpler ways to kill one man but history loves a mystery and the success of this venture's gonna depend on the confusion of interests," Hughes said, smiling seraphically. Romulo, Collins and Gay were gathered in Hughes' Bungalow 4 at the Beverly Hills Hotel, eating McDonald's burgers and fries. Gay, in his perpetual beige suit, was kneeling before Hughes, carefully applying red nail polish to Hughes' pinky toes. "There's got to be too many motives for too many political groups," Hughes continued. "That way, if we're lucky--and I've made a lot of luck in my time--they'll get so confused chasing their own tails, they'll pin it on someone convenient."

At Romulo's urging, they selected Lee Harvey Oswald from the dossiers of American malcontents in the anti-Castro groups active in 1959 during the Bay of Pigs invasion.

One of Romulo's associates helped the unwitting Oswald and his Russian wife Marina get settled in Dallas and secured employment for Lee in the Texas Schoolbook Depository. When Oswald asked, they told him that he would be involved in important undercover work for the government and to be patient.

When Romulo had first become friendly with Whitey, he perceived him as a basically moral individual who objected to crime and violence. Romulo was surprised at the ease with which the man could be bought. Money was an antidote to each of his few scruples.

"They'll pay you $100,000 to do something very dangerous, and you'll have to kill somebody," Romulo said to Whitey over coffee and eggs in the wardroom one morning.

"$100,000? You got a deal," Whitey answered gleefully, as though he were taking a bet on a football game. "I'd do about anything for that much money."

Romulo was buttering his toast. He licked his fingers. "You're going to have to."

"Sheba! Get down!" Jack Ruby, a pudgy man in a baggy suit, was tugging on his dachshund's leash as it growled at Aurora.

"It's ok." She leaned down and petted the dog on the hot Dallas sidewalk.

"Say, you want a job?" Ruby was looking her up and down. "You like to dance?"

Aurora shrugged. She could see the bald spot under his slicked back hair as he stooped to pick up his dog.

"I gotta coupla clubs." He pressed a card in her hands. "Classy places. No nudity. Just dancing and maybe hustling drinks. Pays good." He smiled again. "You'd make a killing."

November 1, 1963

Dear Romo,

I'm glad I came to Dallas as you suggested. It is not as bad as I had feared, although the men are crude and stupid. Mr. Ruby hired me on the spot just like you said he would. Let me know what I must do. I am anxious to get back to school.

Love,

Aurora

The President didn't decide to come to Dallas until November 18th, leaving less than a week for Romulo and Collins to set up. Oswald was in regular contact with Collins who controlled Oswald with veiled threats to have Marina deported if he didn't cooperate. He was a rat being led through a maze.

On the night of November 19th, 1963, the *Thresher* anchored five miles off the coast of Texas and dispatched her launch carrying Romulo and Whitey, his face surgically altered to look like Oswald. Agent Collins met them at the harbor in Galveston.

Whitey posed for photographs the next day, holding up the soon-to-be infamous *Mannlicher-Carcano* hunting rifle in one hand and copies of the *Militant* and the *Daily Worker* in the other. He was enjoying himself.

"Don't smile so much," Collins said and clicked the shutter release.

These photos were added to the other forged documents and identification papers that would be "found" by the Dallas police as part of the mounting "evidence" against Oswald. One of them would be the cover of *Life* magazine two weeks later.

It didn't take long for Collins to meticulously establish Oswald as a psychotic. Towards the beginning of November, Collins spent an afternoon at the Dallas Sports Drone rifle range firing at everyone else's targets and hitting their bull's-eyes each time. He told anyone who'd listen that he was Lee Oswald and he knew what was wrong with America. The management finally evicted him as a nuisance, but not until his rifle clip was empty.

A few days later, he went to a used-car lot, introduced himself as Oswald, and took the salesman for a test drive on the Stemmons freeway at 94 mph. When the man refused to sell him the car on credit, Collins babbled about all the money he was about to be paid "for being a hero" and that if that wasn't good enough, he'd go back to the Soviet Union "where they know how to treat workers like men."

On November 22nd, Romulo and Whitey woke early and ate breakfast with Collins at the Cup n' Spoon coffee shop in Dallas. Whitey wore sunglasses and acted like he thought a celebrity might act, though nobody paid attention. They soon would.

"Look at this," Collins said and passed his folded newspaper over to Romulo. "They've published the whole goddamn motorcade route except for the Main to Houston to Elm Street zigzag. At this rate, someone else will shoot him before we can."

"Are you certain about the zigzag?" Romulo asked.

"It'll be official this morning. I primed the Secret Service boys last night. We stayed at the Cellar past 2 a.m. There'll be a few hangovers today. I got rid of the press car too. Usually, it's right in front of the presidential limo so they can get pictures of him waving, but today their car is going to be sixteenth in the motorcade."

Collins leaned back proudly. Romulo was unimpressed.

"So what? Reporters never hurt anybody."

“No pictures of the shooting. No one will know what hit him or from where. They'll think it was just Ozzie.”

They split up after breakfast and each man traveled to his respective position by a different route. Whitey carried the disassembled Mannlicher-Carcano rifle wrapped in brown paper. Collins had arranged for Oswald to be carrying an identically wrapped package to work that morning. Romulo picked up his weapon from a bus station locker: a hunting rifle with a high-powered scope that fired 6.5 mm soft ammunition, the kind that mushroomed out into shrapnel. He joined the crowd that had been gathering on Elm Street to watch the presidential motorcade drive past. It was noon.

Five minutes later, agent Collins, wearing a dark suit, moved into position by the Stemmons freeway sign. He was carrying an umbrella though there wasn't a cloud in the sky.

Like a serpent gliding through tall grass, Romulo casually made his way through the crowd and walked up onto the grassy knoll. He vaulted the retaining wall and huddled behind it. It was 12:10 p.m.

Across Dealy Plaza, inside the southeast corner window on the sixth floor of the Texas Schoolbook Depository, Whitey knelt in front of the window and opened it slightly wider than a foot. He looked out over the triangle of intersecting crowd-lined streets. The rifle felt cool in his hands.

Across Houston Street, on the roof of the Dal-Tex building, David Ferrie lay on his stomach at the edge of the parapet, holding a Savage hunting rifle loaded with a clip of 6.5 mm soft rounds. Ferrie lifted his rifle, and looked through the sight, scanning the restless crowd for Collins.

He found him easily, standing near the curb on Elm Street, his umbrella casually resting on his shoulder like a soldier with a rifle. It was 12:25 p.m.

Kennedy hadn't wanted to come to Dallas, but he knew he risked alienating Texas voters in the upcoming election if he didn’t. Only a month before, Adlai Stevenson, one of the nicest guys in politics, had been booed and heckled when he spoke here and badly jostled in the parking lot later.

On the morning of November 22nd, after addressing a Fort Worth Chamber of Commerce breakfast meeting, Kennedy and his entourage flew to Dallas. On the plane, he was glad his visit to Texas was nearly over.

*Our young country is still so divided. Will it ever change?*

He knew Jackie felt the same way. She had been upset by an ad in that morning's *Dallas News* sarcastically headed: WELCOME MR. KENNEDY TO DALLAS. It was a mean tract of anti-presidential trash that listed twelve "counts of treason." He'd learned in the early days of his political career, campaigning on the streets of Boston, not to let mudslinging stick, but it rankled him when the dirt bothered Jackie.

*She's a better wife than I deserve...*

He squeezed her hand as their procession of black limousines left the airport at Love Field. It had rained that morning, but now the sun was out, and the Secret Service decided to remove the bubble top from the president's limousine so he and the First Lady could enjoy the fine Dallas weather: sixty-seven degrees and sunny. Jackie smiled, then pulled her hand away to wave at the first group of spectators. A large woman in a Stetson hat spat in the dirt and glared as the Kennedys glided past in their open black Lincoln.

Governor and Mrs. Connally were pleasant. They were always pleasant. Kennedy liked the governor, though frequently disagreed with him over Mason-Dixon line matters. Jackie was equally fond of Nellie Connally. Nonetheless, Kennedy wished he hadn't brought Jackie to Texas. The atmosphere of hatred was too much for her, though she did look splendid in her new pink suit.

*She's an ace.*

Thankfully, the crowds were friendlier approaching the city center, and Kennedy began to enjoy himself, waving to the families and hoisted-high children. Jackie, too, seemed happy and proud at his side.

The Secret Service operations manual states that whenever the protective bulletproof bubble top is removed, the motorcade must drive at a speed of no less than 44 mph, and, in such an event, a cordon sanitaire of police sharpshooters should be placed atop the higher buildings along the route and the windows of all such buildings should be sealed.

The procession of limousines, led by Dallas Police Chief Curry in a pilot car, was traveling at 12 mph as it turned onto Houston

Street in the first band of its zigzag route. Lee Harvey Oswald stood in the depository's entrance watching the motorcade's slow approach. He was wearing a white t-shirt with a torn neckband over the orange t-shirt in which he would later be arrested. As the president drew closer, James Altgens, an Associated Press photographer, snapped a photograph. His picture would show Oswald leaning in the doorway, nowhere near the assassin's nest on the sixth floor.

Through their rifle scopes, Romulo, Whitey, and David Ferrie watched Collins as the motorcade slowed to 8 mph rounding the corner onto Elm Street. Strapped into his ever-present corset, Kennedy's back ached as he waved to the crowd who cheered and fist pumped back. Smiling, Nellie Connally leaned over and said "You can't say Dallas doesn't love you, Mr. President!"

Kennedy laughed. Then, for no reason, the incantation sung by Catholic priests prior to offering communion came into his head: *The mys-ter-y of faith...*

The pilot car, followed by the presidential limousine, passed the Stemmons freeway sign. Collins opened his umbrella, twirled it clockwise, then pumped it up and down.

On the grassy knoll, Romulo swung his rifle to take aim. There was a whirring sound close behind him. Startled, he peered through the bushes concealing him. Abraham Zapruder, a middle-aged children's dress manufacturer with sweat circles under his arms, stood a few feet away, an eight- millimeter movie camera pressed to his face. Romulo decided to kill him quickly – a bullet to the heart – but then heard the first gunshot - Ferrie's - crackle across Dealey Plaza. He found Kennedy's contorted face in his rifle site and squeezed the trigger while Zapruder, numb and horrified, continued filming, unaware of his proximity to an assassin.

In the crossfire, the first bullet tore into Kennedy's shoulder and the second splattered the side of his head across the car trunk. He collapsed into Jackie's lap.

"Oh my God! They've shot my husband!" she cried out.

Six floors up in the depository, Whitey shot but missed, his bullet striking the pavement near the limousine's front tire. *The rifle sight's off.* He aimed again, and fired, hitting Governor Connally in the wrist.

"Oh, no, no, no! My God, they're going to kill us all!" the

Governor yelled as his wife pulled him onto the car floor. Jackie was scrambling out onto the trunk. Secret Service agent Hill vaulted onto the rear bumper and forced her back into the bloody passenger seat. He banged on the side. “Let’s go! Let’s go!”

Spectators on both sides of Elm Street ran for cover as Collins folded his umbrella and walked towards the depository. The shooting lasted six seconds. The motorcade, sirens screaming, roared off to Parkland Memorial Hospital where doctors would try to save the president's life.

On the depository’s sixth floor, Whitey tossed his rifle onto the linoleum next to three spent cartridges. He peeled off and pocketed his plastic gloves as he ran to the stairwell.

The plan had been to stay by the open window long enough for people to see him and identify Oswald's face later. But Whitey was scared. None of his shots struck Kennedy, yet he noticed a policeman jump off his motorcycle and run into the depository. What if he was to be the dupe, not Oswald? But a pipefitter named Howard Brennan had seen Whitey in the window and would identify him as Oswald later.

As Whitey bounded down to the third-floor landing, he heard footsteps running up the stairs and excited voices on the floor below. He slipped behind the open passageway door and held his breath.

Police Sergeant Marrion Baker had discovered Lee Harvey Oswald sipping a Coke in the second-floor lunchroom and was questioning him at gunpoint when depository superintendent Roy Truely rushed in and said “He's okay. He works here!”

The two hurried out and raced up the stairs past Whitey still behind the third-floor door. When they reached the landing above, Whitey sprinted down. That's when Oswald turned and saw himself descending the stairs. A feathery chill tickled his spine. *That guy’s wearing my clothes!*

In the parking lot, Whitey dove into the back of Collins' mud-splattered Chevy and pulled on blue coveralls, a hat and sunglasses. Collins circled the lot and was about to pull into the rapidly forming traffic jam when Dallas Police Officer Joe Smith sprinted up to the driver’s side and held his revolver to Collins' head.

“Alright, where you goin'?”

"Secret Service," Collins brusquely flipped open his wallet to an ID card. "Get out of my way!" He floored the gas and the Chevy peeled into traffic.

"Jesus! That was close!" Whitey gasped.

"No it wasn't. Dallas cops are morons," Collins said, spinning the wheel hard and speeding ahead several car lengths. "Did you get him?"

"No. I guess Romulo or one of the other guys did. That was some head shot!" Even Whitey didn't know the exact number of shooters in the killing zone.

"What do you mean 'no'?" Collins asked. "You were supposed to leave a bullet in him from that gun so they can trace it back to Oswald. That was the plan!"

Collins had mail-ordered the Mannlicher-Carcano and had it sent to Oswald's P.O. box where Collins picked it up with his duplicate key.

"I think I got Connally in the wrist," Whitey offered.

Collins braked to avoid hitting a sobbing woman who had wandered into traffic. Everywhere on the streets, people were gathered, many with portable radios, listening with horror to the breaking news.

"You idiot," Collins said, referring to both Whitey and the woman he nearly ran down.

"I think we've got bigger problems than that," Whitey said.

"What do you mean?"

"He saw me. He was in the lunchroom on the second floor."

"Who saw you?"

"Ozzie."

Collins let out a little whistle; he pulled over by a phone booth and fumbled for a dime.

David Ferrie took the elevator down from the seventh floor of the Dal-Tex building and was walking along Elm Street, carrying his disassembled rifle in a large briefcase. That evening, Ferrie would be sipping Bloody Marys on a plane back to New Orleans.

Behind the retaining wall on the grassy knoll, Romulo stuffed his rifle parts back into his bag. He looked at his watch: 12:03 p.m. *I've got 'til seven or eight tonight. No longer...*

When Zapruder's camera stopped whirring, Romulo darted into the street as though seeking cover. He didn't stop running until he reached a phone booth two blocks from Dealey Plaza. Its ring startled him.

"This is Catholic Avenger. Who are you?" Collins asked.

"This is Black Magic. What's the frequency, Kenneth?"

"Your idiot friend missed with Ozzie's rifle. None of his bullets are in the target."

"Shit," Romulo said.

"And that's not all. He ran into Ozzie face-to-face, if you know what I mean."

Romulo thought quickly. The immediate evidence against Oswald had to be sufficient to get him arrested.

"Go to the second killing zone," he said. "Ozzie's got to know something's wrong."

"I know what to do." He glanced back at Whitey, chewing gum.

"You do what you have to," Romulo said. "I'm going to Parkland to put a bullet in the target."

*Something isn't right!* Oswald left the depository and went straight to a pay phone where he dialed the emergency number Collins had given him. Nearly hysterical, he identified himself to the voice on the other end as A. J. Hidell, his cover name, and demanded a meeting. Immediately. The voice told him to sit in the 10th row of the Texas Theatre at 1:30 p.m.

"What's playing?" Oswald asked, but the line was already dead.

Hughes, through his wealthy Texan co-conspirators, had secured the involvement of key figures in the Dallas Police Department. During the days around the assassination and its subsequent investigation, their function was primarily passive. They let a lot of things happen: the afternoon of the shooting, the security around Dealey Plaza was lax; later, evidence was gathered and docketed slowly, some even fabricated; and no testimony from Oswald was ever recorded between the time of his arrest and his killing four days later.

The police department's only active participation was Police Officer J.D. Tippit's killing. He'd been cruising alone in his radio car several miles from Dealey Plaza. At 12:10 p.m., his dispatcher ordered him to proceed to the Oak Cliff area "to be at large for any emergency that might arise." It seemed a peculiar instruction, but Tippit obeyed and at 12:54 p.m. radioed back to Central that he was in position.

Whitey hailed a cab five blocks from Oswald's rooming house at 1026 North Beckley in Oak Cliff and sat upfront so the driver would be sure to remember him. He hurried into the rooming house, taking care to be seen entering Oswald's room by his landlady, Earlene Roberts. He rushed out again moments later wearing one of Oswald's windbreakers. Oswald's 38-caliber pistol was tucked into his waistband. Collins met him around the corner and drove to the intersection of 10th and Patton Streets where the police department contact had told him he'd find Officer Tippit. Whitey looked out the Chevy window at the parked radio car. The policeman inside was so young.

"It was different up in the building. I wasn't so close," Whitey said. He was scared to death.

"Go take care of business," Collins growled. "Go on. While there's witnesses."

Whitey looked at Collins, searching for sympathy.

Legs shaking, Whitey got out of the car and approached Tippet who rolled down his window.

"Is there a movie house near here, officer? I'm looking for a movie."

Several people passed by on the sidewalk as the policeman got out of his cruiser.

"About eight blocks that way. I don't know what's showing but...."

Whitey fired four bullets from Oswald's .38 into Tippet's chest and stomach. A woman pushing a stroller screamed. A man dropped his groceries to pull her and her child away. Whitey scattered the spent cartridges into a nearby bush, then tossed Oswald's pistol into the front seat of the police car.

He sprinted up a side street, tore off Oswald's windbreaker and dropped it less than a block away from the dead policeman. Collins was waiting in the Chevy around the next corner.

Eight blocks south, the Texas Theater was playing *Cleopatra.* The girl in the ticket booth hardly glanced at him as she took his money. Oswald entered the theater at 1:25 p.m.

Collins pulled up a block away.

"Alright, do your stuff," he told Whitey. "And make sure someone sees you."

Whitey got out and ran splay-legged down the street, stopping a few doors away from the theater. It was lunchtime. He looked around, trying to make eye contact with people hurrying to and from work. Finally, he noticed a young man in shirtsleeves, Johnny Brewer, watching him from inside a shoe store. Whitey moved closer to the shop window. He caught Brewer's eye again and rubbed his crotch deliberately, then turned and sashayed towards the theater. Brewer followed him.

"What you lookin' at?" Whitey said in a low seductive voice. 119

Brewer blushed, looked away.

"You want some of this?" Whitey was rubbing his crotch again.

Brewer smiled hesitantly.

Whitey hurried into the theater without buying a ticket. Brewer's face was crimson. He stalked over to the ticket taker who had his back to the door, a portable radio at his ear.

"Did you see that?"

"See what? "

"That guy just snuck in for free."

The ticket taker opened the theater door and peered into the gloom.

"Maybe it's the guy the cops are lookin' for. Shot one of them on Patton Street," he said.

Inside, Whitey hurried down the aisle towards the exit sign.

He passed Oswald in the tenth row slouched in his seat, staring at the movie. Dressed in gold, Elizabeth Taylor was holding a snake.

"Psst," Whitey said. Oswald glanced over. "Stay put. Someone will be along in a minute."

Oswald sat up, confused; he watched Whitey leave the theater. *It's that guy who looks like me.* His knees began to knock. Collins was parked out back.

Whitey pulled on the coveralls, hat, and sunglasses again as Collins drove them away.

Five squad cars pulled up, responding to a call that the suspect in the police shooting was in the theater. The house lights went on, the movie stopped, and policemen rushed in with Brewer who immediately pointed to Oswald in the tenth row.

"That's him! The mousey one."

Two cops approached Oswald, one from each side of the aisle, guns drawn. The conspirators' plan was for Oswald, presidential assassin and cop-killer, to be shot while resisting arrest. One of the policemen had Oswald's .38 which Whitey had left at the scene of Tippett's murder. He tried to put it in Oswald's hands.

"I am not resisting arrest!" Oswald screamed as he struggled with the burly cop. The .38 dropped to the floor where officer M.

A. McDonalds picked it up. Later, he would claim that Oswald pulled it out during his capture, and that McDonalds wrestled it away from him, jamming his finger into the firing mechanism to keep Oswald from shooting.

News of the arrest flooded the airwaves. It was 1:51 p.m., less than an hour after the president had been declared dead.

Parkland Memorial Hospital was pandemonium when Romulo pushed his way in wearing coveralls from an air conditioning repair company. Newsmen, radio interviewers, Dallas police, Secret Service agents and members of Kennedy and Governor Connally's entourages filled the emergency room admissions area. There was little attempt at security. Even schlubby Jack Ruby, the man who would lurch across television screens four days later to murder the president's murderer, lingered near the coffee machine, drawn to the tragedy. He had fallen head over heels for a blonde dancer at his club. In the hours to come, between sobs, a weepy Aurora would press him relentlessly to do something about that little rat Oswald.

Romulo vaulted down the service stairs to the utility room and set the air-conditioning as cold as it could go.

Jackie was sitting on a folding chair, breathless and brave in her bloodied pink suit. She was the center of the world. No one could stop looking at her, even when they tried.

Romulo lingered at the nurses' station, fingering a mangled bullet in his pocket. An orderly wheeled Kennedy's body on a gurney back from the operating room. A newspaperman was taking flash photos. His camera pointed at Romulo, who froze. A Secret Service agent put his hand up. "No pictures."

*That was close.*

Jackie was staring at Trauma Room One while she twisted her wedding ring and shivered in the now cold air.

I insist you let me in. Jack needs me." She pushed past Secret

Service into the room where Kennedy's back brace lay on the floor with its laces cut.

Romulo saw his chance. A light mattress with blood-stained sheets was on the gurney. Romulo slid his hand beneath the sheets and left the bullet from Oswald's gun. The bullet, fired two days ago at one of Whitey's practice sessions (and hereafter referred to in the Warren Report as "Commission Exhibit 399"), would be the principal evidence for the single bullet theory "proving" that Lee Harvey Oswald was Kennedy's lone assassin.

Late that afternoon, Collins, Romulo, and Whitey flew separately out of Dallas: Collins to New Orleans and, at Romulo's insistence, Romulo and Whitey to Washington. Collins had wanted to eliminate Whitey and his incriminating face in Texas.

"He works for me, and I still need him," Romulo insisted. "But by the time Ruby terminates the original, the copy will be destroyed."

Romulo and Whitey met in the parking lot at Dulles Airport shortly before dusk. Air Force One had landed less than an hour before at Andrews Field with Kennedy's body, Jackie, Robert Kennedy and now President Lyndon Johnson.

"I've been thinking," Whitey was pale as they climbed into Romulo's rented Lark. "My face is going to be famous." He knew he was a cornered animal.

*Poor Whitey*. Romulo spoke in what he hoped was a soothing voice. "After the funeral, we'll rendezvous with the *Thresher* and I'll give you another new face."

Whitey considered this. "Could you make me look like Elvis?"

"I'll make you look better than Elvis. But right now, you need a disguise." He pulled a ginger-colored mustache and spirit gum from the glove compartment. Whitey grinned like a birthday boy as he placed the mustache on his upper lip.

It was after 5 p.m. Time was running out.

At a payphone in Georgetown, Romulo looked up the numbers of Washington funeral homes.

"Brady's funeral home. Good evening," said the woman who answered.

"This is the White House calling. I'm Mr. Kennedy's aide. Have your people left to collect the president's body yet?" Romulo spoke in his most unctuous voice.

"You're sick, mister." She hung up.

Romulo got lucky on his third call.

"No sir, we're not scheduled to pick up the remains until after six. The gentleman we spoke to, a Mr. Reed, I believe it was..."[122]

"Yes, that's right, Mr. Reed." Romulo noted the name.

"Mr. Reed said the autopsy wouldn't be finished at Bethesda before 6:30 p.m."

"Excellent. Just calling to double check. Thank you."

On the way to the Naval Medical Center at Bethesda, Romulo and Whitey purchased two black suits. There was no time for alterations; the clerk hemmed their trouser cuffs with a stapler.

Kennedy lay on his stomach, naked and clinically dead on a stainless-steel table. Commander Humes, the pathologist, was examining the bullet wound in Kennedy's back with a rubber-gloved finger. It went in past his second knuckle.

"There's no bullet or fragment in here, and no exit wound on the other side."

"That can't be right," Colonel Finck, chief of wound ballistics pathology for the Pentagon, frowned over his bifocals. "Let me see." He probed the hole six inches down from the neckline to the right of Kennedy's spinal column. There was nothing—just a wound. "Angle of entry is about forty-five to sixty- five degrees... But I'm damned if I know where the thing went."

Agent O'Neill, one of the FBI observers, came into the room. "Excuse me, gentlemen. I just got off the phone with our Dallas team. An orderly at Parkland found a 6.5 mm bullet on the president's stretcher mattress."

"Thank Christ," Finck said. "That's our mystery solved. Probably forced out of the wound during cardiac massage."

"The bullet's been sent to ballistics to see if it matches the School Book Depository rifle." O'Neill was trying not to look at the saddest sight in the world lying on the table.

"Thank you," Finck said. "Let's turn him over. We're through with the back wound." He shivered. The room was so cold.

Just before 6 p.m., a sentry stopped Romulo and Whitey's car at the naval hospital gate. Romulo rolled down his window. He wore a flower pinned to his new suit lapel. Whitey wore a black fedora.

"I'm Crowley. We're from Joseph Gawer's Sons Funeral Home in Washington. Our hearse will be along in a while. We passed them on the road."

The guard looked at Romulo blankly. "You're supposed to go to Pathology and wait. See Captain Sweeney. Just keep right and park in the lot."

Captain Sweeney sent them to the second floor where a Secret Service agent stopped them at the elevator. "I'm Agent Silbert and you are...?"

"We're from Gawer's Funeral Home. Captain Sweeney sent us up. Is Mr. Reed around?"

Silbert frowned. "Reed's not here. I'll need to see identification."

"We left it with the desk downstairs. They insisted." Romulo leaned close. "My name's Crowley. If they've finished the autopsy, I need to view the body as soon as possible." He took the agent's arm and spoke in a low voice. "Mrs. Kennedy asked us to do everything we can to make him...presentable. And that takes time."

"I don't know about this, Mr. Crowley..."

Romulo and Whitey followed the agent down the corridor. The autopsy was complete. Kennedy lay stitched up under a sheet on the dissection table.

After clearing it with Agent Hill, Silbert left Romulo and Whitey alone with Kennedy's body. Outside, a young agent guarded the door.

Vent fans whirred as Romulo turned up the air conditioning. He pulled back the sheet: Kennedy's eyes were closed. Romulo pressed two fingers against his now lilac cheek. "Nice and cold." He studied Kennedy's wounds, memorizing them.

Hovering by the door, Whitey sipped from an airplane whiskey bottle, trying tried to stay calm.

"I don't know why I came. This is crazy! We could go to prison forever! Longer!"

"Give me a hand. We don't have much time."

Romulo pulled a large garbage bag from his coat pocket and began fitting it over Kennedy's head and shoulders. Whitey looked squeamish.

"Lift him, " Romulo said. "One, two, three!"

They carried Kennedy in the bag to the windowsill.

Outside, a floor below, the parking lot was deserted. Romulo opened the window and peered down. There were bushes at the base of the building.

"Perfect. Come on."

They hoisted the body, partially stiff from rigor mortis, and lowered it as far as they could before dropping it the last few feet into the bushes. The leaves rustled as the corpse crumbled to the ground.

"What're you going to do when they find him gone?" Whitey was wringing his hands. Footsteps were approaching the door.

"Quick. Get on the table!"

"No!"

"Do it!"

Shuddering, Whitey climbed onto the steel surface.

Romulo pulled the sheet over him just as a weary Agent Hill walked in.

"Your hearse is outside." He was squinting at Romulo now. "Everything okay?"

"As well as can be expected under such terrible circumstances. He was a great man." Romulo's voice was quavering. "I'm so sorry..." He steadied himself. "Send them up whenever you like."

"They're on their way. Where's your friend?"

"Using the facilities."

Hill was staring at the covered figure on the table. The sheet rose and fell with Whitey's breathing. Hill rubbed his eyes. "Now I'm seeing things. Will this day never end?" He stepped out, closing the door behind him.

"Is he gone?"

"All clear." Romulo produced a pistol from his waistband and screwed a silencer onto it. "But stay there just in case."

Romulo found Whitey's temple with the gun barrel. He whisked the sheet back.

"What are you doing?!"

Pop! An oozing red hole appeared in Whitey's forehead. Quickly, Romulo pulled off Whitey's clothes, peeled off his false mustache, then pop, pop, pop, fired the pistol into Whitey's face. He turned Whitey onto his stomach, shot once into his back, then twice more into his head, tearing away some scalp. Now Whitey's wounds approximated Kennedy's. He pulled the sheet over the naked body, dropped the clothing out the window into the bushes and stepped out of the room.

"Back in a moment."

The agent guarding the door nodded.

"If you see my people, please send them in."

"Yes, Mr. Crowley." The young man shifted his weight uncomfortably. He'd been there for hours.

Romulo hurried along the hallway, nodding curtly to the various guards at each turn, and rang for the elevator. When the doors opened, Agent Silbert stepped out with four men in black suits. Two of them rolled a coffin on a gurney.

"Mr. Crowley, your men are here."

The four undertakers looked at Romulo, puzzled. One of them started to speak, but Romulo cut him off. "Gentlemen, Mrs. Kennedy has requested that you do your work as quickly and with as much consideration for the president's appearance as possible."

Agent Silbert led them back down the corridor towards the examination room. When he and the men carrying the coffin were out of earshot, Romulo turned to the undertaker at his side. "Name's Crowley. I'm your Navy Security Liaison. I'll be with the body until you leave the base," he said in a low voice.

"Pleased to meet you, Mr. Crowley, although I regret the circumstances. I'm Phyllis. Peter Phyllis."

Silbert looked back suspiciously.

"I thought you knew these men?"

"Why? Is there something you don't like about them?" Romulo snapped.

"No. I just thought...."

"Somebody's got to do this work, you know. Perhaps if you'd done your job a little better, we wouldn't be here now."

Agent Silbert turned white.

"I flew in from Baltimore this afternoon," he said. "If you've got a complaint, mister, take it up with Agent Hill. He was in Dallas. But don't blame me if he breaks your face for you."

They entered the room where Whitey's body lay. The undertakers opened the coffin.

"I don't know what you've heard, but his face didn't come through too well." Romulo told Phyllis. One of the men removed a rubber body bag from the coffin, then pulled back the sheet. There were gasps at the gory mess that was Whitey's head.

Phyllis nodded. "It'll have to be a closed coffin. Will you tell

Mrs. Kennedy?"

"Of course."

"He's still warm," a mortician said with curiosity as they eased the corpse into the bag, then sealed it. Romulo worried that Silbert would notice the difference between Whitey's and Kennedy's bodies, but he didn't. He was still fuming over Romulo's remark. He glared at Romulo as they rode down in the elevator with the undertakers and the coffin. Mr. Reed, the White House aide, Captain Sweeney, and four sailors with automatic weapons accompanied them past the reporters and bulb-popping photographers out to the parking lot where they loaded the coffin into the back of a hearse.

"Very good, Mr. Phyllis. Proceed whenever you're ready. I'll follow at a distance," Romulo's words formed puffs of smoke in the cold evening air. Captain Sweeney signaled the main gate that the procession was leaving, and the hearse, preceded by two policemen on motorcycles sped off, sirens blaring.

Romulo drove the blue Lark to where Kennedy's body lay, barely concealed in the bushes. He checked his watch: 6:45 p.m. In barely an hour, his efforts would be in vain. He turned the car's air conditioning on high, then carried Kennedy's body over his shoulder fireman style to the car and eased him into the passenger seat. He dressed him in Whitey's black suit and propped him in a sitting position.

The sentry at the gate shone his flashlight on Romulo, then over to Kennedy. Whitey's hat was pulled low on Kennedy's forehead. The frigid air inside the car steamed through the cracked window. It was hard to see.

"Your friend doesn't look so good."

"He had a bad day at work."

"Didn't we all?" The sentry waved them through.

A few blocks away, Romulo pulled over. He removed the Sanjivani flower from his lapel. He parted Kennedy's blue lips and carefully placed the stem into his mouth like a teat for a baby. The petals glowed bright as Romulo drove down to the sea.

# 29.

On November 22nd, 1963, McCoy had been aboard the *Thresher* for nearly six months, accustomed to life amidst the stink of men and machines, robotically performing his duties, smoking pot and reading to pass the time when he wasn't dreaming of Katie. Most of the crew spoke in languages he didn't understand—Senegalese, Haitian and various Spanish dialects. He was guardedly friendly only with his cabin mates Floyd and Derek Ts'Me. They spoke English and practiced decent hygiene. McCoy was sitting alone in the wardroom sipping coffee when Floyd hurried in. "President Kennedy's dead! I heard it on the radio."

McCoy forced himself to think about the world outside. "What happened?"

"He was shot in Dallas. Johnson's going to be sworn in on Air Force One."

"Oh, no..." McCoy felt his shock turn to sadness.

"Do we tell the crew?"

McCoy shook his head. "They'll find out soon enough. Most of them won't give a damn. Kennedy was first world, not third." The floor rumbled. The engines were starting up below. "Are we going somewhere?"

"East. To Washington. The captain's going to meet us there."

*Romulo had been in Dallas on Hughes' business, now he's going to Washington?*

"They got the guy that did it. Lee Harvey Oswald. Shot JFK from the top of a building."

"It's good they caught him," McCoy said. *Why is that name familiar?*

"Pretty strange that some nut shoots him in Texas and now we've got a Texan for President. You know what I mean?"

But McCoy had left the compartment.

The photograph was in sick bay, still on a clipboard beneath a stack of papers. He'd meant to give it back to Romulo after Whitey's plastic surgery but forgot. He pulled it out. The face, so ordinary, so forgettable, stared back at him from beneath Romulo's blue penciled arrows and curves. He turned it over. On the back were three initials: "L.H.O."

There was a lump in McCoy's throat. He'd liked President Kennedy. He liked the Kennedy family. They were an American success story, proof that opportunity was a reality: from a booze runner to the White House in one generation.

He closed the curtains around his bunk and poured himself a shot of J & B. *I let Romulo use me.*

"I need you to assist," Romulo had told him. "I will be the knife."

McCoy never asked why Romulo wanted to alter Whitey's face to match the man's in the photo.

*How could I have known?*

It was only the chins and eyes that were different. At Romulo's direction, McCoy had injected lidocaine into five separate sites on Whitey's face. Whitey was conscious throughout the procedures: silicone chin implant, blepharoplasty to adjust the eyelids, some artificial coloring and an appropriate haircut. After the swelling and bruising subsided, the young man unmistakably resembled the man in the photo: L.H.O.

*Am I a co-conspirator? A henchman? If I go to the media, they'll think I'm crazy. I'll spend the rest of my life in a psych ward, and if they believe me, I'll be arrested. It's only Romulo's word against mine.*

He thought about the books he'd read and the movies he'd seen where the hero prevailed. He wanted to be a hero, to make himself (and Stephen) proud. But, above all, he wanted to go on living.

It was 97 degrees at Port-au-Prince airport. From her window, Madonna watched the propellers chug and thrum as the Pan Am flight to Miami rose through an insect cloud into the skies. The tiny old gentleman sweating in a three-piece suit and seated next to her smiled reassuringly as Madonna gripped the arm of her seat. It was her first time on an airplane. She was praying.

At first, she had resisted Aurora's invitation to come to America, but life in Cuba was growing worse and worse under Castro. There were food lines and shortages. Parents who could afford to were sending their children away on "Peter Pan" flights to foster families in Florida. Madonna decided the time to leave had come.

"Would you like to help Irish hospitals?" The man next to her smelled of whiskey.

"Do they need help?"

"Aye, they do," he answered. He had yellow teeth. "Do you mind if I smoke? It will help pass the time."

By the time they landed, Colonel Malay had sold her an Irish sweepstakes ticket.

Miami Airport, Latin America's gateway to the U.S., had long lines at immigration and customs. Madonna's feet hurt. She struggled to haul her heavy suitcase, but a handsome young flight attendant helped her to the crowded arrivals gate.

*"Oh, gracias, Senor. Tu eres mi angel!"*

Tall and blond with a twinkling smile, he spoke in a slight accent. "You will love America. I came from Canada. I love it here."

*"Gracias, señor."*

"Please call me Gaetan." His gaze shifted. "Is that your daughter?"

Aurora was hurrying towards them. "Mama! I'm so glad you're here." She hugged Madonna and made eye contact with Gaetan. He looked like a pilot in his blue uniform. "Thank you for helping my mother."

"It's my pleasure." He bowed. "Let me assist you with her luggage."

In the steamy parking lot, he loaded Madonna's battered suitcase into the trunk of Aurora's Volkswagen. They said goodbyes. Gaetan tipped his cap as he strode away.

Two weeks later, as she and Aurora sipped Cokes on the beach, Madonna opened the *Irish Echo* to check the list of sweepstakes winners. She had won $387,466 which arrived in the form of a check to her P.O. box the next week.

*God has chosen me*, she thought. *But for what?*

Days later, Gaeten saw Aurora in the produce aisle of Food Fair. "Excuse me. I'm looking for a hot tomato," he said. Aurora blushed, but couldn't help laughing at Gaetan's stupid joke. He was out of uniform, but still handsome— almost pretty. He was flying to Atlanta that evening, but would be back in Miami next week. Could they have dinner? His smile set her heart pounding. She said yes. Of course, Gaetan became Aurora's fantastic foolybear.

# 30.

Romulo had been biding his time. In the *Thresher*'s retrofit, Hughes allowed him only one small operating theater, a meagerly equipped laboratory and, instead of a walk-in freezer, a refrigerator. Clearly, Romulo's research was a low priority for Hughes; he really only wanted the submarine.

Visiting day: A crew-cut and obsequious Agent Collins in madras pants and a Lacoste shirt (looking like a vacationing Florida dentist, Romulo decided) helped the grumpy billionaire in his gray suit and bedroom slippers gingerly climb down the conning tower ladder.

Romulo clicked his heels and saluted. "Welcome aboard, Admiral Hughes."

"Not funny," Hughes huffed. "Show me around."

Collins rolled his eyes at Romulo, feigning sympathy, but he knew better. Only that morning Hughes had told him "I've got the boat. Get rid of the wetback." Romulo's days were numbered to the tune of one hand.

Hughes glumly picked his way through the control room, the nucleonics room, and the missle room, saying little, nodding his reluctant approval from time to time.

In the laboratory, McCoy was examining a skin scraping under a microscope, trying to understand how Romulo rejuvenated cells. From his perch on a corner shelf, Remus watched Romulo and his two visitors step in.

"You work too hard, Dr. McCoy," Romulo said, knowing that the doctor strived to learn what he must never know. "You should spend more time with the crew. Make some friends." Remus flapped down, lighting on Romulo's shoulder. "There's my beauty." The rat parrot nuzzled his ear.

McCoy stood. "Hello, Howard. How're you feeling?"

Hughes looked pain-worn and agitated. "Nice little laboratory, eh Wiley?"

"It's OK... for a high school." McCoy sided with Romulo on the facilities issue.

"I'd like to show you something, Howard," Romulo said.

Collins's stomach lurched. "I'll just wait outside..."

"No, no." Hughes took Collins's arm. "Let's see it then." He wanted this meeting to be over.

They stepped into the compartment next door. Romulo flicked on the lights.

A gaunt figure sat in a wheelchair at the center of the tiny operating theater. Although Kennedy's wounds were healing thanks to the *Sanjivani* flower and *mambo* paste, he looked like the corpse he should've been.

*Behold the conscience of our nation,* McCoy thought.

"Wait a minute! What's going on? I paid good money to have him..." He stopped speaking. Kennedy's eyes were on him. "Can he hear? I mean...?"

Romulo smiled. "For now, the president is a vegetable. A portion of his brain was destroyed by the gunfire that "killed" him. I...brought him back."

"You... 'brought him back'?" Hughes looked from Romulo to McCoy who nodded grimly.

"Oh my God, " Hughes said, as though he had one. And then he smiled.

They took a color photograph of Kennedy holding up that day's *Herald Tribune* and wearing a new Brooks Brothers suit, sitting in a rocking chair before an American flag (lest anyone miss the point). They pressed his ink-smeared fingers onto the back of the photo, proof positive that America's 35th president still breathed.

President Johnson took Hughes' call an hour after receiving the snapshot. The billionaire got right to the point. "Lyndon, you gotta keep the world safe for democracy! A country at war means a humming economy and that's what you want."

Not long after the call, Johnson escalated the conflict in Southeast Asia and, as a consequence, increased Hughes' companies' orders for military aircraft and other tools of warfare twofold. Hughes would use his power over Johnson only twice more: once to make him pick up his basset hound by its ears to upset Hughes' wife Jean Peters (an animal lover), and once to make Johnson display his abdominal surgery scar on TV because Hughes wanted to see it.

Nobody knew what to do with Kennedy. Hughes wanted to hide him in a penthouse in Las Vegas with around-the-clock security. McCoy wanted to administer intravenous sleeping drugs to let

Kennedy peacefully die. Romulo had another idea. He had received a letter.

> December 22nd, 1963
> Dear Romo,
> You no longer seem to care what happens to our mother, but you might as well know she's no longer in Cuba. She's living in a house she bought in Miami.
> Your sister, Aurora

From the outside, Madonna's house was another rundown pueblo revival house with too much vegetation clinging to umber stucco walls and a one-legged metal flamingo looking out at a dusty street on the edge of Miami Springs, not far enough away from the airport. Its shutters were always closed. Its small patchy lawn was rarely mowed. A freestanding terra cotta-topped wall concealed a tiny garden to which there was no exterior door. The neighbors who had watched its occupant move in had long since left for other aviation industry jobs in other communities. Now, so many months later, the little house on Nightingale Avenue was of interest to no one.

When Aurora visited her mother there, Madonna initially refused her daughter's request.

"I can't care for a sick gringo in a wheelchair who can't feed or bathe himself." She made the sign of the cross. "Even if he is a Catholic."

"But Momma," Aurora replied, "You left Cuba for the new world. This man was its leader. You have been chosen by God to help him."

Madonna frowned. "How do you know that?"

"God sent you the money for this house. You said so yourself."

Madonna thought for a moment. "And how is your brother involved?"

"I'm not sure. But he must have been chosen, too."

Madonna met her daughter's gaze. "And you? You were chosen as well?"

Aurora shrugged, nodding.

A week after Aurora's visit, Silver and McCoy drove Kennedy to Madonna's house and, after a few hours of instructions, left him in her care. Christmas of 1963 was the first Christmas Madonna didn't feel lonely with no family at her side. Kennedy sat medicated in his wheelchair by the fire near the tinsel-covered tree. She was in her new country with someone who needed her. Madonna was even rich: money from somewhere appeared in her bank account every two weeks. She had been chosen.

That winter, while the Beatles invaded America, the *Thresher* cruised off the Florida coast in the Bermuda Triangle, where, close to supplies and civilization yet concealed by fog and high seas, Romulo studied the boundaries of life and death.

In 1965, he discovered a treatment for several cancers—a mixture of seawater, almond skins, calcium, and a fungus similar to penicillin. He revealed no details of his breakthroughs, not even to Hughes or McCoy, preferring to keep his secrets in his notebook, documenting the rescission of cancerous cells in a rat and a house cat.

All this, but still no cure for sleep.

## 31.

"No, Foolybear, we mustn't," Aurora moaned. They were in the back seat of her car; Gaetan had his hand up her denim skirt and was kissing her behind the ear.

"Oh, god... Why not? Come on, Aurora..."

"Because I'm not ready."

"But I love you."

*He spoke the words.* They had been seeing each other for months now, whenever he had a layover in Miami. She knew that she loved him--*but was he the one?* He wasn't the first boy she'd kissed and more, but she was still a virgin.

The following Saturday night, after a walk on the beach and most of a bottle of Chardonnay, she lit a scented candle in her apartment and let him have his way.

Gaetan wrapped his arm around her and she smiled. *He is the one. What could be wrong with loving him?*

Aurora was not expecting his letter:

> Dear Aurora.
> My supervisor changed my route and I won't be laying over in Miami any more. I have enjoyed the time we spent together and I will miss you. Think of me kindly.
> Love always, Gaetan

*Is that love? Succumbing, then being discarded?* Her anger turned to resentment, then resignation. Her period came and went. Gaetan's flame had cast no shadow.

The sky was creeping dark. Summer lightning flashed, then--one, two, three--thunder and rain started, quick-as-a-thief, turning to sheets as Aurora crossed a parking lot

She broke into a run towards her car, squinting into the downpour. As she fumbled for her key, she heard a familiar voice.

"Hey, Rory. What's shakin'?" It was Maisie, who quickly took her arm. "Payback time, honey."

A hand with a chloroform-soaked towel covered her mouth and nose as two men in hooded sweatshirts hoisted her onto a mattress in the back of a van. She heard Maisie say "I'm counting the money and you're short five hundred."

"My buyer wants tits and hips. This chick's an ironing board. Take it or leave it." And then the lights went out.

She came to in a cabin on a private jet, tied to a seat with a rag in her mouth. A man with kind eyes but a resigned look removed the gag and gave her water. He wore a robe, smelled like incense, and spoke with an accent.

"You have been betrayed," he told her. "You must accept that. If you don't struggle, you will be treated well when we arrive in your new country."

*My new country?*

The scent of patchouli musk. Aurora's feet were tied and her wrists were bound to bedposts when she came to. The mattress was covered in plastic. She twisted, trying to pull her arms and legs free.

"Don't do that. You'll hurt yourself," said a blonde middle-aged woman, seated in a chair at the foot of the bed. She was wearing a silk blouse and pearls. She lowered her glasses with a resigned smile. "It won't help. And if you struggle too much, we'll put you back to sleep."

Aurora pulled at her ropes again.

"Untie me!"

Again, the resigned smile. "You will have to earn that privilege."

Aurora took a deep breath. She was in a cool sunlit room. An air-conditioned breeze blew from vents high in the stucco walls. She could hear muffled voices and footsteps in an adjacent room.

"Where am I?"

The woman looked up from her book—*Sense and Sensibility*.

"Just outside Riyadh. In a private home." A patient smile. "Very private."

"How do I earn my way off this bed?"

The lady nodded, pleased. "That's the right question." She moved her chair closer. "You're pretty. You are a concubine now—a slave. Until you learn to do what is expected, your movement will be restricted. Other women have earned their way off this bed." She rested her chin on her steepled red fingernails. "I did. And I can show you how. If you cooperate."

"And if I won't?"

"Then you will be sent away." A regretful smile. "To I don't know where."

Lunch arrived and the veiled woman helped Aurora raise her head and fed her brown rice with steamed vegetables. The blonde woman left the room, not to return for three days. When the woman reappeared, looking at her tank watch like a busy doctor on her rounds, Aurora was ready to talk.

"You are not a virgin," the woman said. "This need not be so difficult."

Aurora nodded. She was sitting up in bed now, her hands and feet untied. "I have only been with one man."

"One too many." The woman was wearing a pale blue linen suit with Chanel high heels. Her gold bracelets clinked as she gestured. "This may not be so different, provided you give them pleasure. They will be clean, there will be no violence." She wagged her finger as though scolding a dog. "The happier you make the men, the more privileges you will have. If you think about it, " she said. "It's no different outside these walls."

Aurora soon learned that "these walls" were a desert compound in Saudi Arabia belonging to Prince Fereydun, a minor Saudi royal known for his unostentatious wealth and his devotion to Islam. The compound, one of the prince's several residences, was occupied in equal parts by a Wahabi mosque and madras and a building housing a concubine harem. Angie, the blonde woman had been one of the first girls to be taken, snatched from the Sands Hotel in Las Vegas where she'd been working as a hostess and unknowingly caught Prince Fereydun's eye at a Frank Sinatra performance. The Happy House, as the harem's building was called by Fereydun and his male family members and friends, was effectively a small luxury hotel where as many as six young women lived. In recent years, the harem had been overseen by Angie who had matured past Fereydun's point of desire but not his affection. He kept her on for her company and her den-mothering skills. Only Prince Fereydun's inner circle had access to the pleasures offered by these women, who lived in plush suites with generous clothing allowances and stipends proportionate to their enthusiasm for what was expected of them.

Madonna had told her many times "God has a purpose for you and when you find that purpose, you will be happy."

But was this God's purpose? Her priceless virginity stolen by a faithless boy? Her youth and beauty sold to (mostly) silent nervous strangers who grunted on top of her, then slipped away?

For the first year, Angie and Aurora maintained a wary familiarity until Prince Fereydun had a heart attack. In bed with Aurora. She thought he was climaxing, but then his moans of "Oh, Allah, Allah!" became gasps and pleas as he grabbed at his chest. Aurora ran to Angie's room, screaming for help.

The dust-spewing Mercedes drove at 90 mph to a private hospital outside Al-Masif, where doctors, lidocaine, and paddles saved Prince Fereydun's life. Although grateful and solicitous of Aurora thereafter, he associated her with his near death and no longer physically desired her. Now Angie and Aurora were both exiled from the royal bed but not from royal attention. Angie became Aurora's protector. Only clean, kind men were permitted to choose her.

Aladdin bin Hamid was the son of Prince Fereydun's oldest friend and an American-trained CPA with a degree from Wharton.

After his father's death, Aladdin became the prince's financial advisor. They would meet regularly to review his holdings, which included restaurants, gas stations, real property and U.S. securities. Aladdin liked Aurora and visited her often. Once, stepping out of her bathroom, he found her reading the *Wall Street Journal* he'd left on the bed. Soon, the newspaper arrived for her daily.

As always, Angie had advice. "Aladdin's smart, but lazy and over-confident. And his wife is a harridan. Watch your step."

At first, her conversations in bed with Aladdin after she serviced him were wide-eyed questions to her wise lover about how basic financial investments worked. Aladdin would prop an ashtray on his flabby stomach while he smoked and held forth (he didn't know, of course, that Aurora had a brokerage account with a U.S. company in Riyadh). Soon, her questions became more sophisticated; so much so that he followed one of her "hypothetical" stock picks (IBM: she had bought shares) and watched it double. He bought some for the prince who was very pleased a few months later when the investment had grown by ten percent.

"Why don't you pick ten stocks, *Liebling*? (Aladdin had spent a semester in Dusseldorf and loved to hear himself speak German). "We can follow them and see how you do."

Aurora's choices all performed well and Aladdin (secretly) bought them for the prince and for himself. Angie, too, bought shares of IBM and quickly realized Aurora's capabilities. Going over her housekeeping budget with the prince one afternoon, Angie told him about Aurora's potential. Prince Fereydun, who had grown grayer and rather haggard since his heart attack, listened attentively.

"Aladdin, you didn't tell me you have a new assistant." It was a starry night outside one of the prince's meeting tents where they sat together, drinking Johnny Walker Blue after reviewing a real estate deal.

"We must pay her what she's worth," the prince continued "and give her more responsibility."

Aladdin held out his palms and smiled. "But she's a woman."

"Are not half the people on earth women?"

Aladdin looked confused. "Yes, but...she's a *woman*."

"In my small kingdom, anyone who contributes is compensated.

Besides—she's pregnant. It's yours. If you want her to lose the baby, you'll have to give her something." This was a lie, but the Prince wanted to see Aladdin squirm.

"I see. Well..."

"Alternatively, we could tell your wife and the two of you could raise the child." Aladdin did squirm this time. The prince went on with a magisterial wave "Or I could just have her killed."

Aladdin looked hopeful. "If you had Aurora killed..."

"I meant your wife."

"Oh..." he said, rubbing his chin and nodding. "How much should we pay her then?"

## 32.

Four Years Later (1969)

Ten pounds heavier, depressed and disappointed, Wiley McCoy lay in his bunk, leafing through a magazine. He came across a photo of the Ponte Vecchio in Florence, taken through a window in the Uffizi. It was like hearing a sad old song.

Italy, right after the war. Mussolini long garotted; Tuscany open for business again. McCoy's father's Italian beverage client had summoned his American lawyer, and that turned into a family vacation over Thanksgiving break. Happy in her camel hair coat and Grace Kelly sunglasses, McCoy's mom took him for raspberry gelato and then to the tourist-choked corridors of the Uffizi Gallery. She savored every sculpted saint and gilt-framed noble. Teenage McCoy in his brass-buttoned blazer and penny loafers stopped before a small 16th-century painting: *Allegory of Fortune.* Fortune is a slender naked woman standing with one foot on a globe in space while small beating red wings on her opposite ankle try to topple her. A falling crown and coins float just out of her reach—the fleeting nature of power and wealth. He stared at it a long time, barely noticing the man in the red hotel uniform pushing through the crowd.

"Signora!" The man said, taking McCoy's mother's arm, leaning close, speaking intensely.

"Wiley. We have to go. Daddy's hurt."

It had been quick—an aneurism in the back of a cab—dead at fifty-two.

McCoy never forgot that painting. Good fortune one day, bad the next. Fortune's like that.

Life aboard the *Thresher* was an intellectual dead battery. Because decent conversation was in such short supply and disagreement was preferable to boredom, both Romulo and McCoy enjoyed debating over weekly dinners in the captain's tiny cabin.

"Humanity is just another disease," Romulo proffered. "Look at our evolution. We were waterborne organisms that became fish. We grew legs and learned to walk, breathe air. We grew arms to swing through trees, formed tribes with a common language. Now we think we're better than animals. We're not even a successful disease because we limit our populations by making war on each other. The only evolutionary step we've taken in thousands of years will be this Apollo moon mission. But instead of leaving a man and a woman up there to reproduce, we're going to send three guys and bring them right back. Don't preach to me about humanity. We're just seed carriers and egg cases. Give me cancer spores any day. They're efficient."

"You ever think about getting out of this rat race? Find a nice girl. Settle down. Raise a truly strange family?"

A seaman with dreadlocks entered to clear the meal. "Pardon, Captain. There's a Comsat call for Dr. McCoy." He tried to take Remus's plate, but the rat parrot lunged, barely missing his fingers.

It was Hughes – who else? – demanding a meeting. He sounded agitated. Hughes Aviation had been working non-stop to complete the Apollo 11 lunar module. McCoy hadn't heard from him in months.

In the penthouse at the Desert Inn in Las Vegas, McCoy was told to wait. Finally, Bill Gay appeared and led McCoy out to the patio to speak privately.

Gay seemed agitated." The boss has been using doubles for years. We encouraged it." He was confessional, his voice barely audible. 'At first, there was a random series of guys about his weight and height. Put 'em in a hat and raincoat, rush 'em out to the car. The press or Hoover's guys, whoever was watching him, bought it. 'There goes Mr. Hughes. Better follow him.' A few minutes later, the coast was clear and we could take the boss wherever he wanted to go. *Sub rosa* like that, with no one the wiser. But then we found Mr. Randall." Gay rolled his eyes. "He really looked like the boss and once he grew that little mustache, the resemblance was spooky. Soon he was moving and speaking like him. The boss loved it. Maybe too much." Gay looked uncomfortable and leaned closer. "You know how it is with him." He was trying not to be specific, waiting for McCoy to get it.

"No, I don't. How is it with Mr. Hughes?"

Gay moved closer. "He goes both ways. All hot for Ava Gardner one minute—shacking up like newlyweds. Then he's all over the pool boy."

"He's bisexual. I know that."

"Well, at first he had a thing for Brooks Randall. I guess it was like making it with himself. So Randall became the only double we used and fine. But after about a year, it started getting weird."

"You mean weirder." McCoy tried not to grin. "Like how?"

"Randall had been sleeping over, but then one day he never left. He and the boss wore all the same clothes. The boss had us set up another bedroom and soon there were two of them and now... We can't tell them apart."

"That's ridiculous."

"We can't tell them apart, Dr. McCoy. Can you? You've been with each of them."

Gay showed McCoy into the suite next door where Hughes was smiling expectantly. "Thank God you're here." He strode across the room and clasped McCoy's hand. He appeared fit and well-groomed, eyes bright, skin clear, wearing a crisp white shirt and gray slacks.

*But is it Howard Hughes or Brooks Randall?*

Gay hovered at his side like an odor. "The plane's ready, boss." He looked at the Timex on his pink wrist. "If we leave now, we can fly in daylight."

McCoy felt Hughes hand on his shoulder. Again, the big smile. "I don't like to travel. You know that, Wiley. I especially don't like to travel without a doctor present." He winked. "You're it, big boy." The smile dropped like a stone. "We have to go."

*So I'm a doctor again. What is this lunatic up to now?*

The flight from Las Vegas to Los Angeles took slightly under an hour. At first, McCoy was afraid Hughes wanted to pilot the twin engine, but he climbed into the back with him and Gay.

"I'm directing a new film. It's about space travel." Hughes was staring out the window at the clouds and the thrumming propellers. "We're shooting at night in the desert. Lots of insects, but I have to be there." He turned to McCoy, searching his face. "Are you afraid of insects, Wiley?"

"No more than anybody else." *And less than you.*

"Good. Then you can keep them away from me." He nudged Gay, who had begun to doze. "You brought the Benadryl?"

"The Benadryl, penicillin, amphetamines, Valium and those suppositories Jean gave you."

"Jean's not coming, I won't need them."

Gay eyed McCoy. *Who knew?*

It was sunset when Hughes' baby blue Chrysler New Yorker pulled off Route 118 for Topanga Canyon, then headed south. The car's entire trunk was taken up by an air-conditioning system, the only one of its kind in the world. The Beatles were singing *Taxman* on the radio. Gay was driving.

"This moon thing is gonna be huge. Everyone's making money off it—watch companies, car companies, even that orange powder crap Tang. The astronauts are taking Tang to the moon!" He was drumming his fingers on his armrest now. "A lot of money riding on this. Nothing better go wrong. Nothing." He frowned. "Turn that crap off!" Gay turned down the radio. Hughes lowered his window, scowling in the warm summer air. "Make a right at the light for Santa Susana Pass, then keep going 'til you see a church on your right."

"Where'd you find this place?" McCoy tried to seem interested.

"It's an old cowboy ranch. They used to shoot Westerns and commercials there. Now it's a shithole."

They turned onto a dirt road under scraggly trees. A man holding a rifle stepped out of nowhere and checked their license plate, then waved them through. Somewhere, dogs were barking.

Suddenly there was a glow like hellfire and they drove into a clearing where a white sand field dazzled beneath the light of a dozen arc lamps surrounding its perimeter.

Suspended above in the darkness, a small bright green and blue orb glowed in a spotlight—a model planet earth, as viewed from the surface of this ersatz moon. All around, out of the lights, were tractor-trailers, throbbing generators and men wearing headsets. A tall crane dangled something large and metallic high above the lights.

Gay held the door for Hughes, who emerged stiffly, shifting his shoulders to crack his back. One of the headset men stepped forward, his face strained.

"I want to start before these lights..." he spoke with an Eastern European accent, waving his hands "before they attract attention from nosy neighbors."

Hughes took the man's arm. "Let's see the set-up first, Wojy Fry."

McCoy had been to shoots with Katie. *God, don't think about Katie...* The endless retakes, the waiting for lights and cameras to be reset. *There's something furtive about this shoot.* McCoy couldn't put his finger on it. He followed Hughes up the metal steps into a tractor-trailer aglow with TV monitors and more people in headsets.

"It will be a problem if you don't tell him," Wojy was murmuring to Hughes. "Me? I would warn him." Again, the broad hand gestures.

At the back of the truck, a handsome dark-haired woman was watching Hughes intently from her perch on a stool.

"Hello, Abigail." Hughes smiled.

McCoy stepped out of the trailer. In the floodlit circle outside, two men were carefully raking the white sand, creating a dimpled glowing surface.

"You know what's outside the lights?" McCoy had barely heard the man approach. Sad-eyed and scruffy, not much more than thirty, he pushed tangled brown hair out of his eyes. "I mean *really* outside the lights?" A smirk appeared through his five-day beard. "Desert, man. And things with wings." He was cackling now and holding up a joint. "Smoke?" His eyes twinkled; he was a head shorter than McCoy.

Bored, McCoy said yes, and on that moonless night, he followed Charles Manson into the desert to get high.

His battered Zippo brought the spliff to life. Manson inhaled deeply, then passed it to McCoy. "I'm Charlie. I run this place for the old guy."

"Hey. I'm Wiley."

McCoy's face tingled. A dreamy smile played on his lips. *What old guy?*

"Good shit. Right, man?" Manson whooped, waving the flashlight he'd produced as he stepped off the rough path they were following up a scrub-splattered incline. McCoy followed, glad to be wearing his Frye boots. They stopped at the top of the rise. Manson, a whippet-thin scarecrow silhouetted against the purple desert, took a deep hit.

Manson's flashlight beam found what he was looking for: a battered dune buggy with fur-covered seats. Manson stumbled towards the vehicle.

"Come on, Wiley. Let's go for a ride!" Again, the whooping laugh as he started the engine and punched on the lights. McCoy was barely in before the stripped VW chassis lurched forward and they were rumbling across the desert, their headlights leading them like electric eels in a churning pool. McCoy eyed the machine gun mount before him and the driver's side machete jutting out of its scabbard. *Why do these guys always find me?*

"I've got a fleet of these," Manson was shouting over the engine. McCoy gripped the iron tubing at his side, as the buggy vaulted a rise, bouncing on its big tires. "The engine's air-cooled." Manson looked comic-book shrewd. "No water in the desert, Wiley."

Movement behind him – a hand gripped his shoulder – shrieking laughter. McCoy twisted in his seat. A girl in her twenties was kneeling in the back where she'd lay hidden. She smirked at McCoy, red hair blowing in the wind like a frayed blanket, and snatched the last of the joint. She inhaled deeply. A loopy vixenish smile with a few broken teeth.

"I'm Squeaky. You want a boner?"

Manson cackled, nearly upending the speeding buggy as he reached back and pulled up her T-shirt. A ragged scar showed over the top of her jeans. She pushed him away, smiling shyly at McCoy.

"Why do you have a fleet of these?" McCoy shouted over the roar. Manson shifted gears and the dune buggy ground to a stop. The desert was level all around them beneath the stars. He switched off the ignition. Now there was only the sound of the wind.

"I have a fleet of dune buggies because I'm gonna run a taxi service after the Apocalypse." He wasn't smiling now. He spoke with conviction. "After Helter-Skelter. In the war between blacks and whites, my army is going to need a way to escape. Across the desert."

Again the wiry strength as he swung himself up out of his seat and onto the hood, standing there in battered Keds, his hands folded, face turned heavenward.

"We will escape to the bottomless pit." He met McCoy's gaze. "It's all there in the White Album, man. Foretold, like. All you have to do is listen."

Squeaky's fingers were tickling McCoy's neck again. She was breathing in his ear.

McCoy would replay what happened next many times over the course of his life, reliving the moment that could have changed so much. He leaned away from Squeaky's mousy breath as Manson hopped onto the ground. A thrashing in the scrub brush by his feet, a swirling speckled bolt shot up at his calf and he screamed.

The snake shot into the brush and was gone. Manson was hopping on his left foot now, clutching his right calf, gasping. "A rattler! Oh shit, a rattler!"

"Stop moving," McCoy ordered. "You'll spread the venom faster." McCoy led him whimpering to the back seat. Squeaky helped him, fearful-eyed. Manson's color was dropping. McCoy pulled off his belt to tourniquet Manson's leg above the right knee. "Keep him still. He's going to be all right."

"You a doctor?"

"From time to time." McCoy ground the gears, the buggy spewed sand, then made traction. Within moments, they were back at the trailer-ringed clearing.

McCoy sprinted past technicians back to the parked New Yorker. He tried the handle. Locked.

In the trailer control room, Hughes and the Eastern European, Frykowski, were huddled in front of a TV monitor. Gay was by Abigail, holding a phone to his ear. He looked tired and frustrated— not his usual self.

"Bill, I need the car key."

Gay glared at McCoy. Abigail stepped over to Frykowski and rubbed his shoulders.

"I'm in the middle of something, Wiley." The annoyed grown-up.

"You're on hold. Give me the key." McCoy glanced at his Rolex. The venom puncture was eleven minutes old.

Gay rummaged in his pocket, but someone spoke on the phone and he sat up, ignoring McCoy. "Yes. Ready?" A pause. "What's the frequency, Kenneth?" Another pause. "Ok? Good. Can we talk about the broadcast, Dan?" The key was in his hand now. McCoy snatched it and squeezed past the people at the control board.

In the car, he grabbed Hughes' medical bag with "HH" in gold on its side.

Squeaky was still holding the belt tourniquet tight. Manson was pale and dim-lidded, masticating deliriously. McCoy opened the bag and took out a syringe. He tore the plastic wrapping with his teeth.

"He doesn't look so good, mister."

Manson was blue-lipped, but breathing. McCoy found the anti-venom. He pierced the rubber top with the needle and drew a dose. A sprinkle in the air to engage—he plunged the point into Manson's thigh and squeezed. "Ok. He should come around." McCoy felt for a pulse. *Not much...getting weaker.* Squeaky's hands were at the side of her head. She looked like Munch's *Scream.*

"It's not working."

"Give it time." *Christ, he should be reviving by now.*

But he wasn't.

*I'm losing him. I can't lose another one.*

It was automatic. He heard the voice in his head—Romulo's voice—and he began murmuring "*J'ai eno, J'ai mau mau, J'ai eno evil...*" over and over.

Manson's pulse had stopped. He wasn't breathing. McCoy placed Manson's lifeless hands across his chest. Squeaky was sobbing. *The anti-venom should've worked...* And the incantation was useless. Science had failed and there was no magic.

Then Manson sat up.

Squeaky screamed "Christ, Charlie! Don't do that!

He was retching over the side of the dune buggy now. Squeaky produced a dented canteen and Manson gulped water. He looked blearily at McCoy like a dog at its master. “You saved my life, man.”

McCoy shrugged. *Did I? What really happened?*

“I’m gonna write a song for you.” Squeaky had her arm around him. “I owe you, man.”

“I’m not sure who you owe.” *Don’t overthink this, Wiley.* “Stay off that leg. It’s going to hurt for a day or so.”

Still high on Manson’s pot, McCoy was walking back to the lit clearing when the arc lights came on. The sand and air glowed white.

“Here we go!” Frykowski's voice crackled over the P.A. “M.O.S. Take one! Aannd action!” The forty-foot crane's winch whined as a hexagonal shape the size of three cars descended from the overhead gloom, smoke blasting from its base as the quadruped descended onto the sand. The words “NASA, Apollo 11” and an American flag were stenciled on its bronze metal side.

“That's good. Wind please!”

A huge fan blew from outside the circle of light. Someone tossed sand and stones into the gale, buffeting the space capsule as it “landed.” Its cabin door slowly opened and an “astronaut” emerged in a white spacesuit with a spherical silver helmet. A small TV camera was strapped to his chest. With exaggerated slowness, he worked his way onto the ladder between two of the craft’s four-podded legs. Then he missed his step and fell six feet to the ground.

“Cut!” Frykowski was not happy. “Eddie! What happened?”

The crew was helping the “astronaut” to his feet. “Fuckin' A! Those steps are loose!”

Frykowski walked over. “We do it again. Only this time slower. Much slower.”

A headset man began tightening screws at the side of the ladder. McCoy walked back to Hughes’ car and collapsed into the backseat, gazing up through the open sunroof at the moonless sky.

# 33.

She often wondered what he thought about as he rocked slowly before the fire. His bearded face, lit by the flickering, was almost as handsome as before the shooting. *If only he could speak.*

The flames flared, lighting his eyes and disfigured temple. She saw perspiration on his forehead. He wasn't due for pain medication for over an hour; he'd just had his salt pills and antihistamines. She walked in her bent-over way to the air conditioner, wiped dust off its cover with her sleeve, then turned it to High Cool. At first, it seemed foolish to have a fire in the summer, but when she saw how much he liked it, she let him have that sometimes instead of the television.

One rainy night, Mr. Gay came to the house with a little cake.

She answered in her broken English. Gay passed her the cake in its cardboard box and wished her a Merry Christmas. He patted her arm and passed her a bulging white envelope. "This is $10,000. Your mortgage for the house has been paid for the next year and your daughter has been given her stipend."

He smiled as he rose, and looked at Kennedy. Tears welled up in his eyes. "Goodbye. God bless. I'll see you next Christmas."

For supper, she often gave Kennedy what she thought to be his favorite dessert, pureed apple cobbler.

After his sponge bath, she rolled his wheelchair in front of the big mirror and gave him a haircut and trimmed his beard. She rubbed cold cream onto his face, massaging it into the scar tissue along the right side of his head.

*Oh, he was in there.*

Sleeping, dreaming, then briefly awake, and always in a medicated haze to suppress the pain, Kennedy knew who he was. He heard the television: *Bobby was shot dead; King, too. Lyndon was President, then Dick.*

It was the 4th of July. On TV, the newscaster was describing the impending flight to the moon. Even in the half-darkness, she could see the fear in his eyes whenever the television or the fire was extinguished. Madonna wheeled him to the dining table. Her gnarled fingers lit the four sparklers on the cake, decorated like a flag in red, white and blue icing to celebrate her new country's birthday.

The front doorbell rang three times. She saw a man's silhouette through the screen door. *What's that on his shoulder?* She was expecting a courier with fresh drugs and syringes. She opened the door, and Remus flew screaming into the house. The boy she had raised to become a man stood red-eyed and gaunt before her.

"Hello, mama."

"What do you want?'

"To say thank you." Romulo shifted his feet on the doorstep.

She let him step past her and closed the door. Inside, Remus was perched on the back of Kennedy's wheelchair.

*What do you want?* But she knew.

Romulo took color photographs of Kennedy in his wheelchair wearing his blue sweater, his graying hair neatly combed, and the wedding band on his left hand clearly displayed. He was holding that morning's edition of the *New York Times*. Just as he had done with the photos he sent President Johnson a few years earlier, Romulo inked Kennedy's fingers and pressed them against the backs of the pictures, then mailed them to Jackie Onassis with a typewritten letter:

> Dear Mrs. Kennedy,
> Congratulations on your illegal marriage. Here are some recent photographs of the man you are still married to. If you and Mr. Onassis do not want the world to know of your bigamy, be on board the *Christina* off the eastern coast of Jamaica at 6 p.m. on July 10th. I will contact you there.
> Sincerely,
> An old friend

## 34.

Kool Silver, the aeromatic predictor of weather, navigator and manager of all things nautical aboard the *Thresher*, was in love. The object of his affections was a young man, once a middleweight boxer in Yugoslavia who'd turned to crime, then fled to Haiti. Anatol Dragic was a pretty boy with "HOLD FAST" tattooed, letter by letter, across his knuckles.

Silver had been at a shantytown bar near Petion-Ville that hosted cockfighting out back. Tonight, the sounds seemed different. Puzzled, he carried his *cerveza* past the corrugated bathrooms into a dusty square marked by party lights. Twenty or so boozed-up laborers were cheering, then groaning as two men, stripped to their waists, maneuvered like dancers, bare-knuckle boxing. One was nearer 50 then 40, with large flabby arms and a watery squint. The other man, younger, bobbed comfortably, occasionally striking out with a jab of his well-defined right arm. A short woman, with gravy bag breasts, moved through the onlookers, taking their bets in her red plastic cup. The older man's powerful swings weren't connecting. He was growing tired. Silver eased through the crowd and made eye contact with the young fighter, who flinched at Silver's mauled half face. The dance continued, but then the younger feinted with a right jab to his opponent's head followed by a left uppercut to his jaw. Teeth spewed out as the older man dropped to his knees. The fight was over. Silver nodded approvingly at the winner and raised his *cerveza* in a toast.

"Waa gwaan? You need a job?" They were talking quietly at the bar.

"Maybe." Dragic sipped his *cerveza.* "What's it pay?"

"Pay's good. A tru-tru." Silver looked away. *What am I doing? Jeezum pees. I'm repulsive...*

Without flinching, Dragic touched Silver's cheek. He ran his fingers along the scar mask. "You wear so much pain." He smiled. "Be careful or it will own you."

At the next re-provisioning cycle at Port-au-Prince, Dragic joined the ship and became Silver's bunkmate.

Either due to magic or science, Romulo's surgeries were not possible without saltwater, so Romulo converted six of the *Thresher*'s twelve missile silos into a sealed operating room connected to an antechamber by a water-tight sliding glass door.

Romulo and McCoy wore white neoprene wetsuits and scuba masks with mouthpieces. Their air hoses ran to tanks which Ts'Me monitored from outside the water-filled glass theater. A bank of video monitors displayed the vital signs of the doctors as well as of the patient. If the doctors drowned, so did the patient.

It was difficult to see underwater. The saline solution became so murky that it had to be changed every four hours, a time-consuming process involving pumps and filters. The liquid was particularly cloudy today, after only—Romulo looked at the digital display—twenty-three minutes. McCoy peered out at Ts'Me who checked Kennedy's oxygen and made a slight adjustment to a valve before him. He gave McCoy a thumbs up. McCoy thought of Sam Selzer during Katie's operation. *Please God. Not again.*

Kennedy lay face-up on the underwater operating table, held steady by canvas-wrapped lead weights slung over his arms, legs, and midsection. His head and neck were clamped into a stainless steel, basket-like apparatus that supported his cranium and upper spinal column. *A lifetime of* ulcers, *colitis, Addison's disease, ravaged by back surgeries and a lifelong cocktails of steroids, painkillers, and anti-spasmodics… and now this.*

Romulo finished tracing a line with a tattoo needle around the circumference of Kennedy's shaved skull. He paused to regain his composure. The Valium he'd taken less than an hour before had mostly calmed his shaking hands. This would be his first cerebral tie-in on a human.

Romulo squeezed his laser scalpel and a red beam shot out of its handle. He aligned it with the line he'd tattooed around Kennedy's skull. Flesh and bone particles spat out as Romulo traced an incision, only stopping at the occipital protuberance. Now came the difficult part.

In an operating room with an oxygen atmosphere, Romulo would take a surgical hammer and chisel to gently break the internal table of Kennedy's skull. But here, underwater, he would have to use a tiny electric jackhammer to pry loose the skullcap without injuring the investing membrane or touching the metal plate attached to the right hemisphere of Kennedy's brain since the shooting in Dallas.

Romulo flipped on the jackhammer and tapped loose Kennedy's skullcap with two swift motions. The tie-in could begin.

McCoy held up the first of twenty color-coded wires with surgical plugs at their ends, leading to the bank of monitors and sensory recorders Ts'Me was watching in the control room. With his finger, Romulo traced the fissure of Rolando across the surface of Kennedy's brain, then inserted the first plug into the section controlling Kennedy's opposite arm and hand movement.

"I have number one. Verification, please."

Ts'Me turned a dial and Kennedy's right arm and hand quivered. Romulo nodded. McCoy passed him the second tie-in. They repeated the procedure, testing each time, until all twenty tie-ins were live. The right hemisphere which affected vision and hearing on Kennedy's left side had been badly damaged. His ability to speak may have been lost, as well as his sense of smell. Otherwise, Kennedy's brain, including his memory of fifty-two years, responded perfectly and Kennedy's thoughts appeared on one of the video screens.

Romulo and McCoy re-entered the control room to see the monitor with the visualization of Kennedy's brain activity which, for now, was a crackling fire in a stone hearth.

"He thinks he's in the safe house in front of the fireplace," McCoy said.

The video image went black, then new images.

*I'm overboard! Where's my crew?!*

Flaming gasoline was all around him. The Japanese destroyer had sliced PT 109 in half. Kennedy was treading water. *Where's MacMohon?* A white shape bobbed up ten yards away. His back in agony, Kennedy drove under and swam. He reached MacMohon, conscious but burned, and towed him in the crook of his arm over to what was left of their PT boat. Two tattered crew members helped Kennedy ease the machinist's mate onto the broken bow as a shrieking flare lit the night and a Japanese battleship powered by. Its wake rocked their plywood wreck.

"He's reliving his war experience." McCoy marveled.

The fires were dying out as the last flames consumed the gas and oil slick. Kennedy and his men clung to their shattered bow.

"I should've had both engines on," Kennedy gasped. "We could've turned faster, maybe fired our torpedoes. I should've known."

The image faded and the flickering hearth again filled the screen. Kennedy had lost his memory's thread.

Romulo frowned. "Something's wrong." Ts'Me squinted at the

monitors. "He's got a breathing problem."

He tapped the glass of the oxygen display. "Could be a lung infection."

McCoy looked up, startled. "Better give him an antibiotic. If an infection gets hold, he'll be dead by morning."

Romulo pushed through the airlock into compartment A through the saline to where Kennedy lay on the table. Romulo injected the antibiotic into Kennedy's arm. *This body he's worn so long can't last...*

Lately, Kool Silver's cock of the walk, Rasta-meets-the- Navy demeanor had changed. His shoulders drooped. He no longer hummed reggae under his breath. He was unhappy in love.

Romulo heard pounding and shouting in the crew quarters. With Remus on his shoulder, he hurried through the rows of bunks until he came to a dozen sailors, some standing, some watching from their berths. The quarters stank of man fug. On the floor, Kool Silver had his bearlike hands around Anatol Dragic's throat, his half face so distorted with anger that it appeared to be melting as he strained to break the younger man's windpipe.

"I mash you up, rasshole!"

Now Dragic was hacking at Silver's rib cage with a straight razor. The Jamaican roared, spraying blood, and loosened his grip. Romulo flicked the safety off his pistol. Silver was too valuable to lose in a brawl.

Silver grabbed a broom and advanced on Dragic until he had him against the hull wall.

"Nuh romp wid mi!" Silver hissed. The side of his shirt was crimson. Dragic tried to dart past, but Silver caught him and pushed the broom handle crossways up against his throat. There was a crunching and his neck broke. Silver stepped back, aghast. Dragic slid onto the compartment floor, lifeless.

Remus's cackle broke the silence. The men noticed Romulo for the first time.

"Pick him up, Silver, and come with me. The rest of you get back to your bunks."

"Jus a word, captain, we were bredren and he..."

"Pick him up!"

The crew scrambled to their quarters as Silver hoisted Dragic's body over his shoulder and followed Romulo to the surgery. Tears streamed down his half face.

McCoy was scrubbing up as they entered.

"What happened here?"

"An accident, McCoy. He's been dead almost two minutes. Put him in cold suspension, B-compartment, and wire him for recharge. Silver, do what he says. When McCoy finishes with you, get back to your cabin and stay there. You're confined until further notice."

They lay Dragic on the B-compartment operating table and McCoy placed an oxygen mask on his face, while Silver lay weighted bags across Dragic's limbs. He stood wringing his hands. "Can the captain bring him back with an *obeah*?"

"No idea," McCoy responded. "I don't do magic, Kool, just medicine." McCoy tore Silver's jumpsuit away. His torso was a cat's claw of razor cuts. He dabbed the wounds with iodine, then bandaged and taped them shut. All the while, Silver stared at his dead friend.

"He was a samfy man. He stole from me." Silver looked at his shoes. "It's a tru-tru."

"Go to your cabin, Kool, and be happy you're not facing murder charges."

"Bless up. Tanks, doc."

In A-compartment, Romulo and Ts'Me surveyed Kennedy's vital functions. Kennedy's infection was dissipating and his breathing came with less difficulty.

The video screen was alive. Kennedy was in the Rose Garden of the White House, bathed in sun. A little boy in short pants was running with a hose.

Kennedy reached down and turned on the faucet. John John's hose spewed everywhere, nearly knocking him into a flowerbed. He aimed the hose at his father, who was laughing as hard as his son, and soaked him. Kennedy hoisted the boy in the air, grimacing with pain as he swung him over the roses.

The screen changed again: an enormous crowd in Madison Square Garden. Handsome in his tuxedo, Kennedy sat behind the podium among politicians, movie stars, and international dignitaries, all in formal dress.

The crowd grew quiet. The house lights dimmed and a blue spot lit the lectern. Marilyn Monroe, shimmering in white sequins, approached the microphone as a lone pianist began to play. Marilyn sang "Happy Birthday," playfully, breathlessly. On the third line, she turned to Kennedy. Her dress was cut low, exposing her bare back.

"Happy Birthday...Mister President. Happy Birthday...to you." She was looking into his eyes as she breathed the lyrics. He returned her stare, transfixed.

The audience applauded wildly. Kennedy approached Marilyn at the lectern and kissed her cheek, then spoke into the microphone. His words became distorted as the image faded to black. Now there was the sound of water running as though from a tap in a nearby room. Romulo checked the life monitors. Kennedy's heartbeat and pulse had quickened perceptibly.

"We're watching history... from inside his brain," Ts'Me said in awe.

The water stopped. There was silence and blackness. Then Marilyn opened the bathroom door. Light fell across the bed where Kennedy lay, tiny-pupiled and jacketless, his collar and bow tie undone. He watched her spray herself with perfume. She still wore the shimmering dress.

"You should sing more often. You have a great voice."

"I'm glad you liked it," Marilyn said from the bathroom.

"There're some pill bottles in the medicine cabinet," Kennedy said. "Would you hand them to me with a glass of water?"

"Demarol? Ritalin? Gosh, there's a lot."

"Those'll do," Kennedy stretched out his hand for the water glass, swallowed the pills, then pulled her onto the bed. They kissed, then finally stopped to breathe.

"That's better." His back spasm was subsiding. Kennedy reached for the zipper of her dress.

"May I unwrap my present?" Marilyn stood. The dress fell to her ankles. She wore nothing underneath.

Ts'Me was hugging his legs with his chin on his knees. "We just saw her tits. Oh my God."

McCoy leaned into the control room. "Dragic's wired for recharge. I'm ready to fill the chamber."

"Then fill it." Romulo couldn't take his eyes off Kennedy kissing Marilyn's stomach, now her navel.

The screen went blank. The life-support board beeped urgently.
"He's dying," McCoy spoke quietly.
"I say who dies on this ship, doctor." Romulo re-zipped his wetsuit and grabbed his facemask. "Suit up. We're going back in."

The procedure took all night.
Hughes Research Laboratories had built Romulo an alpha version of an artificial circulation system he designed (based on Dr. DeBakey's roller pump), which had yet to be tested on a human being.
In A-compartment, they separated Kennedy's living head and spinal column from his dying body while a maze of tiny plastic hoses ran through a pump the size of a football and kept him medicated and alive.
The B-compartment intercom beeped. Romulo was ready to begin the second procedure.
It took three hours and fourteen minutes in fluid suspension to separate Dragic's dorsal veins from the muscles in the vertebral grooves and away from the integument at the back of his spine. McCoy marveled at the finesse with which Romulo, as though disassembling an orange, unthreaded the delicate vein network, carefully packing each system back into the dorsal cavity lest a single thread float out into the saline solution and be damaged.
Reattaching Kennedy's head and spine to the young sailor's body took longer. First, Romulo sealed the spinal column at the fifth lumbar with mambo paste and what appeared to be ground eggshells. Then, after Dragic's back was set in a brace, Romulo re-wove the musculature and veins. He worked without stopping, hunched over the table in the murky fluid, muttering incantations, speaking to McCoy over the intercom to request clamps or sutures. He instructed McCoy to raise, lower or angle the hydraulic table to facilitate his fingers' access to the gaping dorsal cavity. At last, Kennedy's head was attached, and Romulo directed McCoy to sew shut the trench-like wound from the base of the neck to the coccyx.
"We'll reanimate him outside the tank. He's been in the solution too long as it is."
Squinting, McCoy began stitching at the base of the spine while Romulo disengaged Kennedy's cerebral tie-ins. McCoy was tired. He needed to urinate. His fingers shook as he disconnected the

wires from Kennedy's head. Particles of bone, skin and core hung suspended in the hazy liquid, the liquid that gave life.

"It's pea soup in here," McCoy said over the intercom.

"I should've changed the solution hours ago. I've never gone this long without fresh saline."

"What happens if you don't change it?"

"*Gardez silence*," Romulo said wearily. He rarely answered McCoy's questions and when he did, he purposefully answered obtusely.

On the other side of the glass, Ts'Me was trying to attract their attention.

As McCoy unattached the last tie-in, he saw something move at the back of the tank by the oxygen hose outlets. Ts'Me was gesturing and pointing.

"Do you see something over there?"

Romulo looked up. It moved again, more like a shudder this time.

"You mean by the air hose? No, that's just the..."

A lump of flesh about the size of a human lung darted out fishlike from among the red and white hoses. It flickered to and fro, then zig-zagged back into the shadows.

"What the fuck was that?" McCoy stood staring.

"We've got to get him out of here. Hurry!" There was panic in Romulo's voice.

McCoy stabbed the needle in and pulled the thread through, then stopped again. Particles of gore from the surgery were flowing towards the thing in the corner as though pulled by a magnet.

"No. I want to know what that is."

"That's life itself." Romulo's eyes were wide behind his face mask. "You're looking at evolution gone mad."

The thing propelled itself into the light again. It had grown larger in less than a minute. The bits of bone and tissue in the fluid were attaching themselves to it in a steady pinkish stream.

"I change the saline solution to keep the mambo paste from animating the flesh particles. If it's not controlled, that *diab* will grow larger and larger, incorporating all the flesh in the tank. Including us.

McCoy's hands raced to finish sealing the wound. He glanced

up. The liquid was remarkably clear now. He could see Ts'Me's terrified face outside pressed to the glass. The *diab* had amassed nearly all the tissue in the tank and had grown to the size of a large calf. Romulo grabbed his laser scalpel and stepped out in front of McCoy and their patient. He squeezed the scalpel trigger, shooting its red beam, sharper than any razor. The *diab* turned on its side and glided away. Rows of human fingers and toes jutted out from its pale belly like legs on a centipede.

"This won't keep him away for long. Its parts are human because it's made of human flesh, but the *diab* has no DNA to decipher the genetic code. That's why it has fingers for legs."

Something flickered, "Look out!"

The *diab* swooped towards them, its tail straight out like a stinger. Romulo thrust the laser beam into the *diab*'s back. It scuttled up the side of the tank to hover somewhere above them.

"It'll take a moment to regenerate. I gored him pretty badly."

The *diab's* red blood floated back up to where it waited, healing itself. McCoy's hands were shaking. He could barely cut the surgical thread.

"I'm finished. Let's go!"

McCoy brandished a pair of surgical scissors like a dagger as Romulo pulled the first weights off Kennedy's new young body.

"I'll drain the chamber," Romula pushed a button. The liquid lurched as the drains in the metal floor opened and began to suck the fluid out into the sea.

"Hold on. Whatever happens, don't let him get near Kennedy."

The liquid was draining rapidly. Their heads were clear of it now.

"We can move faster out of the water. Maybe I'll get a shot at him." He reached up and pulled off his mask.

"No!" Romulo screamed, but it was too late. The *diab* broke the surface of the water and launched itself at McCoy's face like a bolt from a crossbow. Instinctively, McCoy held the scissors out in front of him stiff-armed and closed his eyes. It was squirming, sucking up his arm, twisting on the blades deep in its gullet. The thing had engorged his fist and forearm up to the elbow.

Suddenly, the *diab* slid down his bleeding arm and fell back onto the water, the scissors still inside it.

They carried Kennedy to the airlock and out into the

antechamber, sealing A-compartment behind them.

Later, when the chamber was drained, they returned with a can of gasoline and burned the diab, watching it shriek and flop like a dying manta ray.

## 35.

Port-au-Prince twinkled in the distance, its lights growing brighter as the *Thresher* approached. A haggard Romulo stood alone on the winged conning tower, his face splashed by the ocean spray.

Kennedy lay sedated in his new body, strapped to a sick bay bunk lest he awaken unsupervised. Romulo thought about the *diab* again. He'd been careless. In prison, Papa Zobop had warned him about the errors committed by practitioners of *la science.* One man used *mambo* paste to make birds. He created an entire aviary filled with beautiful flying creatures, each more unique and exotic than the next. One day, he let a drop of paste smear over a cut on his hand. He awoke the next morning with a little wing growing out of his palm, flapping and quivering. It grew stronger until midday when it could raise his arm above his head. Soon, the man's nose and mouth became soft and mushy and a hooked beak grew out of his jaws. That night, while he could still move his fingers (they were now webbing, his nails thickening into claws), he clumsily wrapped his beak around the barrel of a shotgun and destroyed himself.

McCoy's alarm went off at 0400 hours. He'd slept for only ninety minutes, still in his clothes from the day before. He hurried to the sick bay to relieve Ts'Me. Silver stood waiting outside with red-rimmed eyes.

"I'm sorry, Kool, you can't go in there."

"Did captain cast an *obeah*? Will me bredren be back?" He meant Dragic.

*I can't explain this now.*

"We'll see." McCoy patted Silver's arm. "Let me talk to you later." He cracked open the sick bay door. Peering past him, Silver saw Dragic's hands (for they were Dragic's) clasped on the cot blanket—the words "HOLD FAST" tattooed on his fingers.

Kennedy's head lay in shadow on the pillow. Silver winced as McCoy closed the door.

Ts'Me was exhausted. "Life signs are strong. Pulse is steady. Breathing raspy but close to normal. Temperature's running 99 to 99.5." He was shaking his head. "This isn't possible. He should be a pile of organs and bones with a head on top."

McCoy confirmed Ts'Me's evaluations. An IV with a powerful sedative ran along a tube to Kennedy's (Dragic's) right hand. An oxygen mask covered his mouth.

"I'll see you in three hours." Ts'Me got to his feet. "We're either on the cutting edge of science... or the front page of the *National Enquirer*."

McCoy watched Kennedy gently breathing. A knock on the door. "Come in."

Silver slipped in before McCoy could stop him.

"Jus a word. I have to know, mon." Silver took Kennedy's hand, straining to see Dragic's face. "He not right..."

"He isn't. He's someone else."

"No! Captain saved him!"

McCoy shook his head. "The captain saved his body."

"Nuh romp wid me."

"Look at his face. Is that your friend?"

Silver leaned close. "Jeezum pees. He's a mash up."

Silver let go his hand like it was a hot coal. "Why didn't captain save him?"

"I'm sorry, Kool. Captain had a different idea."

Silver was nodding. He'd decided something. "You my bredren. Captain a samfy man! A bumborass!"

Romulo had secured clearance from the *Capitainerie du Port* to anchor the *Thresher* in a remote part of Port-au-Prince Harbor to take on supplies.

Port-au-Prince is built on tiers around the lush hills overlooking its harbor. The presidential palace, an awkward hybrid—the White House crossed with a gabled Victorian mansion—is at the city's center. Its streets are wide and sunlit, planted with flowers and small public parks; its buildings are a sampling menu of architectural styles: a Chinese pagoda faces a South American ranch house next to a Beaux Arts office building. Port-au-Prince is the capital city of a country so unsure of itself that it sheds kleptocratic rulers like snake skins every few decades.

On shore leave, Floyd and McCoy picked their way through the business district towards the sour smell of the marketplace, their steps still spongy from being so long at sea. They bought a bottle of rum and flagged down an old Ford pick-up with a pink canopy across the back where several women sat on benches clutching coffee sacks. McCoy and Floyd climbed up front with the driver.

"We wanna go to the Carrefour. Okay?" Floyd said.

The driver grinned. He had a gold tooth. "*Oui, oui. Vous voulez frapper?*" He had noticed their uniforms and was jamming his right middle finger in and out of his left fist. He knew a whorehouse.

The women were pounding on the cabin roof.

"*Cent gourdes, Messieurs,*" he said apologetically. They agreed to his price and he put the truck in gear.

It was dark when they reached the *Carrefour* and they and the driver had finished half the bottle of rum. "*Merci, Monsieur.*" He pointed at the aqua blue house before them. "*Les bousins sont la bas.*" With a lurch, the truck rumbled off down the road.

"He drives better drunk than sober." McCoy looked wistfully at their rum bottle, then led Floyd by the arm into a courtyard planted with mango trees. Moonlight showed an ill-kept gravel path leading to a veranda lit with paper lanterns. The tinny sound of swing music was barely audible over birds cackling in the trees and crickets chirping.

"They're playing Art James!" Floyd said as though recognizing a friend.

A mulatto woman with grizzled hair and breasts nearly bursting out of her cocktail dress approached as they climbed the steps onto the veranda.

"Oo la la, kiddies. Look what *le bon dieu* has provided! Good evening, gentlemen of the sea. You have come looking for sweet women?" She asked in a singsong voice.

Too drunk to speak, Floyd bowed at the waist. McCoy grabbed his belt to keep him from falling over.

"*Suis* Josephine. Welcome to pleasure." She clapped her bejeweled hands.

"What vessel has the good fortune of your working on it?"

"We're off the *Thresher*. You know—the big sub?" Floyd spoke before McCoy could stop him.

The woman, Josephine, was less delighted to see them now. "There's only one girl here for you, and the price is fifty dollars."

"That's fine. Fifty dollars." McCoy wanted a woman. *I'm sorry, Katie.*

The *Thresher*'s reputation obviously had preceded them.

"You go first," Floyd said. "I gotta sit down."

Josephine pushed through the dancers, only pausing to whisper in the ear of a tall man with a prominent Adam's apple. He frowned at McCoy as a giggling young woman pulled him back to the music.

"Upstairs. Second door on the right." Josephine pointed up the rickety banister. McCoy started up but she put a hand on his sleeve. "Pay now."

He counted off five tens. Josephine sullenly tucked the money into her cleavage.

Upstairs, McCoy peered into a little room. A lamp glowed red on a corner table. A towel and a water bowl lay on the floor next to it. On a battered iron bed, a pretty woman in a blue nightgown and high-heels sat curled against the wall. McCoy was expecting a toothless old maman.

"*Suis* Delice," she said, smiling.

"I'm Wiley. Nice to meet you, Delice." She poured him a rum and Coke.

"You are American?"

"Yes."

"You don't look so evil. Gerard said you were an evil spirit from the black boat."

"I'm not. I'm a doctor. Are they afraid of me?"

She nodded.

"Josephine gives me to the *mal eduques*, the ones no one wants. She thinks I am a *zombi*."

McCoy laughed. "A *zombi*? What's that?"

"They say I died before, and a wicked *houngan* brought me back to life. Here, see?" She held up her leg, displaying a scar on her ankle. "That's where they say the candle fell over and burnt me when I was laid out to be buried."

"And is that what that is?"

She shrugged. She stood up and pulled her nightgown over her head. She wore only her shoes now and pink cotton panties. Delice unzipped his pants and began to wash him. She kneaded his thighs with her fingers. McCoy fell back onto the mattress and watched Delice's head bobbing up and down. He closed his eyes, groaning, back arched as he came. *Why does her cheek suddenly feel rough?*

She reached under the bed, pulled out a Coke bottle and spat into it. He opened his eyes. She was a man – an old black man in a white robe.

McCoy sat up heart pounding. Papa Zabop was laughing now as McCoy struggled to pull up his pants. "You look surprised, white doctor? It's okay. I was her." A flickering, and he was Delice again, hand outstretched, smiling softly; then he was the old man, grinning.

McCoy threw him onto the mattress. "You put something in the rum to make me hallucinate!"

Zabop's face was inches away. "You're meddling with the end of days. Who is really evil? Maybe he has a big submarine? Maybe he has a billion dollars? Maybe he is a she?" A new thought. "Did you ever wonder when you would die? Secret time! It's tonight."

Now he was Delice. She screamed theatrically. McCoy heard footsteps running down the hall. He stood, lurched through the open window, and scrambled onto the veranda roof. It was a twelve-foot drop to the bushes below. Behind him, the door burst open and a bald-headed man, naked to the waist, stood brandishing a machete. McCoy hopped off the ledge and plummeted into the foliage.

Floyd pushed up from his chair on the veranda, looking around confused.

"It's me," McCoy whispered. "Let's get out of here!"

Floyd stumbled down the wooden stairs.

There were men on the roof now shouting in Creole. The one with the machete was lowering himself down.

"Come on!" McCoy yelled, already running. Floyd trotted drunkenly behind him. They made it out of the courtyard and cut across the road into the trees. Floyd was gasping. Men were running and calling to each other close behind. A flashlight swept through the trees. McCoy pushed Floyd along. They came to the edge of a sugarcane field, then thrashed through the sea of green plants. Their pursuers swept their beams across the field. McCoy pulled Floyd to the ground.

"Keep still. If they go past, we can double back to the road," he whispered.

One of the men was heading right towards them. McCoy listened to the whizzing and thrashing coming closer.

"They're clearing the field with machetes," Floyd whispered, his drunkenness now terror.

McCoy squeezed Floyd's arm. He hated himself. *You're going to die right here and take Floyd with you. You waited too long for a chance that never came.*

McCoy hugged the ground as the machete whistled and smashed its way towards him. Panicking, Floyd leaped to his feet directly in line with a swinging blade. It caught the side of his head and clove halfway through his skull as though stuck in a coconut.

McCoy tried to crawl away, but a booted foot landed on his back. He scrambled to his feet, glimpsed a uniform--Tontons Macoutes or Services d'Investigation--then a flashlight cracked him on the back of his head. McCoy collapsed into the dirt and everything went black.

On board the *Thresher*, perspiring in polyester suits, Haitian security men stood silently at either end of the officers' mess where Romulo was dining by candlelight with president-for-life Francois "Papa Doc" Duvalier and his private secretary (and rumored mistress) France St. Victor, despised by the other Duvalier women (especially by Momma Doc) for her beauty, fair skin, and control over the diminutive dictator.

Now in his early 60's, Papa Doc was full-lipped and toad-faced, with a white brush cut jutting up over goggle-eyed glasses. His slow, whispering speech oozed menace. The Haitian people believed he was a powerful *houngan*, the successor to *Baron Samedi,* Lord of the Dead. He dressed formally in black suits to conceal his sidearm, usually wore a bow-tie and always carried a gold-headed cane, said to have once belonged to the *Baron.*

"I have great ambitions for my people," Papa Doc murmured as Romulo poured him more Cabernet. "Soon there will be color televisions in every village."

France looked away, bored. Whenever Papa got drunk, he boasted. She crossed her tan legs under the table. Romulo was staring at her. She feigned a smile. *Wait 'til you see what Papa has for you...*

In his black jumpsuit with gold buttons, a skull and crossbones on one lapel and an upside-down Caduceus—a winged staff with two serpents—on the other, Romulo, the doctor from hell, was here to do business.

"But, Mr. President, shouldn't the Haitian people have a powerful Navy?" Romulo asked.

Papa Doc had been trying to expand his eight boat Haitian armada for years with little success. The United States refused to grant its shipbuilders export licenses for Haiti. "There is more power in a single television than in all the might of a battleship," he replied.

"The *Thresher*, for example, could protect Haiti from attack by any nation in the world. With her nuclear weapons, you could stand up to Russia, China, even the United States."

"Are you making me an offer, captain? What would Mr. Hughes think?"

"Mr. Hughes does not command this ship. I do."

"And what makes you think I would betray my old friend?" Romulo lit France's cigarette; their eyes met.

"Because he'd betray *you*."

France looked away. *Those red eyes...doesn't he ever sleep?*

Papa Doc drained his glass. "Let's see the rest of *your* ship.

"France's never toured a submarine, have you, *cherie*?"

"No, Francois." Her figure strained at her Chanel dress as she eased herself out from behind the table. *And I've never wanted to.*

Footsteps pounded in the corridor outside. It was XO Silver and two policemen with automatic weapons.

"Jus' a word, captain. Mr. St. Cloud be dead and Dr. McCoy hurt bad. Police bring 'em aboard."

In sick bay, Romulo and Ts'Me hurriedly examined McCoy. His unconscious body was all cuts and scrapes; one eye was swollen shut; a jagged wound gushed below his navel. Ts'Me looked up from taking McCoy's pulse and shook his head. McCoy's heart had stopped.

Papa Doc finished questioning his policeman in Creole.

"Your men were at a brothel; they frightened one of the *bousins*. She went into a trance and claimed these two were evil spirits. You can imagine the rest."

At a glance from Papa Doc, Romulo gestured for Silver to clear the room. They were alone now with McCoy's lifeless body.

"I'm sorry about your man," Papa Doc whispered.

"He can be repaired."

"Now what would you want for the services of your ship?"

Romulo thought, then said "Safe harbor, shipyard facilities and a million dollars. A year."

It was a good offer—not that Romulo would honor it. Once he'd made repairs, restocked his stores, and taken the president's money, the *Thresher* would disappear, never to return to Haiti again.

Papa Doc spoke very slowly. "I have heard of your success with *la science*. They say you are a great *houngan* and you can travel beneath the waters of death."

"All true. May I show you?" Romulo led Papa Doc into the adjacent sick bay compartment where someone lay sleeping; he switched on the light.

"Do you recognize him?" Romulo watched Papa Doc's puzzled face. "One president to another?"

The dictator slowly nodded, stunned. The scraggly ginger beard had thrown him off, but then he saw the blue eyes and the scar tissue at his right temple.

"Impossible. My curse killed him six years ago."

"No. I killed him, then *I* brought him back." He peered into Papa Doc's bug-eyed glasses. "*My* magic is stronger than yours."

Romulo flicked off the light, then closed the door behind them.

When logic and skill fail, power takes over. Papa Doc pressed a gold-plated revolver to Romulo's heart. "I ask you. Can you heal yourself?" Romulo froze.

A smile flashed on the dictator's face. "Presidents-for-Life never die." He squeezed the trigger. Romulo collapsed to the floor. From his perch above, concealed among the pipes and cables, Remus clutched a *Sanjivani* flower in his claws and cried out miserably.

# Part Three:
# New York City, June 1969

## 36.

"It is the summer of change: hot and sultry with new forces ascendant; new music and new ideas."

The Real (which was the byline he'd chosen in the hopes he'd ever have a byline) pocketed his pen and notebook and stood thinking outside the West Village bar where he'd stopped on his bike to scribble. The temperature was over 90 degrees and the night smelled like cheese. Sweat glistening, bare-chested men swaggered in and out of the Stonewall Inn. Inside, *Satisfaction* was pounding. Young men in tank tops danced outside on the pavement, laughing and sucking on bottles of beer. Distant sirens grew louder. As the Real leaned on his pedal to push off, a squad car, lights flashing, rolled to a stop, blocking his way. Two weary-looking cops got out, handcuffs and badges glinting, and slowly pushed their way with distaste through the partying men. The Real stayed to watch.

A crowd of angry patrons, some in studded leather pants, others in feather boas and lipstick, was forming on the sidewalk. A second police car lurched over the curb. A thrown beer bottle exploded glass and suds, spattering a ducking officer. The Real moved closer just as the bar doors swung open and a handcuffed fortyish woman (or was she a man?) was wrestled onto the street by the policemen. Another beer bottle hit the pavement and shattered.

"Lay off, pigs! We're not doing anything!" a shrill voice shouted. The crowd was closing in on the cops now. Two more squad cars screamed up Christopher Street, forcing the crowd back onto the sidewalk. Again the partiers pushed forward and this time the policemen retreated into the bar, where they remained trapped for over an hour. The Stonewall riots were underway.

Two days later, the *East Village Othe*r published the Real's eyewitness account and paid him enough to buy a refurbished IBM Selectric typewriter with an erase key. His life had finally begun.

On Fifth Avenue across from Central Park, dawn turned into a smudgy grey morning. Jackie had been running much longer than her usual half hour. She stopped to put on dark glasses just past the zoo path that led out to the Plaza fountain. A few blocks north in their penthouse at the Pierre, Ari, in his Sulka robe, would be awake by now sipping mint tea and reading *the Times* through his hooded lids. *He's a wise old owl,* Jackie thought. *Then why don't I tell him? It's too crazy...*

Last night, when she'd opened the note, the photograph fell out. At a glance, she thought some sentimental acquaintance had sent her an old picture of Jack they supposed she'd want. She frowned trying to figure out when and where it'd been taken. She read the note and her fingers froze, she felt a wash of shame for whoever sent such an evil thing. But then she picked up the photo again...

Dumpy Ron Galella was lurking outside *A La Vielle Russe* on the corner of 59th and Fifth. He raised his camera as she jogged by.

"Hey, Jackie. Morning!"

Jackie grimaced, picking up her pace. His Leica flashed as she sprinted by.

People on their way to work stared in charmed recognition as she ran the two blocks to the Pierre's canopied entrance. Her sudden breathless burst had helped her decide. She would talk to Ari. Today, before Caroline and John came home from school. Ari was good with crazy. He would know what to do.

His nose itched. He scratched it. His fingers felt rubbery. With nobody to refill his drip, the effects of the chloral hydrate were receding. Breaking through the surface, he opened his eyes and breathed deeply. *Something is different.... What?*

Kennedy shifted his legs and lifted his head to look down his body. Sure enough, the blanket moved where his foot moved. *I can feel my legs!*

He grabbed the side of his bunk and pulled himself up. *Whose hands are these?* There was no crescent scar from where Teddy's dog bit him; his fingers were calloused... *and tattooed!* The letters forming "Hold Fast" were inked above each knuckle.

Awkwardly (again the rubbery fingers), he carefully swung himself into a sitting position. He looked at his arms, held them out before him. His skin was *young* looking.... Kennedy clumsily disconnected the IV drip from his right forefinger. He looked down at the floor. *Can I walk?* He put a tentative foot (*did my foot get larger?*) onto the floor. Then the other. He took a step. Then another. He crossed the small compartment to the bulkhead door. *Oh sweet Mary and Joseph, I can walk! That Cuban doctor has...what?*

The blat blat of automatic gunfire sounded from somewhere in the ship.

*War? Mutiny?* A rush of exhaustion caused his knees to bend. *I need that doctor (if he is a doctor). Concentrate!* He shambled back to his bunk.

Silver had had a bad feeling ever since France St. Vincent came on board with that Haitian pig. Women on a ship caused erections and other troubles. His concern increased at the sight of Papa Doc's larger than usual coterie of foul-smelling policemen.

After leaving Romulo and Papa Doc in the sick bay, Silver hurried back to his compartment and strapped on his pistol. It wasn't so much out of loyalty to Romulo as fear of Papa Doc. *The bumborass I know is better than the bumborass I don't know.*

A gunshot, then commotion--more gunshots. Silver slipped out into the hallway.

Jack-booted *Tonton Macoutes* – Papa Doc's dreaded storm troopers–were rounding up the *Thresher*'s crew at gunpoint and herding them into the mess room. Ordered to check every compartment, two blackshirts stomped into Kennedy's berth. The larger of the soldiers prodded Kennedy with a black-gloved forefinger.

"*Reveilles-toi!*" Kennedy didn't budge.

"*Il est malade.*" The second thug sniffed the rank air and grimaced.

Romulo's lifeless body lay on the empty compartment floor. Remus perched on his master's chest, the glowing *Sanjivani* flower held in his beak. The rat/parrot slipped the stem between Romulo's blue lips and waited. Minutes went by. Nothing. But then there was a rippling beneath Romulo's bloodstained jumpsuit and the bullet lodged in his heart rose out of its wound. Romulo blinked.

Chewing on the flower now, he murmured: "J'ai eno. J'ai mau mau, J'ai eno evil."

The soldier outside Kennedy's compartment gasped as Silver grabbed him from behind and snapped his neck. Through the open doorway, Kennedy watched Silver vault up the steps to the deck above.

In his compartment, Kennedy pulled off his gown, eying the reflection of his body. He was about the same height, six feet or so, but muscular now and much younger than his forty-six years - *wait – I'm older than that now. How long have I been... what? Hospitalized?* He touched the leathery scar tissue on his right temple. A faint necklace of nearly dissolved surgical stitching encircled his lower throat. *Where have I been and who's done what to me?* He tried to speak, to hear his voice, but the words came out as only moans.

One deck above, Silver saluted a puzzled Haitian soldier, then dropped him with a blast from his gun.

Kennedy walked to the next compartment.

There was a fresh corpse on a gurney in the next compartment. A white man. Kennedy peered at McCoy. I *know him from somewhere.* A Hughes Industries calendar on the wall caught his eye. *July, 1969. Six years... I'm fifty-two! Where have I been?* His head was swimming. He barely caught the side of the gurney as he blacked out onto the floor.

*Cold, very cold. But warm at my middle. It's the bleed not stopping. Syncope setting in....*

"Wiley?"

*Surfacing, blinking, seeing nothing.*

"It's me, babe."

"Katie?"

"It's okay. You're "after" now. You're with *me.*"

*I've died. This is heaven....* "I'm so sorry for everything that happened... For what I did to you, Katie."

"Oh, no, Wiley. You didn't do anything." Her formless embrace held him tight. "My IV was in, but I was still awake. That horrible nurse whispered 'Your magic is no match for mine. You will die on this table.' Then the anesthesiologist told me to count backwards. I was so scared. You came in and I could hear in your voice how tired you were."

"I was exhausted. I shouldn't have operated."

"No, Wiley. That nurse made you flinch. She did it twice. She made your scalpel slip."

"It was black magic?"

"What? Top hats and bunnies?" She laughed. "It was some crazy lady who rattled you. There's no such thing as magic. I oughta know—I was a magician." Her smile was comforting.

But something was changing. Her voice grew faint. He was falling.

Silver watched on the *Thresher*'s control room monitor as a rusty Haitian Navy launch pulled alongside. Several dozen ragged but heavily-armed sailors scrambled onto the *Thresher*'s deck and climbed the sail tower only to find its hatch locked. The submarine began to dive. The would-be boarders all swam, floundering back to their leaky vessel. On board, after several firefights, Silver and his crew overcame Papa Doc's security force. Now, only the despot and his private secretary remained, huddled in the supply compartment to which they had retreated. One of her stiletto heels broken off, France clung to Papa Doc. His suit coat was splattered with blood which he was trying to wipe clean when Romulo leaned grinning into the compartment.

"Aaagh!" Duvalier held France out as a shield, pointing his pistol with a shaking hand.

"Again, Papa?" Romulo grinned, spreading his arms Christ-like. Their eyes locked. *Click, click.* Out of bullets. The president-for-life lowered his weapon, defeated.

Romulo rubbed his hands together like a delighted host. "It's been a perfect evening. I can only think of one thing that could make it better."

Within an hour, Jean Claude Duvalier ("Baby Doc," Papa Doc's oafish son and eventual successor) roared up in a Riva Lamborghini speedboat. Several suitcases of cash were passed aboard the *Thresher*, and France, Baby Doc, Papa Doc, and his remaining *Tonton Macoutes* (each of whom would be executed the next morning for his failure) sped away.

Romulo kept the dictator's gold-headed cane.

An orb took shape. A human face. Romulo.

"Welcome back, McCoy." He smiled like a governor granting a pardon. "Who's a crazy witch doctor now?"

McCoy lay in the sick bay, his teeth chattering from the cold. He was bandaged from his chest to his hips. The *Sanjivani* flower tasted bitter at the back of his throat. A somber Ts'Me cranked him into a seated position and held a cup of water to his lips.

"Your wounds are coated with mambo paste, or mambomycin as Mr. Hughes would like to call it at a $1,000 a tube. You will heal quickly."

*Damn him. He saved me.* "Thank you."

Kennedy awoke again. This time he was clear-headed. His IV had been removed and the blond doctor who he remembered tending to him sometimes was taking his pulse. He smiled. "Hello, Mr. President. How are you feeling?"

The other doctor--*if he was a doctor*--stood scowling at the side of the bunk. A smile crawled across his lips when he saw Kennedy looking at him. A nudge in his rectum and Ts'Me stood holding a thermometer to the light. "Ninety- eight point six. We have normal."

Kennedy moaned. *Nothing here is normal. Why can't I speak?* He tried again, but only grunted.

"Don't try to speak," Romulo leaned in. "Your vocal chords haven't healed yet. But they will."

McCoy let go of Kennedy's wrist. "Just under sixty BPM." He flashed a reassuring smile. "You're doing great, sir. Can you stand up for us?"

Kennedy pushed away Ts'Me's helping hand and clambered out of bed, clutching his green gown. He held up his fingers in puzzled outrage, displaying the "Hold Fast" tattoos. He gestured like a charades player desperate to convey his clue.

"Please be patient while we examine you, Mr. President. I'll explain everything," McCoy lied. *Or as much as I can.*

Ts'Me passed the otoscope to Romulo who examined Kennedy's retinas under the light. McCoy considered how to explain Kennedy's journey from the Dallas motorcade to standing in another man's skin aboard the hijacked U.S.S. *Thresher.*

"You've been through a lot, sir."

Romulo rolled his eyes and Ts'Me feigned coughing to hide his laughter.

After the neurological work-up was complete and Romulo returned to the control room, McCoy sat with Kennedy as he devoured a plate of meatloaf and mashed potatoes.

"I can't tell you much about Dallas," McCoy said. "I had nothing to do with it. You were shot, supposedly dead. The next morning, Dr. Da Vinci brought you aboard and somehow– I still don't understand it– he preserved your life. You're presently on board the U.S.S. *Thresher* which was hijacked, not sunk, by Howard Hughes' operatives."

Kennedy stopped eating, eyes narrowed, as McCoy described Kennedy's half-life, sedated under Madonna's care, and the Johnson and Nixon presidencies and the murders of Kennedy's brother Bobby and of Dr. King. " I honestly don't know whether Mr. Hughes' group took part in either event." Kennedy was nodding, moist-eyed. They sat in silence. McCoy leaned close and whispered "I'm going to get you out of here. Trust me."

Kennedy shook his head with a groan. He was staring at McCoy. *Who are you? Why should I trust you?*

Ts'Me backed into the compartment carrying a tray. "Now, Mr. President, here's something to help get your voice back." He passed Kennedy a paper cup of milky liquid. "Mambo juice cocktail."

McCoy nodded encouragingly. Kennedy drank it, enjoying its sweet and salty flavor.

"How about a haircut and a shave?" Ts'Me pulled back the white towel covering the tray to reveal scissors, electric clippers, and a comb. "We're not the Carlyle Barber Shop, Mr. President, but we can make you look handsome enough." Kennedy smiled gratefully. "We'll leave the beard, but trim it, I think. That'll help with your... bad parts."

Kennedy made a writing gesture with his right hand.

"Oh, sure." McCoy pulled a pen and paper out of a drawer.

He and Ts'Me watched Kennedy write a note, then pass it to McCoy, who laughed and showed it to Ts'Me.

It read: 'Is this a dry ship or can I get a drink?'

That night, McCoy was late for dinner in Romulo's cabin; he'd stopped to make a Comsat call to Howard Hughes. The voice on the other end sounded rational and interested. Very interested.

*At last, I will do some good.*

## 37.

A hapless moon for sailors lost hung above the horizon. The Atlantic Ocean was choppy this July night.

*Christina*, Aristotle Onassis' luxury yacht, lay anchored at the appointed spot. The floor of its forty-foot swimming pool glowed with an orange and blue mosaic depiction of Theseus and the Minotaur, symbols of ancient Greece.

*The waves look like rows of marching nuns*, Jackie thought, pulling her cashmere wrap closer. Bundled in an Hermes sweater, Onassis took a sip of Courvoisier and placed his hand on her thigh. The dozen oysters he'd had for dinner were working their magic. He winked at the *Christina*'s bar man, who retreated below deck instantly. The £5,000 bar stools covered in minke whale foreskin did it for Onassis every time Jackie perched on one.

"Your mystery date is late." Onassis scanned the horizon. "We have been at the appointed bearing for over half an hour, my darling." His eyes crinkled as he smiled. "I see no sign of your former husband." His hand slid up to squeeze her thigh. "But your present husband is showing signs of life."

"You old goat, Teles," she sighed. "You're right. No one's coming."

Onassis helped her off the barstool and kissed her. His children and business associates may loathe her, her cultural haughtiness may annoy him, but his body still wanted her. *She is my prize.*

Bemused by his lust, her eyes failed to focus at first on the massive shape emerging from the ocean alongside. Dark figures swarmed the deck before the *Christina*'s crew or owner could react. Romulo leapt aboard. Silver lurked behind him.

"Good evening, Mrs. Kennedy. I believe we have an appointment."

"She is *Mrs. Onassis,"* Onassis said, laying a protective arm across Jackie's shoulders. "And I demand you leave my ship this instant."

"Precisely my plan." Romulo bowed formally, gesturing to Silver who seized Jackie. "The lady will be my guest. No one will harm her." Jackie was shrieking.

The ship's crew had been neutralized at gunpoint. Onassis thought quickly. "I'll give you each a $100,000 to release her."

Like King Kong, Silver dropped onto the *Thresher*'s deck and began hauling Jackie up the conning tower ladder.

"A half million! I'll pay you each a half million dollars!" Jackie screamed.

But Onassis couldn't hear her over the ocean roar. "$200,000 each," he shouted, confident he'd sealed the deal.

Cursing in Greek, Onassis watched the massive submarine with her guest aboard submerge beneath the roiling waves.

Kennedy awoke to the sound of a long-lost familiar voice, soft and breathy, often following her English words with French ones as though she were surrounded by Gallic spirits in need of translation.

"It isn't him. *Ce n'est pas lui.*"

"Oh, but it is." Romulo turned up the sick bay lights. Kennedy's eyelids fluttered. McCoy was taking his pulse while Ts'Me reduced the tranquilizer load in Kennedy's IV. "Please take a closer look, Madam. I assure you this is your previous husband."

Lips pursed, Jackie shook her head. "My husband is dead."

Kennedy turned his head to look at her. *Jacqueline... why is she here?* He groaned.

"This is absolutely grotesque! I do not know who that man is."

She held her breath, studying his worn face. *Oh, Bunny, is that you?* The eyes were the same, sleepy and wise. The gnarled scar at the temple looked about right. The hair, graying now, but plausible. The mouth she (and God knows who else) had kissed so many times. He smiled weakly. Her heart pounded, knees trembled.

Kennedy tried to pull himself up. He reached out, fingers wavering.

Jackie was staring at Kennedy's fingers, at the tattoos: "H- O-L-D" across the tops of the left fingers, "F-A-S-T" across the tops of the right. "Those aren't his hands. *Ce nest pas ses mains.*" She drew herself up.

"No, those aren't his hands." Romulo glowed with pride.

"I preserved his life in Dallas and now--finally-- I've given him a new body. I've done something no surgeon, witch doctor or priest has ever done before."

Jackie considered his boast. "Like Dr. Frankenstein."

"That was fiction. This is reality."

Jackie seemed to notice McCoy for the first time. "You look normal. Is what he says true?"

"It is. I assisted at the surgery."

Jackie drew closer. "Why doesn't he talk?"

"The shooting caused neurological damage that affected his ability to speak. In time it may return." He didn't look optimistic.

Kennedy was nodding, hearing all this for the first time.

"Exactly what kind of doctor are you?" Jackie asked.

"No kind. I am a vessel of fate, if you like."

Jackie took Kennedy's hand." Please give me a moment alone with my..." she hesitated, "with *him*."

Romulo was about to object, but McCoy and Ts'Me were already leading him out of the compartment, closing the bulkhead door behind them.

"You were a monster to me, Bunny," she said, touching his hair. He listened moist-eyed.

"It's true." He shook his head.

"Oh, I know you loved us, but you didn't cherish us. You only cared for your power and for yourself. You broke me with all those women. I should've left, but your father... Old Joe persuaded me to stay."

Outside in the corridor, Ts'Me had his ear pressed to the compartment door.

"What if she wants to take him with her?" McCoy asked.

Romulo shook his head. "She won't. She came to satisfy her curiosity. She'll be glad to leave."

Ts'Me looked up. "It's gone all quiet in there." All three leaned closer to the door.

There was sobbing, then a masculine voice that hadn't been heard since late November, six years earlier. "Oh, Jacqueline...." He was weeping.

"Quiet, Bunny. You'll wake the dead."

Kennedy was breathing heavily; he struggled to speak.

"Ah...ah...amends. I want to make amends," he said. "I'm sorry for the pain I caused you." He reached for her.

"No," she said as she pulled away from him. "Bunny, if you *are* Bunny... I don't know *who* you are. You're dead. And even if you are Bunny, you're dead to me." Her eyes glistened. "But thank you for that. *Whoever* you are."

Sitting in the folding chair his driver Rocky set up for him overlooking the sea had brought on a sciatica attack in Hughes' left thigh. He shifted miserably, trying to find comfort. Through night vision binoculars, he'd been watching the scruffy beach below for the past half hour. First, two Jeeps bobbled through the dunes, then parked at either end of a hundred feet or so of shoreline. Six men climbed out and roamed around the immediate area– too far away to see Hughes (or Rocky, asleep in Hughes' car). Hughes heard snatches of Greek as they called out to each other, waving flashlights. They secured the area. A walkie-talkie crackled and, shortly, three other men appeared as though out for a moonlit beach walk. Hughes recognized Aristotle Onassis, the smallest of the three, and next to him Costa Gratsos, his old friend and principal adviser. His brilliantined hair glinting, Onassis was smoking and gesturing angrily.

"Don't call her 'The Black Widow.' She is the woman I love." Onassis flung his cigar into the surf, then spat. The wind carried his saliva back, splattering his trailing bodyguard.

"She is not a good Greek wife, Ari. This expensive little adventure is proof of that."

"The Irish are sharing the cost, Costa." Onassis took his arm. "I must have her back."

"As you wish. But her kidnapping could solve all your inheritance concerns. Alexander and Tina were so..." Costa hesitated. "...enthusiastic about the potential here."

"The Irishman is late." Onassis tapped the crystal on his Patek Philippe. "Twenty minutes late."

Costa was staring over Onassis's head out to sea. "Tell me again what the submarine that took her looked like."

"It had no markings. It happened so fast."

"Did it look like that?"

A long, low shape lay about a hundred yards out from the

breaking surf. It hadn't been there moments before.

"Nikos! James!" Gratsos was waving now, but the security team had seen it as well. With drawn guns, they were wading into the waves. Their flashlights shone on a small silver Zodiac bouncing through the water. Jackie sat at the bow like a patrician figurehead, her anger and disappointment hidden behind the sunglasses she wore even at night.

A last drag, then Romulo flicked his Kool across the waves and hopped into the surf, hauling the inflatable boat up to the low tide mark. Silver turned off the outboard motor. His free hand held a pistol across his knees.

Ts'Me was helping Jackie out of the boat. "There we are, Mrs. Onassis. Careful!" She started to fall forward but Romulo caught her arm and held onto it.

"I have returned your wife, Mr. Onassis. Do you have my money?"

"I have half your money. You came early..."

"I came on time. Would you like half your wife?" Romulo held up a knife.

"They're animals, Ari." Jackie tried to pull away but Romulo gripped her arm.

With crunching tires and sweeping headlights, a car came around a curve and pulled up to the dunes over Wasque Point.

"There's the rest of your money now."

They all watched as a tall man with an untucked white shirt climbed out of the black Oldsmobile. Carrying a briefcase, he picked his way down the beach towards them.

"You made Teddy pay half the ransom for me?"

Onassis looked at her, bored now. He always lost interest once a deal was done. "It's not his money, Jacqueline. Joe Senior gave it to him."

"But he hates me..."

"That may be. But the last thing Joe wants is another Kennedy scandal."

"Are you okay, Jackie?" Teddy asked her before looking the other men up and down with alarm.

"I'm better now. Thank you, Teddy." She looked pointedly at Onassis. "And thank you for asking." Onassis avoided her gaze, busying himself with the briefcase of cash Ted handed him.

"Don't you want to know what those men did to me?"

Onassis glared at Romulo. "What did you do to her?" His eyes were slits.

Romulo considered a moment. "We gave her a private cabin. We gave her food. No one harmed her."

Romulo took the two briefcases from Onassis and passed them to Ts'Me to count the money.

Jackie was peering at the briefcases over the top of her big sunglasses. "How much are you paying for me, Teles?" she asked sweetly. Costa Gratsos looked away, muttering.

"Not nearly as much as you are worth, my darling."

Above the beach, Howard Hughes chuckled as he watched through his binoculars. Several years before, he had proposed marriage to Jackie over the telephone. Her refusal angered him at the time, but not so much today. "You dodged a bullet, Howard." he whispered to himself.

Onassis's party climbed back into their Jeeps with Jackie and sped away along the beach.

Pain shot through Hughes' shoulder and he nearly dropped the glasses.

"You okay, boss?" Rocky was awake now.

Hughes grunted and watched the Zodiac pull alongside the *Thresher*. Bobbing in the chop, first Romulo, clutching the briefcases, then Ts'Me, and finally Silver spider-climbed onto the deck and up the sail ladder into the conning tower. But what was this? Kennedy and McCoy emerged from the shadows and tore the Zodiac away from the sailors trying to stow it aboard. The two men threw the boat in the water, jumped in and sped towards shore.

"Rocky, there's something you could do for me now."

*Well, that went alright*, Ted Kennedy thought as he carefully guided Joe Senior's Oldsmobile car back along the winding road through the dunes. Crimmins, the chauffeur, usually drove it. But not tonight. Tonight was top-secret. He hadn't even told Mary Jo where he was going. He wondered again why she'd left the party. It's hard keeping secrets. He'd wanted to tell Onassis to go eff himself when Ethel told him why he'd called, but Joe Senior insisted. "We're better off with Jackie as a living legend than a dead one. " And so Joe had paid up.

A fork in the road. Ted slowed down, still feeling the booze. *Glenfiddich'll do that.* The road wound so much, he lost his sense of direction. He peered back through the rear window, but there was no exterior light to help him. *What was that pile of blankets on the back seat? Must be Crimmins's stuff. Be decisive, Ted.* He turned right, gunning the big engine through the fog along Dike Road.

Kennedy was helping McCoy up out of the water onto Dike's Bridge when Ted's headlights picked them out only yards away. Kennedy turned and stared down the driver. Ted stomped on his brake. No! In a freeze-frame instant, he recognized his brother as the car's wheels skidded across the sandy boards. He swerved, barely missing the two men, and the Oldsmobile rolled off the bridge into black water. There was a squelching sound. Ted struggled to roll down the driver's side window as water began to engulf the car. The headlights were at a forty-five-degree angle now as the car's tail end sank into the creek.

Rocky and Hughes, gasping for breath, clambered to the top of a dune overlooking the little bridge. Leaning on his walking stick, Hughes squinted into the fog. He recognized McCoy but who was this younger athletic-looking man? *That can't be him...*

Ted had both arms out of the car window and was struggling to escape when the back of the Oldsmobile sank beneath the water. Kennedy crouched, then dove into the foam. The car's hood was submerged; now it's roof. All went dark as it slipped beneath the surface.

Hughes had his night binoculars up again, watching Kennedy's five quick strokes to where the car had been, followed by an otter-like dive. A moment later, he broke the surface holding a writhing Ted and towed him back to the bridge. *He swims like a nineteen-year-old!* Hughes was near tears watching a man who had spent the past six years as a crippled husk, now using his body like an Olympian. *That Haitian shaman did it! My investment has paid off.*

McCoy helped Kennedy, then Ted, retching, onto the wooden bridge.

Behind them, beneath the black water, twisted in a blanket in the back seat of the sunken car, an inebriated young woman, locked her fingers around the edge of the open car window. To no avail.

"You need to leave now." Large and thuggish, Rocky was pointing a pistol with a silencer at Ted.

"Is that really you, Jack?" Ted was clutching his brother's hand, peering at Kennedy's badly scarred temple.

"Somewhat, Ted."

"Nothing to see here. Move along." Rocky was nudging Ted with his gun.

Ted drew himself up. "I am a United States senator, sir."

"And I was the president." Kennedy squeezed his brother's arm. "Ted, go back home before something worse happens."

There was a thomp as Rocky fired at a spot near Ted's feet. Ted backed away up the road, then began to run.

Leaning on his cane, Hughes was picking his way down the dune.

"Mistah Hughes." Kennedy nodded in greeting. "So I'm still your prisoner."

"Maybe not." Hughes looked him up and down. "Please unzip your top, Mr. President."

McCoy nodded and Kennedy reluctantly squirmed out of his upper jumpsuit. Rocky held up a flashlight as Hughes hobbled around Kennedy, inspecting Romulo's handiwork. "You look good." There were light railroad track scars down either side of his spine. "How do you feel?"

"Like a shiny new half-dollar."

McCoy stepped forward. "It's what I told you, Howard. The surgery was only a few weeks ago. He eats, drinks, walks, runs. It's more than a transplant– it's a meld." McCoy helped Kennedy pull up his jumpsuit.

Hughes was squinting like a horse trader. "You pee okay?"

"Like a racehorse. Are we finished here? I appreciate my diminished circumstances, Mistah Hughes, but there are things I'd like to do."

McCoy took a step forward. "He wants to see his children, Howard. They're in New York."

Hughes had no children. Never saw the use. "*See* them?"

"At a distance. At least I can do that."

"He's been through a lot, Howard." McCoy said. "He can't hurt you– he's dead."

“No, doctor. That's where you're wrong.” Hughes had produced a 45 automatic and was holding it to Kennedy's heart. “Too many people would lose their trust in government if this ever came out. I can't have that.”

But Kennedy was not to be killed again. A rock flew out of the high grass and grazed Hughes’ cheek as Ted Kennedy charged out.

McCoy snatched the pistol from Hughes, sidestepping Rocky who looked grateful for the intervention.

The night exploded as gunfire strafed the grass behind them, leveling a ten-foot stretch like a weed whacker. Silver and two crewmen had waded ashore and spotted them.

“This way!” Teddy shouted. “We can swim it and follow the road.” Kennedy and McCoy scrambled behind him up the dune, then down the other side to the edge of the bay. Another blast lit up a tree on the ridge above. They waded into the tide and swam hard for the opposite shore.

“Ted...” Jack gasped as all three floundered out of the water onto the bank. “I want you to promise me something.”

“What is it?”

“I want you to promise me that no matter what anyone tells you—including our father—you will never run for president. I love you and I loved Bobby...” Jack’s voice was cracking. “I want you to last.”

McCoy watched the brothers embrace.

Much misinformation and truth have been written about Senator Ted Kennedy’s actions or failures to act that night and early the following morning. As for Kennedy and McCoy, they dozed on a 7a.m. propeller flight from Martha’s Vineyard to LaGuardia Airport, where they caught a cab to West 23rd Street.

The Victorian Gothic red brick Chelsea Hotel opened in 1884 and by 1969 was a shabby creative hothouse. Tenants’ cats ran in the pot-skanky hallways. Musicians, artists, and writers (both renowned and reviled) passed through its pop art-filled lobby like exotic birds: heartbroken Arthur Miller, Janis Joplin in her feathers and furs, soft-spoken Andy Warhol with his hangers-on, and Patti Smith and Robert Mapplethorpe in black leather. Kennedy and McCoy were sparrows unnoticed.

“We have one single room with two beds. 205, Dylan Thomas’

old room. Will that suit you..." Stanley Bard, the manager/owner, lowered his bifocals and peered at the guest register. "Dr. Spock and...Mister Roosevelt?"

"Perfect."

Their room had two beds on either side of a scarred table, a lamp and stained wall-to-wall carpeting that smelled of dust and nicotine. There was no evidence of Dylan Thomas unless it was he who underlined the word "temptation" in spidery ink wherever it appeared in their Gideon Bible. Their rattly windows overlooked a fire escape on 23rd Street where guests in pursuit of coolness often photographed themselves semi-naked.

After showers in their cracked tile bathroom, they put on the new clothes they'd bought on Eighth Street and went down to the bar at the El Quijote where a noisy crowd had gathered to watch the Apollo 11 moon landing over salsa, chips, and tequila. They sat at a table facing the color TV over the bar. Behind his trim ginger beard, Kennedy was incognito as he ordered a daiquiri from the young waitress. "I know you! " But she was pointing at McCoy. "You're Steve McQueen."

"I'm not actually, but thank you for the compliment."

She gave him a your-secret's-safe-with-me smile, pushing her way back through the crowd. The TV was tuned to CBS where Dan Rather was describing the three Apollo 11 astronauts' daily routines, filling time until the big moment arrived. His words could barely be heard over the roar at the bar.

Kennedy leaned close to McCoy, eyes on the screen. "When Jacqueline and I visited Rome, our guide asked us to imagine that we were emissaries from, say, Greece 2,000 years ago entering the city for the first time. The Circus Maximus held up to 265,000 spectators for chariot races. The entire city of Athens had only 200,000 residents then. Next, we came to the Coliseum, a stadium that could hold 50,000 witnesses to imperial power and cruelty. Finally, there was the Forum, a village of elected government institutions, the cradle of democracy. Here's the point, McCoy. If you were a foreign diplomat visiting Rome, wouldn't you want to make friends with this powerful nation, not challenge or inconvenience it?"

"Of course." McCoy sipped his vodka, but he was bursting with pride. *I'm getting a personal history lesson from JFK.*

"That's why I wanted to put a man on the moon. So every nation on earth would fear and respect us." Kennedy's eyes lowered. "And there are other reasons."

"Such as?"

"Our planet is growing warmer. Our climate is changing. I met with environmental scientists in 1960. We—Man with a capital M—are destroying Earth with our pollution. Our species will need to settle on another planet. Some day. Long aftah you and I are dead. The Apollo program is critical to that effort."

The waitress returned with Kennedy's drink, eying McCoy like a candy bar. "She likes you," Kennedy said. "Want me to stand at the bah?"

The crowd, six deep now, was shushing each other as a bartender turned up the TV. Pencil-pocketed Houston flight controllers in short sleeves and headphones were staring up at an image. Roll bars cascaded through static down the black and white screen as a voice spoke through intermittent beeps. "Ok, Neil. We can see you coming down the ladder now." A shadowy image took the form of the lunar module Eagle and a man in a spacesuit emerged, climbing down its steps. McCoy gasped.

"What?" Kennedy was staring at him. McCoy shook his head, uncertain, yet...

"I'm going to step off the LAN now....That's one small step for a man, one giant leap for mankind." Over 650 million people around the world watched Commander Neil Armstrong set foot on the moon.

McCoy was trembling. The image on the screen looked exactly like the image Hughes' film crew had shot on that ranch in the California desert. *Could it be?*

There was cheering and hugging across the country, including in New York City: at El Quijote, outside appliance store windows, in Central Park. A grinning Kennedy put his arm around McCoy. "What did I tell you, doctah? America does what it sets out to do!"

Kennedy's fever returned after his second daiquiri. He began shivering. McCoy helped him back to their room. He checked his vitals. Pulse and blood pressure: normal. Body temperature 103. *Ok, fever... Bring it down.*

After a cold bath and two aspirin, the fever broke. Kennedy slept fitfully, with McCoy watching him.

*We have taken him where he should not have gone. Can I keep him alive?*

At 9 a.m., Kennedy's vitals were all normal and his blue eyes were clear. McCoy's relief must have shown because Kennedy patted McCoy's shoulder.

"Whatever happens, doctah. I'm living in a pain-free body. I have a chance to see our world and feel things an ordinary man feels even if only for a short while. Whatever happens, thank you for looking after me."

"It's an honor, Mr. President."

"Now tell me *your* secret because I know you have one. Last night when we were watching the moon landing, you saw something. Something that wasn't right."

McCoy described his evening with Howard Hughes on the California desert film set.

"It looked identical to me. Down to the way Armstrong or whoever it was held onto the stair rail."

"So Mr. Nixon discovers that the moon landing I instigated and Johnson supported could not take place for whatever reason until aftah the next election. Rather than admit any delay and risk his popularity declining in the polls, he gets Mr. Hughes to fake the whole thing. Typical Republican cheatah."

"But I could be wrong! Maybe Hughes was just shooting a promo film like he said..."

Kennedy leaned close. There was an edge in his voice. "If you only learn one thing from me, it's this." His blue eyes were flashing. "Nevah. Evah. Undah-estimate the G.O.P. They're weasels!"

## 38.

On a bus ride up newly one-way northbound Madison Avenue, McCoy pulled the stop cord with a ding at 86th Street. They walked one block west to Fifth Avenue, then sat in the shade of Central Park on a bench across from 1040 to wait.

"I've missed six years of their lives," Kennedy sighed.

Nearly an hour passed before a Checker cab pulled up and a

young nanny in a T- shirt and jeans got out with two children. Kennedy stood as though to cross the avenue and go to them, but McCoy held him back. The girl, about twelve, wore a school uniform with a plaid skirt. She was helping the nanny carry a cage with a rabbit in it while her young brother tried to feed it a carrot through the bars. The trio hurried past the doorman in the shade of the lobby and was gone. Kennedy's eyes were red-rimmed.

"They look happy," he said finally. "I'm sure their muthah takes very good care of them."

"Of course she does."

"That's it then." Kennedy swallowed. "We have to go."

He shook off his sorrow like strong men can and, despite the shirt-soaking summer heat, they walked south, then west along Central Park. They dropped tokens into the slots, pushed through the wooden turnstiles, and rode the IND downtown to the new Penn Station.

"My Gahd! They tore down a temple and built a rat's maze."

Kennedy sat in a phone booth while McCoy fed him coins. "Kenny? Is that you? Are you sitting down? It's your favorite Irishman, back from the wrong side of the grave. No! No! Don't hang up. This is not a joke!" Kennedy peered up at McCoy over his new Ray-Bans, shaking his head. "Kenny, I'll explain when I see you. Okay, old friend, ask me a question only I would know the answer to." There was a pause. "That's a good one. The Harvard-Princeton game. At Harvard. Bobby bought us beers. One of your shoes had a hole in it." He smiled, then looked up at McCoy again. "What time do we get into D.C?"

In the new Metroliner club car, McCoy read *The Godfather* while Kennedy pored over *Time, Life,* and *Newsweek* magazines, fascinated. "Ian Fleming's been dead for five years?" he marveled.

A scowling, drink-weathered Kenny O'Donnell, Kennedy's former White House secretary, was waiting for them under the clock in Union Station. Despite the heat, he wore a raincoat over his wrinkled suit and one hinge of his spectacles was taped. He stared at Kennedy who punched him in the shoulder. "Hello, leprechaun. Don't look so shocked."

O'Donnell continued to stare. "I was in the car behind you. I helped lift you out. You were *dead.*" His voice was choking. He touched Kennedy's disfigured temple. "That looks about right." He looked him up and down. “But you grew bigger.”

“It’s me, Ken. I pulled through.” He smiled. “It’s complicated.”

Ken reached out and hugged him, quietly sobbing. Kennedy patted his back a moment, then pushed him away, holding both his shoulders. “I need a favor.”

“That’s *all* you need?” Ken was laughing through his tears.

“Oh, it’s a big favor.”

“Who’s this?” O’Donnell nodded at McCoy.

“A fellow traveler.”

“Wiley McCoy.” The men shook hands.

“He’s Irish.” Kennedy winked. “He looks aftah me. Carries the whiskey.”

O’Donnell grinned.

Of course, Kennedy had a plan, which he laid out over hard-boiled eggs and Jamesons at the Terminal bar.

“What have you got on Nixon? The DNC must have him staked out six ways to Sunday.”

O’Donnell considered the question. “What would you do with that information if you had it?”

“Help our nation in a time of need.” Their eyes met. “With no attribution.”

Fortune had grinned at Aurora. She guided the prince’s investments with considerable success; she bought shares of Coca-Cola and General Electric, carefully redirecting cash wherever she could to increase her own stock holdings.

She longed for news of Romulo and Madonna, but contact with the outside world was forbidden to the women in the Happy House. Using a trusted local merchant’s telephone and mailing address, Angie made a few inquiries through a private investigator in Florida.

“Your mother is still living at the same address.”

“Is she well? Is she living alone?”

“That’s all I could find out. The investigator told me never to call him again.”

And now Angie was not well. Her cough had grown worse and, at Prince Fereydun’s insistence, she was admitted to the hospital outside Al-Masif. After various tests, the doctors informed the prince alone that there were cancerous nodules in one of Angie's lungs. The prognosis was grim. How did he wish to proceed?

It was a warm summer night after dinner. There were stars in the desert sky. "Angie, come walk with me," the Prince said, taking her hand.

"You have a purposeful look, Fereydun." She smiled. "I am so pleased your health will soon improve," he lied.

There was a spot down the path with a sheltered divan where in earlier times they would make love, but now was a place for conversation and quiet.

"I have been thinking about our lives," he said as they sat staring at the mystery of night in the desert. "I'm growing old. Every day, I find more comfort in your company."

"That's very kind, Fereydun." Her eyes were glazed from pain medication.

He took her hand. "It would please me if you would be my wife."

"If I would...what?" She appeared confused.

"Marry me before Allah."

She smiled in surprise, then leaned on one arm and began coughing. He held out a small Cartier box and opened it to reveal a diamond ring.

She laughed, still gasping, overcome with happiness. He placed the ring on her finger and kissed her. "You will spend the rest of your life at my side."

"I'm sorry. This is so unexpected, Fereydun." She didn't see the tears in his eyes as he leaned back to hold her from behind. A shiny new future: she loved him, now she would share his life.

Something hard touched her head. The bullet from his pistol killed her instantly.

A red moon floated over the Eisenhower Executive Office Building, a cherry atop a Second Empire sundae. It was shortly after 2 a.m. when Ken O'Donnell removed a ring of keys from his pocket and let McCoy and Kennedy in through a door on the 17th St. NW side of the building. They were in a dimly lit corridor.

"Brings back memories, eh, Kenny?" Kennedy said, clapping O'Donnell on the back and striding around the corner to another door marked "No Re-entry."

Producing another key, O'Donnell spoke softly to McCoy. "For nearly two centuries now, our leaders have competed to win the office of the presidency. But soon after Inauguration Day, the truth sets in: the White House is the white *prison.* You can't leave without at least a dozen people around you. Your only privacy is on the john."

O'Donnell unlocked the next door which opened onto a small landing with steps leading down to a long, carpeted corridor the width of an airplane cabin. Ankle-level lights softly lit the way.

"Welcome to the Fiddle Faddle tunnel," Kennedy said, grinning as they walked. "Mistah Truman renovated the White House in '49. He built this tunnel to slip out and meet friends. He liked to play golf. I had a more personal use for it." Kennedy winked.

O'Donnell picked up the tale. "LBJ never used it and I don't think anyone ever told Nixon about it. We're under the White House south lawn now." They turned left and, a few hundred feet later, came to a locked door. "This is my last key and this is where I leave you, Mr. President." O'Donnell nodded at McCoy. "Doctor."

"Thanks, Kenny." Kennedy shook his hand, then hugged him.

"If I can ever be of service again..." O'Donnell's eyes were moist as he turned and headed back the way they'd come.

McCoy followed Kennedy up a flight of thickly carpeted steps to a landing which led to a second flight. They crept quietly up to a vestibule outside a large baize-covered door.

"I'll bet Ken's right. They haven't used this passage since I was president." Kennedy spoke softly now. "This door leads to the back of the president's walk-in closet off the dressing room." Kennedy put his finger to his lips, then inserted the key in the lock and eased the door open. A dozen or more men's suits hanging on a rod blocked their way. Kennedy wrinkled his nose as he held up a sleeve. "Too boxy. Nixon's always dressed like an old man."

McCoy smiled remembering JFK's sleek Brooks Brothers suits. They pushed their way through the clothing to find themselves in a large walk-in closet with racks of lace-up shoes and drawers of socks and underwear. Kennedy pushed open the closet door, his arm stretched behind him to keep McCoy back.

It was, as befit the leader of the free world, a large bedroom.

Two six-over-six Prussian blue draped windows let moonlight stream across the king-sized bed in which an unshaven man in a quilted sleep mask lay, fists balled, snoring. An empty martini glass and a partially eaten dog biscuit were on the bedside table.

"Where's the First Lady?" McCoy mouthed.

"Pat must have her own bedroom." Kennedy rolled his eyes. "Wouldn't you?"

As they drew closer, McCoy saw that a sweat mustache like a shiny caterpillar had formed on Nixon's upper lip. The right sleeve of his pajama jacket was rolled up revealing a long red irritation along his arm. *Superficial phlebitis*, McCoy quickly diagnosed.

Kennedy poured himself a glass of water from the pitcher on the bedside table and took a long sip before climbing over the gold counterpane to sit at the sleeping man's side. He crossed his legs and gestured for McCoy to sit in a nearby armchair.

"Oh, Richard? Dick?" Kennedy nudged Nixon, who snorfled and turned over. "You're having a dream. It is I, the ghost of presidents past." Nixon shuddered. "I know you can hear me, Richard."

Richard Milhous Nixon sat up, tearing the sleep mask from his stubbled face and stared bug-eyed at Kennedy. His mossy jowls hung like testicles on either side of his face. "Oh God! Jack! It wasn't me. Johnson had you shot."

"I'm over it, Richard."

"This is a dream?" He reached out and turned on the lamp. Kennedy grinned behind his ginger beard. Nixon stared at him. "You don't look right."

"It is the state of my union, Richard."

Nixon turned to McCoy. "Who's that?"

"My personal physician."

McCoy waved politely.

Nixon wiped his sweat mustache, suddenly fearful. "What do you want?"

"What happened to my moon landing, Richard?"

"*You* never had a moon landing. That was *my* moon landing."

Kennedy leaned closer. "Was it? Did it really happen, Richard? Or was it a hoax?"

"How could it have been a hoax? We watched it on TV!"

"Answer me."

"How the hell would I know?" Nixon barked. "Do you think they always tell me the truth? Did your people tell *you* the truth? No, they let you get shot!"

A tap on the bedroom door and the First Lady leaned in, clutching her housecoat. "Dick, what's going on?"

"I'm having a dream, Pat. And now you're in it." He glared at her.

"Is that possible?"

"Please, Pat..."

She shut the door.

Kennedy was pointing his finger in the president's face now. "You perpuhtrated a hoax on the American people!"

"You want to talk about hoaxes? You published two books, both written by others, which were best-sellers because your father bought a few thousand copies of each. You managed to ram your PT boat into a Japanese destroyer and somehow got awarded a medal for heroism. You won your House and Senate seats because of your father's money. You were mostly absent during your fourteen years in the House. With the help of the Chicago Democratic machine, you stole the presidential election from *me*. You and your brother used the IRS to pressure your friends and enemies. You paid lip service to civil rights but appointed segregationists as judges. You contracted for the murders of Lumumba in the Congo and Trujillo in the DR. You abandoned the rebels at the Bay of Pigs. You brought the world to the brink of nuclear confrontation. Khrushchev backed down. You cashed in. Did I leave anything out?"

Kennedy smiled. "I cared about the American people, Dick. I wasn't just in it for myself and they knew that. But you— you only want what you can get. And they know it."

Nixon glowered. "Are you calling me a crook?"

"Go out one night, take a few Secret Service with you. Go somewhere hallowed where you'll feel safe, the Lincoln Memorial, maybe, and talk to your citizens. They'll tell you what they think."

"I'm not a crook."

Kennedy leaned in close, whispering, "Larry O'Brien and the DNC know all about the $100,000 Mistah Hughes gave Mistah Rebozo so you could renovate your Key Biscayne home. $46,000 of it was for a putting green, a pool table, and a fireplace. All in exchange for favorable treatment for Mistah Hughes' airlines and casinos. That's a *quid pro quo* impeachable offense. The DNC has the evidence and they will use it."

"I don't know what you're talking about." Nixon had grown pale.

"Of course you don't," Kennedy said, "You're dreaming, remember?"

Nixon eyed his empty martini glass.

"It will all come down around you." Kennedy was walking back to the closet now. "And everything you do will only make it worse. You're a disgrace to our founding fathers. And you are..." He paused for emphasis. "A douche baag."

With that, Kennedy and McCoy bounded back through the closet, down the steps, and hurried back along the underground corridor.

## 39.

*Not good.* The cramps and nausea were back. Since the fall, they'd come and gone like bad weather. Aurora had been to a Lebanese specialist who at first told her it was a stomach virus. "Pepto Bismol and only light food until your appetite returns." When she visited him a third time, he looked evasive and wrung his plastic-gloved hands. "You may want to go to the hospital outside of Jazan. I've heard there's a clinic there...."

"What's wrong with me?"

"It's a virus." He steered her to the door. "Try the clinic." A professional smile. "They might help you."

She'd heard of this clinic. Several men who visited the Happy House had been treated there. She'd been with each of them once, perhaps twice. The rumor was that no one was ever cured.

The sun came out; she felt better.

*What kind of virus plays hide and seek like the weather? Forget the clinic, I need an American doctor.*

Boarded and bored economy-class passengers had quickly spread the word: there's a rock star in first-class. A group of American fans had been taking turns walking up to the open curtain to get a glimpse of Jimi Hendrix with his halo of curly black hair, prizefighter's nose, and slender mustache over kissable lips. He stared back through his sunglasses and raised two long fingers in a peace sign. A girl in a Union Jack T-shirt shrieked before the cabin attendant herded her back to her seat. The Caravelle jet was still sitting on the Casablanca tarmac nearly twenty minutes past departure time.

"What's the problem?" Jimi asked his manager across the aisle from him.

"Dunno, mate," Mike Jeffrey said.

Resplendent in a ruffled shirt and velvet headband, James "Jimi" Hendrix, late of the US Army 101st Airborne, had risen from a grateful American kid playing side for a few working blues bands into a world-class headliner with demands, some reasonable, some not so much. It depended on the moment and the narcotic.

Outside, on the tarmac, a long black Mercedes raced up to the plane. A tall figure wrapped in a white *niqab* emerged and strode up the metal stairs as luggage, including a large Louis Vuitton trunk, was swiftly loaded into the cargo bay. A squeaky voice reading phonetically came over the PA: "Royal Air Maroc apologizes for the delay. We will be departing shortly."

Jimi and Mike watched the hooded passenger step aboard, push past a flight attendant and into the WC. The jet's engines started up.

"You shouldn't've come for me, man." Jimi's feather bracelet slid down his wrist as he pointed an accusing forefinger at his manager.

"Needed to be sure you wouldn't do a bunk." They were both watching the restroom door. "This Woodstock gig is important. You're the headliner. There's gonna be ten thousand people, maybe more. And you've got a new band to rehearse."

"You mean I'm your meal ticket." Jimi's beringed left fingers were playing a riff on the seat arm that only he could hear. "I stand up next to a mountain..." he murmured.

The bathroom door opened and Aurora stepped into the aisle as the jet began to taxi on the runway. Wearing hip-hugging jeans and a cowboy shirt, crimson-mouthed and ghostly pale beneath her curly white hair, she surveyed the first-class cabin from behind wrap sunglasses. Her lips pursed. There were only two seats left: one next to a dozing priest and one next to Jimi. She chose Jimi.

"I am seeing myself in the opposite," Jimi said, smiling like a man very sure of himself. "You are my X-ray."

It was true, Mike thought. The effect was unsettling.

With a tight "fuck you" smile, Aurora fastened her seatbelt as the plane started to taxi. *Well at least I still look good.*

Jimmy admired her pale fingers and gold Rolex. "You are a fine woman."

Jimi's fame and music had not yet reached Aurora's radar. She smiled coldly. "Let's understand each other. I don't feel well. We have a nine-hour flight. Please keep to yourself."

Mike smirked. Out the window, a plume of dust revealed two black Mercedes and a red Ferrari convertible speeding towards the plane. Men in overalls tried to block them, but the vehicles tore onto the tarmac in pursuit of the taxiing jet.

"Fuck," Aurora muttered, leaning across Jimi to peer out the window. He rolled his eyes, taking in her Shalimar perfume. "They coming for you, foxy lady?"

The cars were abreast of the aircraft now, close enough for them to see the Ferrari's angry driver, a bearded young man in a suit and a red, checked *keffiyeh*. The jet was slowing down. The Ferrari gunned ahead, then pulled into the airliner's path fifty yards ahead and stopped, blocking the runway.

"They don't look like police," Jimi observed.

"They are servants of a very powerful family who have come to take me back."

"What did you do?"

"I wanted my freedom." *Oh, and I stole over a million dollars in bearer bonds, jewelry, and cash over the past two years.*

Mike Jeffrey stared at her, open-mouthed. But then he sensed a moment. *What would Andrew make out of this?* Andrew Loog Oldham was the publicist turned manager/producer who discovered The Rolling Stones in a London bar and piloted them to fame, promoting every drug bust and dark excess as a laudable rebellion and the polar opposite of The Beatles. Andrew never missed a chance for free publicity. Mike leaned across the aisle and spoke in Jimi's ear.

The plane's captain, sweating profusely, and two cabin

attendants reopened the pressurized door and lowered the emergency steps, waiting for the Ferrari driver and two hulking bodyguards to clamber aboard.

"My father says you are to come with me *now*!" Mr. Ferrari was pointing an imperious finger at Aurora.

"I like your hat, man. But you can't talk to my wife like that." Jimi took an astonished Aurora's trembling hand and kissed it.

"She's not your wife!" Ferrari tried to grab Aurora, but Mike stood up, blocking his way. He was a large man used to being obeyed.

"Mr. Hendrix and I are British subjects. Thanks to the padre there..." He waved at the priest across the aisle, "...these two young people were married only moments ago." He lowered his shades onto the bridge of his nose. "It was a whirlwind courtship. And now the young lady is a British subject."

Jimi beckoned the captain over. "You gonna fly this plane or are we gonna sit here all day?"

The plane's purser was speaking urgently into the cabin phone. He gestured to Ferrari that he had to leave.

A defeated look crossed Ferrari's face. "You have no idea what you're getting into." He looked at Jimi. "Don't turn your back on her or you'll regret it." His men were urging him to follow them back out. "We have a saying in my country: Beat your wife every day."

Jimi got to his feet and was climbing over Aurora. "And we have a saying in my country: Fuck you, mate!" Aurora grasped his thigh and held him back as the men disappeared down the ladder. The cabin door was sealed. The flight took off for New York.

Two burly men in short-sleeved shirts were waiting by Hughes' baby blue Chrysler on 17th Street NW. Rocky was in the driver's seat. McCoy spotted them and pushed Kennedy into the hallway shadows. "I'll lead them away. You go out the other exit and take the rental car." He pressed the keys into Kennedy's hand.

"Thank you, Doctah." He clasped McCoy's shoulder.

"My privilege, Mr. President."

McCoy stepped onto the sidewalk and immediately broke left, sprinting down the block with Hughes' men running after him.

They caught up to him in Farragut Square, tearing his shirt as they forced him into the Chrysler's back seat.

"Where's the other one?" Rocky shouted through the driver's window.

But Kennedy was gone.

McCoy dozed through most of the drive to New York. The passenger doors were locked.

The concrete and glass of lower Manhattan glittered in the afternoon sunlight as the Chrysler *p*ulled up in Brooklyn Heights before a massive East River warehouse. None of the busy stevedores looked twice at McCoy as he was frog-marched onto the *Tiny Marie*, a trashed cabin cruiser whose skipper was neither tiny nor Marie, but a burly man with a Yosemite Sam beard and a Grateful Dead cap.

The skipper pointed. "There's tuna sandwiches and beers in the cooler." As they passed the Statue of Liberty, he turned on his portable radio. The Yankees were beating the Royals five to one. Hurricane Camille was approaching the East Coast. The skipper kept shaking his head.

The cabin looked like a frat house: any original built-ins had been ripped out in favor of a stained sofa. On a table, today's *Daily News* carried the headline "Actress and 4 Slain in Ritual." McCoy began to read about the horrific killings of Sharon Tate and four others on Cielo Drive in Benedict Canyon, a neighborhood he'd visited many times as both a physician and a guest. Blood, nylon rope, a white hood and "PIG" finger-painted on the front door in more blood. His heart was racing. Then he came to this: "Outside the two-story house, sprawled on the front lawn were the bodies of coffee heiress Abigail Folger, 26, and a man tentatively identified as Voityck Frykowski, 37, a writer and photographer." Black and white photographs of the victims ran across the bottom of the page like tombstones. It was the woman he'd seen in Hughes' production trailer named Abigail and the man Hughes called "Wojy Fry," the director of the staged moon landing.

*Is Hughes getting rid of witnesses? Will that include me?*

Aurora slept with her head on Jimi's shoulder most of the way to New York. When breakfast came, he ate hers. She awoke with a shudder as the jet touched down at JFK. *I'm safe. Back in the USA.*

The lines in the arrivals lounge were long.

"You're makin' a mistake, honey. You should come with us. Three days of peace, love and music." Jimi held onto her hand, smiling.

"No can do, music man." Aurora wanted to get her luggage, fly to Miami, and find Madonna. She pulled Jimi close and gave him a hug. "Thanks for what you did." She included Mike in her smile.

She presented her passport and yellow form to an immigration officer. "Welcome home, Miss Lee."

Aurora watched Mike and Jimi lug their bags off the carousel. A group of young fans trailed after Jimi. He patiently signed autographs every few feet as they waited on the customs line ten yards ahead of her.

A porter placed Aurora's suitcases and trunk onto a baggage cart. The customs line moved quickly; she presented her declaration form. The agent looked her up and down, then waved her through. She froze. *Something's not right. Look around...*

Ahead of her, the doors to the arrivals area swung open. Travelers' families and friends waited three-deep behind metal stanchions to greet their loved ones. That's when Aurora came face to face with Maisie. Standing next to her was a much older-looking Duane, leaning on a cane, his face twisted like a broken prizefighter's.

"Hi, hon." Maisie grabbed Aurora's arm with steely fingers. Duane held a small syringe at his side, poised to plunge.

Aurora knocked Maisie into Duane who raised his cane to strike Aurora. Someone screamed.

"Hey, watch it, asshole!" A woman holding a "Welcome Home, Bobby!" sign dropped it and shoved Duane back into the crowd as Aurora abandoned her luggage and fled the terminal.

Outside, Mike stiff-armed a girl in a floppy hat trying to kiss Jimi as he got into the back of a black stretch limo. Still clutching her purse, Aurora pushed through the young fans surrounding the car and dove in after Jimi.

"Changed my mind."

Jimi grinned and kissed her cheek. "Voodoo Chile!"

In the front seat, Mike nodded at the driver and the limo pulled out into traffic.

# 40.

Dusk. The *Thresher* lay anchored a few miles off the New York coastline near Plum Island. Waves washed the submarine's hull as McCoy grabbed hold, spider-climbing up the submarine's netting, then onto its sail as the *Tiny Marie* sped away, blasting *Iron Butterfly*.

"Waa gwaan, bredren? All fruits ripe?" Silver winked at McCoy as he stepped off the ladder into the control room.

"I need a shower and sleep."

"Captain's ashore." Silver lowered his voice. "Mi nuh bizniz, but his new patient wants to see you. He nuh feel right."

Hughes was unshaven, sitting upright on an examining table. His hands were shaking.

"Hello, doc." Hughes' voice was slurred, retinas dilated. His frightened smile became a grimace. "I go to sleep, then I wake up. Every day. Full of drugs. And I'm still in pain. I'm *always* in pain."

McCoy took his wrist, and checked his pulse. Junkie bruises lined his arm.

"All right. Let me give you something."

"No!" Hughes shook his head like a kid refusing cough medicine. "I want a new body." He leaned closer and whispered. "DaVinci can do that. I saw what he can do." His face clouded over. "It's safe, isn't it?" He grabbed McCoy's arm and peered into his eyes. "You'll assist him. You'll take care of me?"

"Of course, Howard." McCoy removed Hughes' bony grip.

*He's old, in poor condition. DaVinci could kill him.*

"I need another chance. I've done a lot of good. My medical institute's done a lot of good. Oh sure, I bent a few rules. I want a new body," he sobbed. "Or I want to be dead."

*What to give the man who has everything...*

"You'll be ok, Howard." He lowered Hughes' seat back, then quickly administered a morphine injection.

"Please set me free," Hughes muttered as he drifted off to sleep.

It had been her idea. The Real (worthy of his by-line at last) was a stringer who had just been promoted to staff writer and features editor, although titles didn't count for much at the new magazine. Tuesday morning, the Real and Amerika met Jann for breakfast at that spot he liked in the Castro.

"Greil's already covering it," Jann said, shaking his head. A waiter dropped a packet of Sweet'n Low on the table.

"There are tens of thousands of people converging on a farm in upstate New York while we're sucking coffee here," Amerika replied, "and you want to send *one* lousy reporter?" She grabbed Jann's pudgy hand. "*Rolling Stone* can't pay for two more plane tickets and a Rent-a-Car? Woodstock is going to be bigger than the Super Bowl!"

Jann Wenner and Amerika Abramowitz were old friends. After graduating from Bard, Amerika had headed to UC Berkeley to get a poli-sci degree "and a perfect tan" as she told Jann the night they met. The sex was terrible but the friendship took.

"You just want to fuck under the stars," Jann countered, eying The Real, the beautiful blond young man, at her side. What was he, six, seven years younger than her? The kid could write though. His Stonewall piece was first-rate. "Okay," Jann relented, rolling his eyes heavenward. "But background stories. Color. Let Griel handle the narrative."

Amerika kissed him on the top of his head before rushing out of the coffee shop with the Real to buy plane tickets.

They weren't lovers, never mind what Jann thought. Sex wasn't something The Real cared about. Not as much as he cared about his body. He'd graduated from UCLA at the top of his class and captain of the tennis team. He thought about turning pro, but the Bobby Kennedy and MLK assassinations drew him to writing about the struggle for America's soul.

Amerika slept during the flight to JFK. The Real drove them up to Bethel in a rental car packed with a tent and sleeping bags they borrowed from Annie Leibovitz's nervous assistant. The roads were so clogged with people, they had to abandon their car and walk the last mile, lugging their stuff.

The VIP passes Jann scored from John Roberts got them close to the stage and The Real pitched their tent while Amerika took photos of Janis Joplin drinking bourbon with a bare-chested guy in American Flag pants. Later, in the tent, Amerika rolled a joint by flashlight.

"Not for me, thanks." The Real smiled apologetically.

Amerika shrugged and took another toke. Rain drops were pitter-pattering on the canvas above.

"Here's the deal. The real deal," she said. "I don't want to be your mother. I don't want to be your wife. And I don't like to fuck." She made a face.

"I'm not sure I understand." But he was interested.

"I only like to do one thing..." She was unzipping his jeans. The Real lay back against the side of the tent, smiling. Camping was fun.

Jimi had the limo pull over in Saugerties so Aurora could dash through the rain to buy a change of clothes. The house Mike had rented was less than a mile from the concert site and came with a chef and a slimy swimming pool. The place was run-down, but large with six second-floor bedrooms and two more small ones with dormers on the third. In the living room, there was a reel-to-reel tape recorder, Vox amps, microphones, and a drum kit which Mitch Mitchell, the only remaining member of The Jimi Hendrix Experience, was playing, bare-chested. Jimi's new band was to be called Gypsy Suns and Rainbows. Two of his new bandmates Billy Cox and Larry Lee were playing beer pong and passing a joint. The room smelled of cigarettes, incense, and spilled beer.

"Jimi's here," Mike announced.

Billy and Larry hugged Jimi, nodded at Mike, and gave Aurora a polite boss's girlfriend smile.

Mitch stopped drumming, eying Aurora. "She play tambourine?"

Jimi's eyes narrowed. "She does if I say so, mate."

Aurora was given her own room on the third floor.

The rain let up enough for everyone to eat Cajun chicken and ribs at a picnic table outside, listening to Richie Havens performing in the distance on the main stage while late summer fireflies flitted through the trees. Finally, Jimi stashed his lit cigarette on the head of his white Stratocaster and strummed the first chords of "Hey, Joe." It was time to go inside and practice.

Aurora stretched her long legs. "I'm turning in. G'night, all."

"I'll stop up later." Jimi grinned. "To say goodnight, Irene."

As Aurora climbed the stairs, a distant onstage voice proclaimed "There's a half million people here! We shut down the New York State Thruway!" The crowd roared.

She attributed not feeling quite right to jet lag, but after an hour of sheet twisting, pillow over her head to muffle the sound of Jimi's band (who sounded *awful*), her writhing turned to chills and night sweats. *It* was back.

At last, there was only the sound of crickets and she drifted into sleep. Later, she heard Jimi come into the room, unbuckling his pants. He placed a hand on her back. "You're hot, girl. You sleep." He tip-toed out.

Aurora's fever broke shortly after dawn. She heard people downstairs. She showered (there was a bruise on her ribcage), then pulled on a fresh t-shirt and jeans. Wishing she hadn't left her amphetamines in her abandoned luggage, she went down to the kitchen in search of coffee.

Jimi and his band were climbing into golf carts driven by roadies with walkie-talkies.

"Two years ago, we were opening for the Monkees...the fucking Monkees!" Mitch Mitchell passed the spliff he'd lit to Jimi. "Now we're headlining in front of a half a million people."

Inside the house, Mike Jeffrey paused in the kitchen doorway. He looked Aurora up and down.

"You ok?"

Aurora nodded.

"Jimi said you were sick last night. You take drugs?"

She shook her head.

"You look sick."

One of the roadies was hovering over his shoulder. "They're setting up. We gotta go."

Mike studied her. "If you can wait, we'll find a doctor later."

"Thank you. Yeah, maybe...."

"There's an EMS station next to the circus tent by the stage. That path through the woods," he pointed through the rain, "will take you right there."

Mike joined the others in the golf carts and Aurora watched the procession bump its way down the puddled driveway.

Miles of happy young people in tie-dye and denim trudged through Catskill rain showers carrying knapsacks and tents along the winding road from Bethel to the festival site on Max Yasgur's farm. With the last of their ticket revenues, the organizers had built a large plywood stage surrounded by four scaffolding towers hung with enormous speakers at the edge of Filippini pond. There was no money left for barriers to keep people out; the event was now free of charge.

Romulo's van was at a standstill. With less than a mile to go, the two-lane road had become impassable from the mud and the abandoned cars. He pulled over to the side, nearly hitting a girl with bobbing body-painted breasts, squelching through the mud. "I love you, man." She waved.

Romulo gave her the finger.

"Time to walk." He opened his door and Remus flew out ahead.

"This shouldn't take long. With all these people, one kid won't be missed."

Ts'Me dutifully followed, holding his medical bag. Silver picked his way behind them, nearly twisting his ankle in a puddle. A post with a painted sign told them they were on "Groovy Way."

Aurora made herself a cup of coffee, then climbed wheezing back up to her bedroom. She took a sip, gagged, then ran to throw it up in her bathroom sink. Her pale sweaty reflection in the mirror stared back at her. *I need a doctor.*

It was raining hard again. Sneakers sliding, clutching her purse (passport, wallet, stolen bearer bonds), Aurora picked her way along the path through the woods towards the concert site and the EMS station. She was coughing violently. The rain stopped; sunlight filtered through the soaking trees. She came to a clearing and sat on a rock to catch her breath. She thought of Madonna, Angie—even Romulo. *No one can help me now...*

Wings pounding, Remus rose over the treetops, high above the tens of thousands of people sprawled across the fields below. Tents, barbecue fires, blankets, tarps and rows of outhouses lay like a checkerboard below. He swooped towards the stage where people were playing steel drums.

Remus dropped down, hovering a few yards over the crowd's heads. A girl in a top hat stopped dancing and pointed at him. Her boyfriend grabbed a guitar and waved it at him. Remus rose once more and flew hissing back to the trees.

He saw Romulo, Silver, and Ts'Me trudging through the forest below.

Romulo heard her coughing before he saw her. He and the others paused in the clearing. Aurora's wet hair hung over her quivering shoulders. She hugged herself with bony arms. Romulo gestured for his companions to stay back as he approached his sister. Her flesh was grey. He saw a lesion on her neck.

Surprise, some semblance of love, and panic coursed through Romulo like drugs running through his system. Aurora gasped, then swallowed her shock at seeing her brother. "I must be hallucinating. I prayed for a doctor and I got *you*." Her bravado fell. "Oh, Romo. I'm so lost..."

Silver and Ts'Me exchanged puzzled looks. *He knows her?*

"I'm here, sister. Let me help."

She stood, then, with a sob, threw herself at Romulo, pounding her fists on his chest. He held her until she stopped, finally resting her head on his shoulder. Her flesh was clammy, her eyes rheumy.

"I'm sick. I think I'm dying. Mama was so afraid you were the evil one. But it was *me*," she said. "Men who've been with me have died, other men are dying. I started a plague. I'm the carrier."

Romulo had heard of this new virus. The Haitian dockworkers called it "the dwindles." It affected heroin users, homosexuals, Haitians, and hemophiliacs--the 4Hs.

"Here's where I stop. I can't fight anymore. I can't live this sick." She was squeezing his arm.

He looked into her eyes like a firefighter watching a house burn down.

He had no *Sanjivani. He had* no *mambo* paste. He had only pills that would allow her to die peacefully and that is what he gave her.

Twelve years later, five young men would be admitted to a Texas hospital with an unidentifiable breathing disorder their immune systems could not overcome. None of them had slept with Aurora or Gaetan, but each had slept with someone who'd slept with someone who'd slept with Aurora or Gaetan. Handsome, feckless Gaetan, her love's first victim (later dubbed "Patient

Zero"), was bisexual and lived his short life to travel and seek pleasure. In the age of free love, someone had to pay the tab. And so the AIDS epidemic began. Aurora was its petri dish.

Three days of peace and music had become three days of rain and rain. The Real had never liked Canned Heat, but their insistent bass notes thudding through the morning mist were good to run to. His mud-splattered Jack Purcells hit the dirt on the beat as he wove his way along the periphery of ragtag tents and thousands of young men and women in fringe and face paint. The Real juked to their left and kept on stride. His hair was coming loose again. Dancing as he ran, hopping over sleeping bags and smoldering campfires, he re-tied his ponytail, then checked his watch. Nearly half way. Time to turn and jog back to where Amerika lay asleep in their tent.

Wet, hungry people had begun to leave. What had been a crowd of a half a million was now less than two hundred thousand. Technical problems and on-and-off again storms had delayed the festival. John Roberts and Michael Lang had urged Jimi and the Gypsy Suns and Rainbows to perform at midnight, but Jimi held out. "I close the show, man. That's what I do."

At 9 a.m. on the now clear Monday, Jimi Hendrix strode onto the stage in a pink bandana and a fringed and beaded leather jacket before fewer than 50,000 stalwart fans. Jimi's white Fender slashed out the opening notes to *Purple Haze*, then shifted into *Gypsy Woman*.

A shirtless young man in running shorts and a ponytail was jogging towards Romulo, Silver, and Ts'Me. He stopped. Bad move.

Silver, who had circled behind him, grabbed his arms.

"Hey!" He struggled as Ts'Me covered the Real's face with a chloroform-soaked towel and his world went black.

## 41.

Like generations of pretty girls born into wealthy families before her, Rosemary Kennedy was high-spirited and neither especially intelligent nor ambitious. But her younger brothers and sisters loved her. Her parents Rose and Joe Kennedy, for whom children were either an asset or a liability, sent Rose to boarding school when she was eleven and then to a convent where the nuns complained she snuck out and drank with men. In 1941, when she was 23, Joe learned of a new surgical technique to treat mental illness. Fearing Rose's promiscuity and mood swings could damage his sons' political careers, Joe Kennedy decided, without consulting his wife, that his oldest daughter should undergo a lobotomy.

On a snowy winter morning, a devoted servant and a chauffeur drove Rose to the Harlem Valley Psychiatric Center in Wingdale, New York, a gloomy assortment of red brick buildings with bars on their windows that squatted in an enormous field across from the train station where passengers waiting for their trains could sometimes hear patients wailing.

Rose was given a tranquilizer, then put on a padded examining table, while the presiding physician and his colleagues strapped her down to keep her "comfortable." Woozy, with no additional pain medication, Rose sang softly to distract herself or counted backwards to ten as instructed during the procedure. On the morning of the lobotomy, Rose had the mental capacity between that of an eight-year-old and a twelve-year-old. By the afternoon, she had the capacity of a two-year-old and was incontinent, unintelligible, and unable to walk.

Joseph Kennedy, who would never see his daughter again, tearfully, if somewhat impatiently, explained to his wife what happened. He paced before her in his three-piece suit on the Aubusson carpet, clenching manicured fingers and implying that Rose's predicament was somehow unavoidable, the sad result of medicine's best efforts defeated by the intractability of Rose's depravity. He did not mention that the surgery was both speculative and dangerous, nor that only 80 or so lobotomies had been performed in the U.S. up to that time. Mrs. Kennedy was distraught. Their marriage turned to ice.

Now, so many years later, in a home in Wisconsin, Rose was having her blue dream again. Blue was her best color. Her father used to say it matched her eyes. Her dreams were simple like that ever since… what? She couldn't remember.

Something woke her.

"Rosie." It was a familiar whisper from long, long ago. "Rosie, it's me."

Her head began to clear. Her bedroom was dark and still. Sister Leona no longer permitted Rose's dog to sleep in her room.

"Who's 'me'?" She asked.

"Jack. Your brother."

Rose gasped. She could make out his form sitting in the armchair across from her bed. "But they told me you died." Her family had told her many things over the years. Some of them definitely weren't true. She felt a headache coming on.

"I lived, Rosie. And I only just got well enough to visit you. It's still a secret that I'm alive but I wanted to come see you and tell you I haven't forgotten you." He took her hand. "Your brother loves you, Rosie. Please don't ever forget that."

"A secret?"

One of the nuns once described Rose as "a secret". She wasn't sure what that meant.

"Will you be president again?"

"No, I won't. My time has passed. But I can still make things better in other ways."

She had always loved the sound of his voice. She was smiling. She knew a secret now.

Downstairs, Sister Leona hurried into the attendant's office.

"I could swear I heard voices coming from Miss Kennedy's room," she reported. Sister Margaret Ann frowned. A floorboard creaked above their heads. When they flicked on the light, Rose was sitting up in bed, smiling.

"Are you all right, dear?" Sister Margaret Ann walked to the open window and closed it.

"I'm very well, thank you, Sister. I know a secret."

The nuns looked at each other.

"Don't ask me, because I won't tell you."

Late that night, the *Tiny Marie* returned through the rain to the *Thresher*'s anchorage with Ts'Me, Silver and an elated Romulo, bearing a person on a stretcher whose face was obscured by an oxygen mask.

Near midnight, Romulo summoned McCoy and Ts'Me into his

cabin. "Good news," Romulo announced. "We'll perform our second procedure tomorrow at 7am. No food or drink for Mr. Hughes. Keep him sedated."

"God help us." McCoy sighed.

"There will be three surgeries: the first, to remove our subject from his relinquished body; the second, to remove the donor from the replacement body; and the third, to unite Mr. Hughes with his new body."

"Donor?"

"A figure of speech, doctor." Romulo smiled at his team. "If the procedures are successful, Mr. Hughes has promised substantial payments to each of us."

"And if it's not?" McCoy asked. "Will there be murder charges?"

"We are on the high seas, gentleman. Murder charges require jurisdiction, evidence and a corpse."

There are unexpected events and there are expected events that happen in unexpected ways. Hurricane Camille was forecast to miss the East Coast or die out before reaching it. Silver had been checking the weather forecast hourly and saw the shifting track of the storm.

A sleepless Romulo was sitting on his bunk, feeding Remus pellets on his perch when Silver knocked.

"Jus a word, Captain. Storm's gonna mash up your boat.

"Can't we submerge beneath it?"

Silver looked dubious. "We can try. Camille got upgraded. She's a hurricane now." Romulo's eyes were unfocused. *How can he make any decisions? He hasn't slept in what? Days? Weeks?*

"Do what you have to do," Romulo replied. "Once we begin the procedures, the ship has to be stable. You understand?"

"Yeah, mon. But do *you* understand?"

Like a crusader with a cross, Romulo carried a glowing *Sanjivani* flower in a small beaker as he entered the surgical antechamber where McCoy was pulling on his wetsuit. Romulo's nose was running and his eyes were animated and watery.

McCoy's heart sank. *Is that his cure for sleep? Cocaine?*

Hughes lay unconscious, already strapped onto the rotating platform, his spine carefully aligned with the long medial slot for surgical access. An external jugular IV ran out the back of Hughes' neck since, once the first procedure was complete, anesthesia delivered through a conventional IV would be useless. A second IV delivered life-preserving *Sanjivani* to a vein on the other side of Hughes' head.

Ts'Me slid the watertight glass door shut. There was a hiss as the seal connected. Remus flapped outside looking in at the two men and their prone patient.

McCoy attached Hughes' breathing apparatus, covering his nose and mouth, then pulled a neoprene collar up over Hughes' jaws and cheeks to rest below his closed eyes, creating a waterproof seal. The patient was ready.

They pulled on their oxygen masks. Ts'Me sat down at the control panel. Romulo and McCoy rolled the table where Hughes lay along its tracks into the operating room. The saline water that had begun puddling at their ankles soon reached their waists. Romulo was flexing his fingers like a violinist about to perform.

McCoy watched Romulo painstakingly mark the pathways alongside Hughes' spine from the cervical vertebrae down to the tip of the coccyx in blue surgical ink. The sedated billionaire's right shoulder was heavily scarred and his spine curved abnormally, one of the sources of his ever-increasing pain.

Using a laser saw, Romulo traced the blue lines, separating the tissue and muscle from Hughes' back. When he tired, McCoy took over. Ts'Me administered Hughes' anesthesia, monitoring his blood pressure, heart rhythm, body temperature, and blood oxygen.

At one hour and nine minutes, they achieved dis-attachment: Hughes' arms, torso, and legs floated free from his spine in the water. Romulo removed Hughes' heart while McCoy severed the connections from Hughes' windpipe to his lungs.

McCoy paused. *Surely we've killed him now.* He looked over at Ts'Me who flashed him a thumbs up. The *Sanjivani* was working.

At two hours and three minutes, they placed Hughes' head into a padded brace and his still-beating heart into a mesh bag. His spine dangled below like the tail of a sperm cell.

So far, there had been only occasional turbulence from the hurricane outside. Silver's efforts to keep the *Thresher* steady below the storm had prevailed. But now, the submarine began to shake violently. Romulo squeezed McCoy's arm and pointed at the table. His eyes were urgent behind his mask.

McCoy opened the airlock and slid a gurney through the water over to the operating table, then lifted the "donor" body into position on its back. It was a fit young man with long blond hair, his face covered with an air hose and a breathing mask. His vital signs were good.

When they exchanged Kennedy's body several weeks before, the "donor" had been a fresh corpse. For Hughes, Romulo wanted to use an even fresher one. "We'll terminate him on the table, right before the exchange."

"I can't do that." McCoy was shaking his head.

"I'll do it." Romulo grunted. "He'll be anesthetized. I'll inject lidocaine into his heart. He won't feel a thing."

"That's still murder."

"Whatever *my* death will be, I'd trade it for that one."

The young man was breathing comfortably. McCoy could see the outline of a smallpox vaccination on the side of his left forearm. *Like Stephen's.*

Romulo had prepared the lidocaine syringe.

McCoy stared at the top of the young man's sleeping face behind the oxygen mask. *He's about the same build and same age as my son...*

The deck shook beneath them. Romulo held the long spinal needle in his right hand while he felt with his left for the fourth intercostal space between the young man's ribs.

*The scar!* When Stephen was eleven, he'd fallen off his bike and landed on his right knee. The resulting scar was a perfect X.

McCoy held up his palm in a stop gesture; he took the syringe from Romulo, who was so startled he let him do it. There was a bang on the side of the ship's hull. McCoy reached down and turned the boy's knee. The scar was there.

Rarely are the damned offered redemption. McCoy held a death-filled syringe in his gloved hand. Romulo stood a foot away, unaware that the young man on the table was McCoy's son. Romulo was nodding insistently, bubbles bursting from his mouthpiece. McCoy looked from Romulo to Stephen. He raised the syringe. *Better I stab my own heart than his...*

But having found him, fortune wasn't finished. The *Thresher* had ridden beneath the hurricane for several hours. But now a massive undersea wave scooped the submarine's hull, lifting it like a hooked fish and sending the surgical team tumbling. McCoy fell into Romulo and as they floated to the floor, McCoy found his anger. He slid the needle through the wetsuit's skin and between Romulo's ribs, flooding the lidocaine into his heart.

Now Ts'Me pointed at Romulo floating like a broken marionette. McCoy grabbed his son's hand and jerked loose the IV from the top of his wrist. He knew the risk: Stephen would awaken immobile, strapped to a gurney underwater wearing a scuba mouthpiece and mask. He might choke or drown in his panic.

Ts'Me was peering through the glass window. McCoy drew his hand across his throat, their agreed-upon signal to terminate the procedure and unseal the compartment door. McCoy set to work freeing Stephen. He unbuckled the gurney straps, then pulled his son into a sitting position. Stephen's eyes flickered open inside his face mask. *Did he recognize me?*

McCoy, fireman-carrying Romulo's body, led Stephen through the airlock. In the murk, Hughes' ashen face loomed, desperate-eyed. *Don't leave me!* The sea outside and Hurricane Camille battered the ship. McCoy pulled off his mask and shouted to Ts'Me: "Get him to sick bay! We'll work on him there." Ts'Me hurried to obey.

"I was running in the woods, these guys jumped me… Where are we, Dad? Stephen asked, looking around. "Is this your secret world?"

"Stay close." McCoy grabbed his arm. We're getting out of here."

Stephen pulled on the scrubs McCoy handed him. He saw Romulo's gold-headed cane and grabbed it. They headed for the bow of the ship. Something was fluttering way ahead in the corridor. Stephen froze. "What the hell is that?!"

Remus, clenching a *Sanjivani* flower in his beak, was jetting towards them.

"Be careful. It bites," McCoy yelled.

Stephen held Romulo's cane like a baseball bat and swung at the rat parrot as it passed, striking it in the chest. Remus cart-wheeled to the floor. Stephen raised the cane and slammed its gold head into the creature's skull. The flower landed at McCoy's feet. McCoy, and now Silver, who'd emerged from the control room stood gaping at the dead creature. A cheer went up from the crew members.

"Big up, boy. Big up!" Silver patted Stephen's arm, smiling. "Who dis?"

"My son, Stephen."

"Bless up." Then his eyes narrowed. "Waa gwaan, Doc?"

"Captain's dead, Silver. You're the captain now. We're outta here."

"Outta here, mon? How?"

"We'll use the Steinke hoods. Help us!"

McCoy and Stephen climbed up into the *Thresher*'s escape trunk.

"You my bredrin, Doc. All fruits ripe." His mask of a face broke into a smile. McCoy saluted and Silver sealed the inner hatch behind them.

McCoy tossed Stephen an orange neoprene life jacket with a cowl. Stephen pulled on the hood and McCoy showed him how to connect it to the air-charging station as the escape trunk flooded with seawater. Their hoods quickly filled with compressed air and gave buoyancy to their rise to the surface. The ship lurched again.

"Ready?"

Stephen flashed a thumbs up. McCoy tore the *Sanjivani* flower he'd picked up in half, reached under the hood and placed a piece in Stephen's mouth.

"Bite down on it as you swim to the surface," McCoy shouted, biting into the other half, then unsealed the exterior hatch. Seawater surged in as they began their ascent into Hurricane Camille.

## 42.

Los Angeles, 2008

Lungs nearly empty of air under pounds of water, McCoy had blacked out when strong hands grabbed him by the armpits and pulled him to the surface. Her blond hair washed against his face as Katie half swam, half dragged him to the shallow end of the

Hockney blue pool.

"Ronnie!! Where are you?" she screamed.

A muscular Black man in a home attendant's uniform ran down from the house and helped her lay her husband on the grass. He held McCoy's nose and administered the kiss of life over and over while Katie pressed on his chest. Ronnie was Nigerian and had Yoruba ritual scars on half his face. Coughing finally, vomiting water, McCoy opened his eyes. He spat something out of his mouth. A flower stem.

Ronnie picked it up. "This was in the bud vase on his tray."

"It would've been Stephen's birthday today," Katie sighed. "That always upsets him." McCoy's son had died of AIDS in 1985.

She reached 911 on her iPhone. "We just pulled my husband out of the pool. I don't know how long he was down there. He wanders. He's nearly eighty." She gave the operator their address. "Holmby Hills. That's right. Hurry, please." She stroked McCoy's cheek. He looked up vacantly, uncertain what trouble he'd caused now.

"Thank you for taking care of me." He always said that.

Katie smiled. Dementia or maybe Alzheimer's had ended his practice, stolen McCoy's well-being at seventy.

"I always will," she answered, kissing his wet forehead and wrapping a towel around him.

He gazed peacefully at the sky. He had long ago lost track of walls and doors; he looked out windows that showed him only what he wanted to see.

"Katie?" he whispered.

"Yes." She leaned close to hear him.

"All things are passing. Don't be disturbed." He was smiling.

A siren wailed in the distance, slowly rising above the sounds of the cicadas in the warm California breeze.

## ABOUT THE AUTHOR

Spencer Compton was raised in New York City. He spent the summer of 1969 working as a bartender at London's Chelsea Drugstore where he watched the Apollo moon landing alongside cheering patrons. After graduating from NYU Film School, he made independent feature films and music videos and was a screenwriter on the cult classic *Cocaine Cowboys* starring Andy Warhol and Jack Palance. He then went to law school and became a real estate attorney. He lives with his wife in Brooklyn, N.Y.

For further information about Spencer Compton and *The Thresher Ghost,* please go to ThresherGhost.com

# QUESTIONS FOR DISCUSSION

1. What are your memories of the events of the summer of 1969: Chappaquiddick, the moon landing, the Manson killings, and Woodstock? How did these events change how Americans viewed themselves?
2. How would the reporting on, and our understanding of, the seminal events of the 1960s be different if they had occurred in the age of social media?
3. Who is your favorite character? Who is your least favorite? Why?
4. The music of the era permeates the storyline. How do the lyrics amplify the scenes they are associated with?
5. It is said that magic is science that has yet to be discovered. Discuss the tension between magic and medicine in the book. Does either prevail?
6. Kennedy's fate at the end of the book is ambiguous. What do you think he did next?
7. When the reanimated Jack Kennedy and Richard Nixon meet in Nixon's White House bedroom, they discuss each other's flaws. Which president has the better argument?
8. In the moral arc of the narrative, are the guilty punished? Are the just rewarded?
9. Quests for purpose, redemption and vengeance are character motivations in The *Thresher* Ghost. Which character (or characters) does each apply to?
10. At the climax of the book, McCoy and his son Stephen escape the *Thresher* and swim up into Hurricane Camille. What do you suppose happens to the submarine and its crew? Are Romulo and Hughes really dead? Go ahead, imagine the sequel (let me know if it's any good!)

Made in the USA
Middletown, DE
26 November 2021

52967228R00116